Praise for *New York Times* bestselling author B.J. Daniels

"Readers who like their romance spiced with mystery can't go wrong with *Stroke of Luck* by B.J. Daniels."
—*BookPage*

"Daniels keeps readers baffled with a taut plot and ample red herrings, expertly weaving in the threads of the next story in the series as she introduces a strong group of primary and secondary characters."
—*Publishers Weekly* on *Stroke of Luck*

"Daniels again turns in a taut, well-plotted, and suspenseful tale with plenty of red herrings. Readers will be in from the start and engaged until the end."
—*Library Journal* on *Stroke of Luck*

"B.J. Daniels has made *Cowboy's Legacy* quite a nail-biting, page-turner of a story. Guaranteed to keep you on your toes."
—*Fresh Fiction*

"I kept reading until I finished it once I started. It was that good."
—*Night Owl Romance* on *Cowboy's Legacy*

"Daniels is an expert at combining layered characters, quirky small towns, steamy chemistry and added suspense."
—*RT Book Reviews* on *Hero's Return*

B.J.
NEW YORK TIMES BESTSELLING AUTHOR
DANIELS

JUST HIS LUCK

HQN™

ISBN-13: 978-1-335-01681-2

Recycling programs for this product may not exist in your area.

Just His Luck

This book is for Jodee Lee, who keeps our quilt club running so smoothly.

I wish I had your organizational skills, girl!

JUST HIS LUCK

CHAPTER ONE

ANOTHER SCREAM ROSE in her throat as the icy water rushed in around her. She fought to free herself, but the ropes that bound her wrists to the steering wheel held tight, chafing her skin until it tore and bled. Her throat was raw from screaming while outside the car, the wind kicked up whitecaps on the pond. The waves lapped at the windows. Inside the car, water rose around her feet, before climbing up her legs to lap at her waist.

She pleaded for help as the water began to rise up her chest. But anyone who might have helped her was back at the high school graduation party she'd just left. If only she'd stayed at the party. If only she hadn't burned so many bridges earlier tonight. If only…

As the water lapped against her throat, she screamed even though she knew no one was coming to her rescue. Certainly not the person standing on the shore watching.

The pond was outside of town, away from everything. She knew now that was why her killer had chosen it. Worse, no one would be looking for her, not after the way she'd behaved when she'd left the party.

"You're big on torturing people," her killer had said. "Not so much fun when the shoe is on the other foot, huh?"

More than half-drunk, the bitter taste of betrayal in her mouth, she'd wanted to beg for her life. But her pride wouldn't let her. As her hands were bound to the steering wheel, she tried to convince herself that the only reason this was happening was to scare her. No one would actually kill her. Not even someone she'd bullied at school.

She was Ariel Matheson. Everyone wanted to be her friend. Everyone wanted to be her, a sexy spoiled rich girl. No one hated her enough to go through with this. Even when the car had been pushed into the pond, she told herself that her new baby blue SUV wouldn't sink. Or if it did, the water wouldn't be deep enough that she'd drown.

The dank water splashed into her face. Frantic, she tried to sit up higher, but the seat belt and the rope on her wrists held her down. The car lurched under her, as it wallowed almost full of water on the rough surface of the pond. Waves washed over the windshield, obscuring the lights of Whitefish, Montana, as the SUV slowly began to sink and she felt the last few minutes of her life slipping away.

She spit out a mouthful and told herself that this wasn't happening. Things like this didn't happen to her. This was not the way her life would end. It couldn't be.

Panic made her suck in another mouthful of awful-tasting water. She tried to hold her breath as she told herself that she was destined for so much more. *The girl most likely to end up with everything she wanted*, it said in her yearbook.

Bubbles rose around her as the car filled to the headliner, forcing her to let out the breath she'd been holding. This was real. This wasn't just to scare her.

The last thing she saw before the SUV sank the rest of the way was her killer standing on the bank in the dark night, watching her die. Would anyone miss her? Mourn her? She'd made so many enemies. Would anyone even come looking for her in the days ahead? Her parents would think that she'd run away. Her friends...

Fury replaced her fear. They thought she was a bitch before? As water filled her lungs, she swore that if she had it to do over, she'd make them all pay.

Ten years later

As Lizzy walked around the desk and sat down in the large leather chair, she gave up trying to hide her grin. Sheriff Elizabeth Conners. By afternoon, those words would be painted on her office door. Still, she wanted to pinch herself. She'd won the election and now this was her office.

She leaned back but didn't dare put her feet up on her desk, although she knew that if the men who'd run against her were now sheriff, *they* would have.

"How's it feel?" Sid Anderson asked from the doorway.

Lizzy sat up quickly, shooting to her feet at the sight of the former sheriff and her mentor. He laughed and motioned her back into her chair.

"Congratulations on your win. You're going to make a great sheriff," Sid assured her. It was so good to see him up and about, although he would probably have to use a cane the rest of his life after his hit-and-run accident.

"Thank you." She noted that he remained standing in the doorway, leaning on his cane. "Want to come in?"

He shook his head as his gaze took in the office with what could have been nostalgia. She hoped it wasn't regret. But he'd made it clear that he'd planned to retire even before his accident. Still, she couldn't help but wonder if he missed it. He swore that he'd been looking forward to the time when all he had to do was hang out in his woodworking shop. That and get married.

"Do I hear wedding bells?" she joked. "I heard that you finally proposed to Dorothea Brand."

Sid broke into a huge grin. Dorothea had worked at Sterling's Montana Guest Ranch for more than thirty years and was like part of the Sterling family. Lizzy had gone to school with Shade and knew that when his mother died, Dorothea had stepped into the role for him and his brothers, Will and Garrett.

"I asked and she said yes. I couldn't get down on one knee to do it. She cried when I put the ring on her finger. I'll admit this to you and deny it forever, but I had tears in my eyes, as well."

Lizzy felt her heart soar. "You two are going to be so happy. Dorothea is perfect for you. I couldn't be more delighted."

"The save-the-date announcement will be in the mail soon," he said. "I expect you to be there."

"You couldn't keep me away."

Sid shifted his weight as he leaned on his cane. "I just had to stop by to tell you how proud I am of you."

She'd grown up next door to Sid. From as far back as she could remember, she'd wanted to be a sheriff's deputy and work with him. He'd hired her out of the police academy and she'd gotten her dream to work as a deputy with him. But that dream had been short-lived.

When he'd been forced into an early retirement because of his injuries, he'd encouraged her to run for sheriff, telling her she was the best deputy he'd ever had. She'd worked hard at the job because the last thing she'd wanted to do was to let Sid down, but she'd also known that he was partial when it came to her.

"You inspired me," she said, wondering if he knew how true that was. "I just hope I can fill your shoes even a little bit."

"You'll do great." He lowered his voice. "Just don't let the male deputies give you a hard time." He winked. The phone on her desk rang. "Best get to work."

"Thanks for stopping by," she said. He had no idea how much it meant to her. "I'm happy for you."

"I'm happy for you," he said.

Her phone rang again. She reached for it and when she looked up, Sid was gone.

"Sheriff…" She cleared her throat. "Sheriff Conners."

There was a moment's hesitation before the man on the other end of the line said, "This is Tiny Fraser. I'm a heavy equipment operator out here on Highway 93, northwest of town. I think you'd better come out and have a look."

Her first thought was a car accident. "What's the problem?" she asked, wondering if there were any patrol officers in the area to assist with traffic.

"I was doing some excavation work near this pond out here… I found a car that looks as if it's been in the water for years. The problem is, there's what looks like human remains behind the wheel and that's not all."

A WARM FALL wind whipped the pine boughs and sent dried leaves from the nearby aspens whirling through the air. A sound in the brush brought his horse's head up with a jerk. Shade Sterling reined in as a grouse burst out of the trees with a flurry of wings. His horse sidestepped under him, but he quickly brought the gelding back under control.

He loved riding on the ranch this time of the year. Very soon winter would come and blanket the land in white. No longer would he be able to smell the scents of fall and enjoy a morning ride like this. Shade savored these days although they came with a little melancholy as they always did. Summer was gone and he could feel another year passing.

As he watched the grouse disappear over the horizon toward the town of Whitefish, he saw the flashing lights of police cars a half mile away at the pond. He'd heard that some kind of convenience store was going in on that corner. The valley was one of the fastest growing in the state. He hated to see the ranch and farmland disappearing because of what some called progress.

More and more people were moving in, the valley changing before his eyes. He wasn't sure he liked change and had to laugh. He was starting to sound like his father, rest his soul.

He studied the flashing lights for a moment before curiosity got the better of him. Spurring his horse in that direction, he rode to the far end of the ranch where civilization encroached.

A combination of law enforcement and construction workers had gathered at the far end of the pond. A wrecker was pulling something from the water. Shade heard the wrecker motor roar to life, saw the cable tighten and vibrate as it began dragging a large moss-covered shape out of the water.

The day seemed to grow darker and cooler as Shade recognized the shape as it broke the surface. An eerie silence fell over the pond as his pulse quickened. Weeds clung to the slimed-over surface of the vehicle, and discolored water poured out onto the ground.

He felt as if he'd been hit in the chest with a sledge-hammer. He knew that car.

I NEVER THOUGHT this day would ever come, though I would have preferred that someone found me when I was still alive.

Well, at least everyone is talking about me again. I thought they'd all forgotten me. It's been a while since the name Ariel Matheson caused a stir in Whitefish. But it is about to.

I'm sure a lot of people thought they'd never hear from me again. They should have been so lucky. Little did most of them know how close I've been all these years. And now I'm about to make national news thanks to being the daughter of my illustrious father, the crooked politician. Otherwise, finding the body of a girl who'd disappeared the night of her high school graduation party over ten years ago would barely get a mention.

So I should be grateful. Thanks, Dad. Funny how things work out. Or don't, in my case, since the one person I hated the most our senior year in high school will be in charge of finding my murderer. Sheriff Elizabeth "Lizzy" Conners. Now there's irony for you.

Now it's up to her to find out whom I tormented enough to make them want me dead. A lover? A friend? A classmate I bullied? That should keep Lizzy busy.

I think I'm going to enjoy this. Much more than I did the night I saw her kiss my former boyfriend Shade

Sterling at the party. The same night my killer pushed me into the pond.

Little Lizzy should be very careful though. I'd hate for anything bad to happen to her before she can discover the truth. After all, there's a killer out there who's a lot closer than little Lizzy knows.

LIZZY FROZE WHEN she saw the car being pulled out of the pond. Memories assaulted her, taking her back to the many hours she'd spent riding shotgun in that once baby blue SUV that Ariel's father had ordered special for her in her favorite color. It had been an early graduation present. The stereo was always cranked up to a deafening volume while Ariel talked over it a mile a minute and drove as if she owned the road. In this state, at least, she had since her father had been the state attorney general—until his arrest.

Not that it often required her father taking care of her tickets. Usually all Ariel had to do was bat her baby blues, twist a lock of her long blond hair and purse those full bow-shaped lips. With that face, she'd breezed through life, laughing at how easy it was to get her grades changed or talk a cop out of writing her a ticket or keep her friends in line and her enemies running scared.

Ariel grew up used to getting everything she wanted and getting out of trouble, guilty or not. It was why some referred to her as Teflon. Nothing stuck to her no matter what she did. At the same time, there was something about her, a shiny brightness that drew people to her and made them want to be her—at the same time they dreaded her. Lizzy knew that better than anyone.

"Sheriff?"

She blinked and pulled her gaze away from the water streaming from the SUV to look at Tiny and the officer who'd approached.

"Remains?" she asked and cleared her throat. "I'm sorry, you said there are remains in the car?"

Tiny nodded. "Hard to say how long the car has been in the water. Long enough for a body to be little more than bones."

She had a pretty good idea of how long the car and body had been in the pond. No one had seen or heard from Ariel Matheson since she drove away from her high school graduation.

"We called in the license plate," the officer said.

"QueenB," she said. "I recognize the car. It and the driver have been missing for over ten years."

"No kidding?" He checked his notes. "Ariel Matheson." He frowned. "Related to the former state attorney general?"

She nodded and looked again at the car. "His daughter." His only child, which explained a lot. Lizzy thought about the day Ariel got the car.

"GET OVER HERE," Ariel had called, laughing. "You aren't going to believe this. Hurry. Tell me I don't have my daddy wrapped around my little finger." She'd hung up before Lizzy could ask what it was this time.

Having been summoned, she'd ridden her bike the few blocks to Ariel's house. She slowed as she saw the bright baby blue SUV sitting in the drive, an even brighter huge red ribbon balanced on top.

She'd been the first person to ride in the car, something Ariel never let her forget. "Being my friend comes with benefits. Remember that."

BEING ARIEL'S FRIEND also came at a price. Ariel would sling an arm over her as they walked down the hall and smile at her. Lizzy had basked in that ray of brilliant light at first. She'd felt special being singled out. She was a part of the in-group for the first time.

Ariel had latched onto her the moment she walked through the doors of Progressive, the small private high school on the edge of town. The school offered more individual attention with smaller classes and a more imaginative curriculum. Lizzy had found it very different from the public high school—there were only twelve in her graduating class.

On Lizzy's very first day, Ariel had insisted she eat with her and her friends. Soon, Ariel was telling her that they would be best friends forever. Ariel used to say it like a promise. Or a threat of what would happen if Lizzy pulled away.

The heavy equipment operator had wiped the slime off the driver's-side window when he'd first uncovered the SUV so he could see inside. She moved to peer in now. She hadn't seen Ariel or the car since their high school graduation party ten years ago. Yellow polypropylene rope was tied to the steering wheel on both sides. A pile of bones, among what appeared to be what was left of her clothing, lay in the driver's seat, the seat belt still fastened.

Feeling sick to her stomach, Lizzy stepped back and cleared her throat again. "We're going to need assistance keeping the area closed off," she told the city cop. Word would get out soon—if it wasn't already, she thought, looking up to see cars driving slowly past, drivers gawking.

She made the call to the state Division of Criminal Investigation. DCI would collect evidence at the scene to assist in her investigation. The SUV would be transported to the crime lab in Missoula. But crime scene tape needed to go up until the investigators could arrive and search the area, and that would have to be done by local law enforcement.

Not that it would stop people from driving by, staring at the pond and speculating. Locals had been wondering for ten years about Ariel Matheson's disappearance. Now they really would have something to talk about.

As the cop walked away, Lizzy recognized the reporter making a beeline toward her.

"Interesting timing," Brad Davis said as he joined her.

"Pardon?" she asked, wondering how he'd gotten in here. Davis had always been pushy even back in grade school when he'd taken her glue stick without asking. He'd ended up at Progressive as well, where he'd been the editor of their school paper and had later gone into journalism after graduating from the University of Montana in Missoula. He'd worked for a variety of papers before starting his own here in Flathead Valley.

"Your first day on the job. The high school reunion this weekend," he said, looking over at her as if to see if she was kidding. "Interesting timing, get it?"

She got it.

"So you think she's been here since the graduation party at my house? Wow. She didn't get very far after the party, did she? This is all anyone will be talking about at the reunion," Brad went on, enjoying this way too much. "But then again Ariel would have loved it. She couldn't stand not being the center of attention, as you might recall." He scratched his head with the corner of the notebook in his hand. "But she wasn't the first one of our class to die. Remember Whitney Clark?"

She did. Whitney had tried to befriend her and warn her about Ariel. But Whitney had died so soon after that the friendship had been short-lived.

"I guess I don't have to remind you that the driver who killed her in that hit-and-run accident was never caught. I hope you do better with this one." Brad took a breath and then said, "So what have you got for me?" as he motioned to the notebook and pen he held.

She'd noticed as he was approaching that he had a camera slung around his neck, leaving her little doubt that he'd been taking photos. Page one news. Missing daughter of former ousted state attorney general found in pond ten years after disappearance.

"You know as much as I do at this point," she said. "Probably more." She would find out who'd let him in and give them hell.

"Congrats, by the way, on your successful run for sheriff."

"Your paper didn't back me. You backed one of my now deputies, I believe. Ace Turner."

"The publisher is a dick, but you know that," he said, laughing. "I bet on the wrong horse, so to speak. Hope you won't hold it against me."

She gave him her best smile. "I wouldn't dream of it."

His smile faltered. "Seriously, I like a good working relationship with law enforcement."

"Yes, I'm aware of your...relationship with former undersheriff Ward Farnsworth."

Brad blanched. "Never saw that coming, although it does make good copy. Ward's trial for his involvement in the former sheriff's hit-and-run is going to be preempted for this though. Ariel Matheson *is* news. How do you think she ended up in the pond?"

She sighed and walked away. Not that she had anything against the media. She believed in the free press. She just didn't like Brad.

"You aren't going to use our past as a wedge between us, are you?" he called after her. "Lizzy—"

"That's Sheriff Conners," she called over her shoulder. "And if you don't get out of my crime scene, I'm going to have you arrested." She motioned to one of the officers to see Brad off the premises.

DEPUTY JOHN "ACE" TURNER finished helping put crime scene tape around the area as the SUV was being loaded onto the flatbed trailer to take it down to the crime lab in Missoula. He wandered over to the vehicle as it was being strapped down and climbed up on the trailer to look inside.

He felt a small thrill rocket through him when he saw the yellow ski rope tied to the steering wheel. *Murder.* He would have given anything at that moment to be sheriff. He'd run for the job but the county had voted in a woman. A young woman with less experience than he had. It made no sense. He would have sworn that the election was rigged.

But he knew that the reason he'd lost was because of retiring sheriff Sid Anderson. The man had put his support behind his favorite—Lizzy Conners. Sid had completely overlooked Ace and gone with his neighbor girl. Ace didn't think he would ever get over that. Sid had clearly lost his marbles. Seriously, maybe his hit-and-run accident had knocked something loose upstairs.

Whatever the reason, Lizzy got the job and this murder—and on her first day as sheriff. It was so unfair. There were so few murders in this part of Montana and this one was one that would get a lot of press. A young woman tied to her steering wheel so she would drown slowly after her SUV was pushed into the pond. Brutal way to die.

Add to that the scandal surrounding her father, who was still doing time in prison in Deer Lodge. It was the kind of murder he could sink his teeth into. The kind that would make a name for a man like him who had higher aspirations than just being a deputy sheriff.

Ace considered who might have done it. What type of mind came up with this particular way of snuffing someone out? he wondered as he jumped down. The trailer began to pull away. He'd seen enough. The pile of bones and clothing in the driver's seat. What was left of the victim. Grisly stuff.

He would have given his eyeteeth to even be involved in this case, but he knew Lizzy would keep him on the periphery. She wouldn't let him near the important stuff. Hell, she had him putting up crime scene tape. Any idiot could do that.

As he headed for his patrol SUV, he told himself that he would get his chance. He had to believe that. In the meantime, he'd find out everything he could about the deceased—behind the sheriff's back.

CHAPTER TWO

LIZZY HADN'T BEEN in her office long when she looked up to find Shade Sterling standing in her doorway. They'd crossed paths over the past ten years since high school graduation but only spoke in passing. After high school, they'd each gone their own ways, her off to Montana State University, then the police academy, him off to the University of Montana.

Now, looking into his handsome face, she had to admit that she'd thought about him over those years. Some men just got under your skin in a way that you couldn't forget. Shade was like that.

Mostly she'd thought about the stolen kiss they'd shared at their high school graduation party—the same night that Ariel Matheson had disappeared. He and Ariel had just broken up. Lizzy'd had a crush on Shade long before that but would never have dreamed of acting on it because of Ariel.

The night of their graduation party, Shade had sought her out, grabbed her impulsively and kissed her, saying he'd been wanting to do that for a very long time. There'd been fireworks, enough to make the kiss something she hadn't forgotten.

She'd seen him again after that, but only when he'd stopped by the house where she lived with her aunt Gertie asking if she'd seen or heard from Ariel. Ariel's mother, Catherine, was going crazy with worry.

That had been ten years ago. After a week without any word from Ariel, Catherine had called the police. Everyone just assumed that Ariel had run away and would come home once she ran out of money.

But as time went on, the police began to suspect foul play. They had questioned Shade at length since he'd been Ariel's boyfriend. Also by then, they'd heard about the fight Shade and Ariel had had at the graduation party before she left. But nothing more had come of it. Until now.

Lizzy cleared her throat and rose to her full height of five-five. The cowboy stood at six-three, his broad muscled shoulders filling her doorway. "Shade," she said, not surprised to see him. She'd known that once he heard about Ariel, he'd come by.

What surprised her was the small jolt she felt at seeing the handsome cowboy again. The past ten years had added maturity to his rugged good looks.

He removed his Stetson and stepped in, his long legs covering the space in two strides. He smelled of the outdoors, a mixture of sweet pine and mountain air. Blue eyes twinkled in a face chiseled by a master sculptor. "I was out riding this morning on the ranch when I saw the car being pulled out of the pond. It's Ariel, isn't it?"

She nodded. "I'm afraid so."

He bowed his head for a moment before looking up at her again. She'd forgotten how blue his eyes were, how intense his gaze. "I feel terrible. I should have stopped her."

"Stopped her?" Lizzy asked, confused.

"That night at the party when she stormed off," he said. "I knew she was drunk, which was bad enough. But in the mood she was in…" He shook his head. "I tried to stop her so she couldn't leave drunk and mad and throwing one of her tantrums. But you know how she was. She probably wasn't paying attention and in the state she was in, missed that turn and crashed into the pond."

Lizzy stared at him. "You think she drove into the pond because she was impaired?"

"Drunk as a skunk. I tried to talk her out of driving that night. She was in one of her moods and had had too much to drink on top of it. But Ariel being Ariel, she wouldn't listen. I even tried to take her keys. She fought me like a wild woman and later took off in a hail of gravel. It's just lucky she didn't kill anyone but herself." He raked a hand through his hair. The sun had streaked his dark hair with gold. "All this time she's been in the pond."

Lizzy took a breath and let it out slowly. Ariel had turned up all right. *Deceased.* Ariel's reign of terror was truly over. One person in particular had seen to that.

"Shade, Ariel didn't accidentally drive into the

pond because she was intoxicated or in one of her moods," she told him. "She was murdered."

He froze. *"What?"*

She nodded as she watched all the color drain from his face.

He lowered his lanky frame slowly into a chair across from her desk. "Murdered? Are you sure?"

Lizzy nodded as she took her own chair, realizing what the past ten years must have been like for him. Since graduation night when Ariel disappeared, a black cloud had hung over him. What he didn't realize yet was that cloud was now a major thunderstorm.

He balanced his Stetson on his knee and rubbed the back of his neck for a moment before his blue-eyed gaze met hers. "I knew Ariel had enemies, but I never thought anyone would… I'm trying to imagine someone who could have despised her more than I did at the end."

Chilling words, Lizzy thought, then reminded herself of how she'd felt about Ariel at the end of their senior year. No love lost there, that was for sure.

"I'm going to be talking to everyone who knew Ariel, especially everyone who attended the party that night," she said.

He nodded, clearly in shock. "Just let me know. I'll tell you what I can remember." He retrieved his Stetson and, turning the brim in his sun-browned fingers, rose to his full height. The long sleeves of his Western shirt were rolled up, exposing strong muscular forearms that were also tanned below a fuzz of blond hair.

She remembered those arms around her and how she'd once yearned to feel them around her again.

But today she was the brand-new sheriff and she had a murder to solve. She got to her feet as he started to leave.

He stopped and turned to look at her. That grin of his still had the power to weaken her knees. "I hate that it's under these circumstances, but it's good to see you, Lizzy."

She nodded. "You, too, Shade." With that he was gone.

Lizzy stared at the empty doorway before it was filled with former sheriff Sid Anderson's familiar shape.

"Was that Shade Sterling?"

She could just imagine the wistful look he'd caught on her face. She felt herself flush as she dropped back into her chair.

"Looks like your first day as sheriff has been interesting," Sid commented.

"That was my number one suspect who just left," she said with a groan. "He doesn't realize it yet."

Sid said nothing for a moment. "What does your gut tell you?"

"To not let Shade Sterling distract me from doing my job."

He chuckled. "That's not bad advice. Any other suspects?"

"Too many to mention. Even though our senior

class was small, Ariel alienated all of them in her own unique way. Myself included."

"I thought you were best friends," Sid said in surprise.

"A lot of people did. I hate to admit it, but I was afraid of her. I'd seen her destroy anyone who got in her way." Looking back, she could see that Ariel had probably suspected that Lizzy'd had a crush on Shade. Ariel had probably known before she did. "She made my senior year a living hell. Worse, I let her."

"She sounds delightful."

"I actually thought that was why she disappeared on graduation night. She wanted everyone to think that Shade had done something to her. She was vindictive that way." Lizzy let out a bitter laugh. "Instead she was at the bottom of that pond."

"Not a bad way to start your new career, though—with a murder."

Lizzy groaned again. "Shade said something interesting. He said that given the way he felt about her, he couldn't imagine who might have hated her so much that the person killed her. It was like we all wanted her gone, but everyone was too afraid to stand up to her. Until someone just lost control?"

"And killed the town bully," Sid said.

"Ariel controlled us all but she did it in a way that was so…calculatingly sweet. You never knew where you stood with her. You just knew to be very careful."

"Did I hear that your class was holding its ten-year class reunion this coming weekend?"

She sighed. "We put it off until fall because everyone was too busy during the summer tourist season. One of the joys of living next to Glacier National Park."

"How large was your senior class at Progressive?" he asked.

"It was one of the smaller ones," she said. "Twelve originally. The reunion is going to be held at Sterling's Montana Guest Ranch. It'll be a good opportunity to get everyone together in the same place. I'm just hoping someone saw something that night that will help find Ariel's killer."

"Are you thinking one of them was Ariel's killer?"

She felt a chill at the thought. "I suppose it's possible, but at least it's a place to start. These were the people closest to her. They would have known her best. I'm hoping to get a chance to talk to each of them separately."

"The timing is interesting," Sid said.

Lizzy nodded. "You aren't the first person to point that out."

CHAPTER THREE

As SHADE WALKED out of the sheriff's department, he was thinking how good it was to see Lizzy again. He'd thought about her over the years. He knew he would have pursued things further after their kiss at the graduation party if Ariel hadn't disappeared. He'd always thought that she'd planned it that way.

Now he felt guilty. If he'd insisted Ariel not leave the party that night. If he'd physically kept her from it… But he'd tried and she'd turned on him, scratching his face. He'd backed off, telling himself he didn't give a damn whether or not she killed herself. He'd had no idea that before that night was over, she would be dead.

As Shade walked into the ranch house the family owned in the valley, he could see that everyone had already heard the news. His brothers, Will and Garrett, looked up as he came into the living room. Clearly they'd been waiting for him to return.

Dorothea rushed to give him a hug. "I'm so sorry."

He looked at the three of them and realized they didn't know that he and Ariel had been over long before graduation night. Nor did they know that there was someone else he'd been interested in his senior year.

"So you've heard," Shade said. "I saw her SUV being pulled out of the pond. Apparently, she and the car have been there for more than ten years—ever since graduation night. But just so you all know, we'd broken up."

"What?" Dorothea said. "But I saw the way you were graduation night, primping in front of the mirror. There was definitely a woman in mind." She looked confused.

"Just not Ariel."

They all three looked confused now.

"I'd had a crush on Lizzy Conners most of my senior year."

"The new sheriff?" Will blurted.

Shade nodded as he plopped down in a chair. "I'm still in shock. For ten years everyone was looking at me like it was my fault that Ariel disappeared. I've been waiting for her to turn up all this time so I wouldn't have her disappearance hanging over my head."

"And now you don't," Dorothea said.

"There is one downside in all this," he said.

"That Ariel is dead?" Garrett asked sarcastically.

He ignored him. His brother had no idea what Ariel had really been like. Shade hadn't either until he'd started dating her, but he'd realized soon enough and then just wanted out.

"I realized after talking to Lizzy at the sheriff's department that some people might think I had something to do with her ending up in the pond," Shade said.

"Some people?" Will asked.

He chewed at his cheek. "It wasn't anything she

said exactly, but I realized that the new sheriff is considering me a suspect."

"Why would she?" Garrett demanded.

"Well, she's wrong," Dorothea said quickly as if that was the end of it.

"Lizzy was once Ariel's friend," he said. "And graduation night at the party, I kissed Lizzy. Ariel saw. She was already in a snit, but that set her off even more. In my defense, Ariel and I broke up long before graduation night. No one knew because she begged me not to tell anyone until after graduation. She didn't want to go to the party by herself, she said. But then at the party, she broke up with me in a loud, embarrassing, drama-filled scene."

Garrett let out a low whistle. "I can see why you're the number one suspect," he said, ignoring Dorothea's pointed look.

"The reason I broke up with Ariel was because I had feelings for Lizzy. Unfortunately, Ariel knew and she made sure there was no way we could be together."

Will cursed. "Sounds like a motive for murder."

"Doesn't it though," Shade admitted and raked a hand through his hair. "I know it doesn't look good. The night of the graduation party when Ariel took off, I went after her. I was worried that she would kill herself. I tried to stop her from driving."

"I'm guessing you didn't," Garrett said.

"I grabbed her keys and she scratched my face and took them back. I backed off and left. That's the last I saw of her. I don't have an alibi since I went for a long drive after the incident. I can't prove where I was."

Dorothea looked worried. "Maybe Sid can—"

"No!" Will and Garrett cried almost in unison.

"Don't involve Sid," Shade agreed. "I'm innocent so there isn't going to be a problem." He ignored the are-you-really-that-naive looks his brothers gave him.

"You've kept this to yourself all these years?" Dorothea said, putting a hand on his arm.

"I always knew Ariel would turn up. Not quite like this though," Shade admitted. "I just assumed she disappeared to hurt me. Now with her murdered…"

"Was she really that horrible?" Dorothea asked.

"She's the kind of woman who tried to make everyone miserable. She would from the grave if she could. We all got trapped in her web, I think, because our class was so small. We were also young and foolish and, truthfully, a little afraid of her."

He saw that his family now looked afraid, as well. "Don't worry, I didn't do anything so I'm sure Lizzy will realize that and it will be fine." He waited for them to agree with him but could see it might be a very long wait. So he didn't add that after seeing Lizzy today, he'd been reminded of their kiss and wondered if the chemistry was still there.

"By the way," he told them. "Some of us are getting together to finalize plans for the class reunion."

"You're going ahead with it?" Garrett asked, sounding surprised.

"Why? You don't think we should?"

"I guess there's no reason not to," Garrett said.

"It could be good for everyone to get together and share their memories of Ariel," Dorothea said.

Shade chuckled. "That is probably what is going to happen. But I'm not sure how cathartic that will be." He glanced at the time. "I'm not sure how many of the class are coming over today to discuss last-minute plans."

Dorothea said not to worry, she'd take care of coffee and tea. His brothers excused themselves to get back to ranch chores somewhat pointedly.

A half hour later Shade opened the door for what appeared to be the last classmate, the one that was always late. As he did, he looked out at the horizon and the dark clouds gathering there. The end of October could be downright pleasant or turn bitter and snowy. Today was nice, but there was a hint of some weather in the air. A promise of what was to come. He could smell it on the breeze.

Ashley Houston let out a sigh as she stepped into the foyer. "This valley just keeps growing. The traffic is terrible. It just keeps getting worse." She held out a manila envelope. "Some printed photos and the rest on a thumb drive."

"Great," he said, taking the envelope and adding it to the others stacked by the front door. "Everyone brought some and Kayla picked up a box from Ariel's mom. I'm going to take them all up the mountain to the guest ranch this afternoon and go through them for the slideshow."

Ashley dusted off her hands before slipping out of her coat to hang it by the door. They'd all decided to meet here today rather than at the restaurant where they normally met because of the news about Ariel. Gossip would be running wild and none of them felt like being quizzed right now.

"I hope you haven't started without me," Ashley said coyly.

"No get-together could start without *you*, Ashley," he said with mock sincerity.

She beamed. "Oh, Shade." Her expression turned serious. "You're certainly taking all of this so much better than I expected you would be. Ariel told me graduation night that the two of you were getting married." She patted her stomach and winked. "Our little secret."

He stared after her too shocked to speak as she seemed to get teary-eyed either over Ariel's death or a baby's as she pushed on past him into the living room. Ariel had told Ashley that she was pregnant with his child and they were getting married? So what was the point of the very public breakup? To make him look like he was bailing on her and the baby? If there even was a baby that Ariel knew wasn't his.

He felt stunned at the lie. But was it possible Ariel really was pregnant with someone else's child?

All his suspicions came flooding back. They hadn't been together for months before the breakup. But he'd suspected she'd been seeing someone else even before then.

WAY TO RUIN my big surprise, Ashley. You always did have a big mouth. You just had to tell Shade, didn't you? Why did you wait all these years though? Afraid I would come back, find out and make your life miserable?

Maybe you did know me.

Unfortunately, Shade won't believe the baby was his—not the way our relationship was going in the months before graduation. He'll know he wasn't the daddy. Worse, he'll tell Lizzy and once she gets my medical records...

Ah, just another mystery for her to solve. Whose baby was I carrying? Another suspect to add to her list? Why not.

One more thing to wonder about at the reunion since Ashley won't be able to keep that trap of hers closed. If she hasn't already told the others, she will and then it will move like wildfire through the group. The father of my baby certainly won't ruin the mystery. He has too much to lose.

The best part is that Shade will know I was cheating on him for a lot longer than even he suspected. I loved the expression on his face when Ashley told him. He really was shocked. Surprise! He thought he was the only one who was lusting after someone else? Fool. I wanted him to know that there was someone else and would have eventually told him—if my killer hadn't changed my plans.

But the thing about karma is that it always comes back to bite you in the butt. At least it did me. I can

*only hope it's got its sights set on everyone who be-
trayed me—including Shade and Lizzy.*

KNOWING IT WOULD be a while before she received
anything definitive from the crime lab or DCI, Lizzy
jumped into the investigation. News of Ariel's death
would make national news after her father's fall from
grace. Nothing like a high-profile case to get national
attention. As sheriff, she would be getting pressure on
all sides to solve this crime.

From social media, she knew where she could find
the reunion committee this morning.

As she drove toward the valley that held Sterling
Ranch, she mulled over the fact that she had no idea
who had killed Ariel. After ten years underwater in a
pond fed by a warm spring, Ariel's skeleton wouldn't
be offering up much in evidence either. If the killer
left any clues behind, he or she could be fairly certain that they had been destroyed by the water over
that span of time.

Lizzy thought it ironic that the killer had used
ropes to tie Ariel to the steering wheel. Otherwise,
she would have believed, just as Shade had, that Ariel
had accidentally driven into the pond drunk and mad.
It was a reasonable assumption; everyone had heard
Ariel leave the graduation party that night, tearing off
angry after having been drinking.

People might even have believed suicide—had she
not been bound to the steering wheel. Although Lizzy

couldn't imagine Ariel killing herself. It would have been more likely for Ariel to kill someone else.

Really, why *had* the killer made it so obvious? All he or she would have had to do was knock Ariel out, push her car into the pond, wait for her to drown and walk away. No one would have been the wiser.

Because the killer wanted everyone to know?

The thought sent a chill up her spine. That she probably knew this killer was creepy enough. She'd been close enough to Ariel that she had a pretty good idea of whom she'd hung around with. The logical assumption would be that the killer was one of the classmates Ariel had bullied. But Lizzy wasn't ruling out anyone at this point.

Right now some of the suspects were together, probably talking about Ariel and her death at the reunion meeting. Ahead, she saw the turnoff to the Sterling Ranch and slowed.

The Sterlings had two ranches: Sterling's Montana Guest Ranch, high in the mountains, an isolated secluded summer guest resort; and the main ranch where they raised cattle down in the valley. While the reunion was planned at the resort in the mountains, the meeting was being held at the home ranch in the valley—not far from where Ariel's car was found.

Lizzy wasn't disappointed as she pulled in and saw vehicles belonging to those she now considered as some of her prime suspects. At the front door, she tapped her knuckles on the wood but didn't wait for an answer before walking in. After all, this was Montana. No one locked doors. Or at least they hadn't always. With the valley growing, the small town's once low crime rate was increasing.

She walked in through the foyer to the edge of the living room and stopped to take in the classmates already gathered without them being aware of her presence.

Ashley Houston and Stephanie Curtis Tanner, blond, blue-eyed and dressed all the way up, were seated on the couch together. Tyler Brent had taken a chair some distance away and so had Kayla Harrison. Short and stout, Kayla had dyed black chin-length straight hair and still wore all black as if she hadn't given up her Goth days in high school. Tyler, in his usual khakis, button-down shirt and loafers, looked bored. Both had been tormented by Ariel in her own special way, while Ashley and Stephanie had been her BFFs, along with Jennifer Fox.

Lizzy was a little surprised that Jennifer wasn't here. Maybe the trio was no longer as close as it had been in high school. They'd been Ariel's best friends before Lizzy had come along.

There was a tray of coffee and tea along with a plate of sugar cookies on the coffee table in the middle of everyone. Standing next to the large brick fireplace was Shade. He was wearing what he had been earlier when he'd stopped by her office, a plaid Western shirt, jeans and boots.

She remembered the way the shirt had stretched across his broad shoulders. She could almost still smell the fresh outdoorsy scent of him. He seemed to be watching the others with interest. No one had apparently heard her come in so she held back at the edge of the room to observe.

"How were the cookies?" Ashley was saying with a laugh as she motioned to the small crumb-filled plate in Kayla's lap. Kayla quickly dropped the cookie she'd been eating on her plate.

"Did I hear everyone brought photographs?" Stephanie asked Shade. "Do you want help going through them?"

He shook his head. "I'm going to edit them later up at the guest ranch for the slideshow."

Ashley turned to Kayla. "You got Ariel's?"

Kayla looked startled to have everyone's attention on her, clearly still uncomfortable even after ten years out of high school to find herself in the spotlight. "You asked me to call her mother and I did. I went up there yesterday before…before they found her." Her voice broke. "It was really sad. Her mother told me and Jennifer that she hoped Ariel would hear about our class reunion."

"Jennifer was there?" Stephanie asked sounding surprised.

"She and Ariel's mom were going through some of Ariel's things," Kayla said. "Catherine said she hoped that her daughter could come home for the reunion."

"She kind of did," Ashley said. "Just in time."

"She always did love making an entrance and

being the center of attention," Stephanie said under her breath.

"Can you believe it?" Tyler said, dropping his voice as if in respect for the dead. "I heard that it wasn't an accident. Someone *killed* Ariel. Tied her to her steering wheel and probably watched her drown." He pretended to shudder. "Can you imagine?"

Lizzy swore silently. Of course all aspects of the case had gotten leaked. She bet she could thank Brad for that.

"Who do you think did it?" Ashley whispered and looked across at the two young women huddled in front of the cookies.

They all glanced around the room at each other. Kayla seemed to realize that most of them were looking at her. Her eyes wide, like a deer caught in headlights, she cried, "Why are you all looking at me? How would I know who killed her? *You* were her friends."

"I wouldn't go that far," Tyler said. "I just did my best to stay off her radar."

Ashley glanced at Shade with an expression Lizzy recognized. She felt her stomach roil. The look was conspiratorial, as if they alone shared some secret.

Shade didn't return the glance. "Sorry, all I know is that I had nothing to do with it." Out of the corner of his eye, he must have seen Lizzy. Or sensed her.

He shifted his gaze to where she was standing at the edge of the room in her sheriff's department uniform—cowboy boots, tan shirt and pants, Western hat and star. Most of the men in the sheriff's department wore jeans instead of standard issue cotton trousers. But today, Lizzy had wanted to be dressed in her full uniform for her first day on the job.

He smiled as if glad to see her. She felt the heat of his look and shifted her gaze away from those blue eyes of his. She'd often wondered if he remembered their kiss the night of the graduation party. From the look he'd just given her, he did.

While Shade had seen her, the rest were still oblivious, giving her the opportunity to continue studying them unnoticed.

"Too bad you didn't do it, Shade," Ashley said. "You had good reason from what Ariel told us. Of course, so did a lot of other people in our class."

"Yourself included," Stephanie said.

Ashley looked over at Stephanie as if shocked she'd say that. "Why are you looking at *me*?" Her hand went to her hair. It was long again after Ariel had insisted she get it cut because long hair made her look haggard.

"Feeling a little paranoid?" Tyler asked and laughed.

"She fat-shamed you enough, Steph, that I'd think you wouldn't be that sad to hear she's gone," Ashley snapped. "Not to mention the hard time she gave you, Kayla, for your…habits."

Kayla's face burned with heat. She picked up her cookie from the plate and took a bite, eyes downcast.

"It wasn't just us," Tyler said, jumping into the fray. "Ariel gave everyone a hard time, including Christopher, Josh and especially Brad. Can you imagine what he's going to write about her in his newspaper?" He glanced over at Kayla and Shade. "There isn't a person in this room who's missed her these past ten years," he said and waited for someone to argue the point. No one did.

"So should we talk about the reunion?" Stephanie said with a sigh. "Or should we just cancel it?"

"Maybe we should consider either canceling it or at least postponing it," Kayla said, without looking up.

"She makes a good point," Tyler said. "Ariel's death changes everything."

"Ariel's murder, you mean," Stephanie added.

Ashley gave them all a shocked look. "Why would we cancel our plans? Just because of Ariel? She ran our lives when she was alive and now we're going to let her come back from the grave to do it? No way. I say we go ahead with our plans. Anyway, it's what Ariel would have wanted."

Stephanie let out a bitter laugh. "Seriously? I thought we didn't care about what Ariel would want?"

"It seems…disrespectful," Kayla said in a small voice.

"She's dead," Stephanie said a little too flippantly.

"We were her only friends," Ashley cried. Ashley, Stephanie and Jennifer. Three Barbie Dolls, Lizzy thought, all so much alike, all best friends.

So where was Jennifer? It seemed odd that she wasn't here. Maybe they hadn't all stayed friends. Lizzy was noticing the fissures between at least two of them as they began to disagree because of Ariel. It amazed Lizzy how Ariel could still wreak such havoc in their lives.

"What will people say if we don't do something to remember her?" Ashley protested.

"They'll say what they're already thinking," Stephanie said. "That one of us killed her. She might be gone, but—"

"She's not forgotten," Shade added and everyone seemed to notice that he was no longer looking in the group's direction. Instead, his intent gaze was on the edge of the room—and Lizzy.

"Well, look who it is," Ashley said with a laugh. "Our new sheriff. Come here to interrogate us?" Her laugh held little humor. "Or are you here to arrest one of us?"

OH, JUST LOOK at all of them down there taking pleasure in my death. Nothing like your best friends. At least now I finally know what they really thought of me. I almost feel as if I wasn't missed. I guess this means that any tears shed at my funeral will be crocodile ones. It would hurt my feelings if I wasn't already dead.

Still, with our ten-year high school class reunion this weekend, I'm looking forward to seeing everyone again. How perfect that my former boyfriend Shade Sterling is hosting the event at his family's guest ranch. The number one suspect in my murder. Don't you love it?

While I can't be there in person, trust me, I'll be there in spirit. Get it? They'll all be looking at each

*other, speculating on who hated me more. Who hated
me enough to do what they only dreamed of doing. But
I know something they don't. Some secrets just can't
be buried deep enough.*

*I would love to see my killer get what's coming. I
hate the way we left things that night after the graduation party.*

*But I hate even more that I'm depending on Lizzy
to make that happen.*

LIZZY REMOVED HER Western hat as she took in her former classmates. She was glad that she'd gotten those
few minutes to study them before they'd become aware
of her presence. It had been years and yet, seeing them
together again had taken her back to high school in
the snap of her fingers. It also made her sick to her
stomach to realize the effect Ariel had had on everyone in this room.

"Just stopped by to see how the reunion was going,"
she told the group, even though it was Shade who had
her attention.

"We're going ahead with it," Ashley said as if it had
been decided. "It's what Ariel would have wanted."

"And we're so worried about what Ariel would have
wanted," Stephanie said and took a cookie.

Lizzy didn't doubt that Ariel would have loved the
attention at the reunion as everyone speculated on who
had killed her and watched each other warily. "Are
you sure that's what the others would want? I'd think

this would put a damper on the reunion knowing that one of you might have killed her."

Ashley laughed. "I suspect it will give the reunion some excitement that would have been lacking otherwise."

"Especially if one of us killed her and that person isn't done killing," Tyler said and laughed.

"Tyler, you're such an ass," Stephanie said. "If you're trying to scare us—"

"It's been ten years," Ashley said. "What killer waits ten years to take his next victim?"

"One waiting for the perfect opportunity—like all of you in one place," Tyler said. "Just like on graduation night at the party. Or maybe the killer was waiting for his or her first victim to be found."

"Stephanie's right," Shade said to Tyler. "Put a sock in it."

Tyler laughed and mugged at face at Ashley. "Just saying that I would be more comfortable with the reunion after Ariel's murderer was behind bars. I don't trust any of you."

"But that could take years, or maybe never be solved," Ashley said, then quickly added, "No offense to your abilities, Lizzy. But we all know how slow the wheels of justice can be."

"You're right," Lizzy agreed. "Finding out the truth could take time. So we all need to be patient. But at least with us all together at the reunion, I'll get the opportunity to question each of you—if I don't get to question you before then. Someone might remember something from that night that will help me find the killer."

Ashley clapped her hands together. "Once we're all together, we can help solve the crime. We'll find the killer for you," she said and laughed. "After all, it might have been ten years ago, but we knew each other really well since it was such a small class."

"Isn't that the truth," Kayla said, sounding not the least happy about it.

Lizzy groaned. They all seemed to want to play detective. The reunion definitely could get interesting if they all turned on each other.

"Fine," she said. "I guess I'll see you all at our reunion." She gave Shade a nod. He gave her a grin. She turned to leave.

"Should she be investigating Ariel's murder?" she heard Stephanie whisper as Lizzy started to leave the room. "I mean if anyone wanted Ariel dead..."

Lizzy turned to look back at the woman who'd spoken. "Is there something you want to say, Steph?"

Her former classmate shook her head adamantly. "I'm good."

"Like I said, I'm going to try to stop by to question each of you about graduation night and your relationship with Ariel before the reunion if there is time." With that Lizzy left. She'd known that it had only been a matter of time before someone questioned her investigation of the case—she hadn't just known Ariel. She'd been in her immediate circle.

She could recuse herself but she didn't have an undersheriff at the moment with Ward Farnsworth in jail awaiting his trial for the hit-and-run of the former sheriff. DCI would be doing all of the forensics work and the prosecuting attorney would be watching over her shoulder like a hawk.

Lizzy told herself that if anyone could find Ariel's killer, it was her. And maybe that was why the killer might want her off the case. She knew all her classmates but not like she'd known Ariel.

So until someone forced her to step aside, she was going to investigate this case come hell or high water.

CHAPTER FOUR

As LIZZY WALKED out to her patrol SUV parked in front of the Sterling ranch house, the reality of the situation seemed to finally sink in. Ariel was dead. She'd been dead since the night of their high school graduation party. For ten years she'd been in her SUV at the bottom of the pond.

Lizzy shuddered, still having trouble dealing with how cold-blooded the killing had been. For ten years, she'd imagined Ariel taking off that night, angry and drunk and probably planning her disappearance—if she hadn't been planning it for weeks.

Her father had just been indicted for misuse of campaign funds. Her mother was said to have gone to a spa for an extended stay for nerves. It would be just like Ariel to make an exit that would have everyone wondering and worrying about what had happened to her. Lizzy had figured that if anyone loved being a mystery, it was Ariel.

Never had Lizzy dreamed that her nemesis was so close by. Sitting behind the wheel of her precious SUV all these years under fifteen feet of water as her body turned to pond scum. She hated to think of what

Ariel's last tortured moments had been like as water rushed in and the vehicle sank.

"Lizzy, wait up."

Startled from her thoughts, she turned as Shade came loping out of the house after her. Even against both her better judgment and her professional one, she couldn't help the small thrill she felt every time she saw him. The handsome cowboy grinned at her as he came to a stop just inches away.

"I was hoping you wouldn't get away before I caught you," he said.

"Is something wrong? Did they change their minds and decide to cancel the reunion?"

He shook his head, a worried look replacing the grin. "The reunion is still on, but there's something you should know. I just found out from Ashley that Ariel had told her she was pregnant. With my child."

Lizzy felt her eyes widen in surprise.

He rushed on quickly. "It wasn't mine. I know that for a fact, but no one knew that Ariel and I hadn't been together for months so they were more apt to believe it when she told them we were getting married. I guess the scene she made breaking up with me was to make me look bad when everyone found out about the pregnancy."

Lizzy knew that Shade was telling the truth. Ariel had been furious at Shade and made excuses for why the two of them weren't spending any time together during those months. As far as Lizzy knew, they'd only seen each other at school. Ariel had tried to convince her that they were fine, that they often got together late at night because they were so busy otherwise. Lizzy had known she was lying and she knew why.

"Whose baby do you think—?" she began.

"I don't know. I thought maybe you might know."

She shook her head. "I'm as surprised as you must have been."

He nodded. "I have no idea how far along she was or if any of this is even true. I figured if she went to the doctor…"

Lizzy saw where he was headed. "There would be a record." Maybe even blood had been taken. Not that there was any chance of getting DNA since, if true, the killer hadn't just killed Ariel but the child she was carrying, as well. "Do you think her mother knew?"

He shrugged and met her gaze. "I was thinking that if she really was pregnant, the father of the baby might have a motive for murder."

"Unless he was in love with her and wanted to marry her."

Shade chuckled and looked toward the mountains. "I suppose anything is possible." Neither of them could see anyone actually wanting to marry Ariel. Not the young woman they knew anyway.

"I have a lot of people to interview before and during the reunion," she said. "But at some point, I'm going to need to ask you some questions about that night."

"Sure," he said and smiled. "Whenever. Just give me a holler. I'll help in any way I can. You look cold."

He took a step closer, blocking the wind with his body. The October breeze had a bite to it and he'd run out without a coat, but he was worried about her getting cold. That was the Shade Sterling she knew.

"I'm taking the photographs up to the guest ranch today if you need to talk to me," he said. "Call the landline. Or come on up. It will just be me up there." He suddenly looked embarrassed. "That didn't come out right." He shook his head. "Just trying to help."

She laughed. "I appreciate that."

He stood there, his hands in the front pockets of his jeans, looking so adorable that for a moment she wanted to kiss him like he had her ten years ago at their graduation party.

She felt a pull toward this man that felt stronger than gravity and had to remind herself that Shade was a suspect. "I should go."

He nodded, but neither of them moved.

"Tell me you haven't thought about me at least once in the past ten years," he said, looking almost shy. "I sure as hell have thought about you."

She opened her mouth to deny it, but then closed her lips again.

He grinned. "That's what I was hoping. And I do love a woman in a uniform."

"Shade—"

His blue eyes locked with hers. "I know, I'm a suspect in your investigation. But come on, Lizzy, there's no way you suspect me. Admit it."

"Shade—"

"Okay," he said, still grinning. "But when your investigation is over…"

She smiled and turned toward her rig. As she did, she saw that Ashley was watching them from the window. "You'd better get back inside. It appears you were missed."

SHADE STOOD FOR a moment, watching Lizzy drive away before he went back inside. What was there about that woman that made him feel like a teenager again? He was thinking about her as he came into the house on a gust of cold air to find Ashley waiting for him.

"The temperature is dropping. We'll be lucky if it doesn't snow before we even get to the lodge this weekend," he predicted.

"What's with you and Lizzy?"

He laughed at the way she skipped niceties without any hesitation. "Let's see," he said as if he had to think about it. "After ten years of everyone thinking I had something to do with Ariel's disappearance, now it turns out that she was murdered. I'm probably Lizzy's number one suspect. So what do you think is with us?"

Ashley cocked her head, studying him. "She told you that? That you're her number one suspect?" She scoffed. "Don't try to kid me. Ariel told me that Lizzy had a crush on you and that she couldn't be trusted."

Shade let out a huff. "Ariel knew darn well that I was the one with the crush on Lizzy. She did everything possible to keep us apart."

"Sounds like a motive for murder."

He chuckled. "There's a lot of those going around. For instance, I know you and Ariel were on the outs at the graduation party that night. Is it true she hounded you until you cut your hair short?"

Ashley immediately looked irritated. "She didn't make me do anything I didn't want to do."

"Right," he said with an eye roll.

"If you're suggesting that I killed her because of a haircut—"

"You left pretty quickly after she did the night of the graduation party," Shade said.

Ashley shook her head. "If you must know, I got a text from her to meet her, but she never showed." When he said nothing, she stomped a foot in frustration. "*I didn't kill her.* I might have been her only friend at the end." She waved a hand through the air as if to signal that she was through with that particular discussion. "I want to do something special at the reunion for her, no matter what the others say. Any ideas?"

"A dartboard with her picture on it?" he joked. "Or is that too close to the truth?"

Lizzy WAS THINKING about what Shade had told her on her way back to the office. Had Ariel really been pregnant? If so, then who was the father? Another one of Ariel's secrets, *if* true. She parked and started toward the sheriff's office.

A female reporter suddenly came running across the

lawn and stepped in her path, shoving a microphone into her face. Belatedly, Lizzy saw the news van parked on the street nearby. She'd been so lost in thought that she hadn't noticed either the woman or the van or the man with the large camera now aimed at her.

"Sheriff, you must be shocked. What can you tell us about Ariel Matheson's murder?"

"It's under investigation," Lizzy said. "That's all at this time." She tried to step past the woman.

"You knew the deceased better than anyone, I'm told," the reporter said, blocking her way. "What was Ariel Matheson like?"

She was the kind of person who if she saw a tiny hole in the stitching along the edge of your couch, she would stick her finger in it. She would do that every time she came over until she'd ripped it wide-open. Ariel loved to find your flaws and pick at them, never letting you forget them but in a seemingly kind, helpful manner that at first fooled you.

"She was like any other high school girl," Lizzy told the reporter. Not her first lie.

Ariel had been like a dazzling spotlight. If she beamed in on someone, there was no turning away. It was as if you were under a spell. Lizzy knew only too well. Get too close though and you were going to get burned. She knew that better than anyone.

"IF SHE SETS her sights on you, run," Whitney Clark had warned her. "She'll draw you in with flattery and kill you with kindness. But if you cross her... I used

to be her best friend. Now she acts as if I'm wearing
camo and she just can't see me."

Ariel had quickly stepped in and pulled Lizzy away.
"You don't want to get in with the wrong kind," Ariel
had told her. "Whitney has...let's just say problems
with the truth and has been known to suddenly turn
violent. Don't worry, my friends and I won't let anything happen to you."

Lizzy had been flattered when Ariel chose to be
her friend. She'd felt honored to be a part of that
circle. To be in the glow of Ariel's personality. She
didn't realize that the popular girl had set her sights
on her. Whitney had tried to warn her again. When
Lizzy told her that she still wanted to be her friend as
well as friends with Ariel, Whitney had wanted nothing to do with her.

"She's toxic. She's already done a number on me. If
she thought that I even tried to warn you about her..."
Whitney had walked away and from that point on, kept
her distance, not even hanging out with Kayla, also an
outsider. It wasn't long after that Whitney was killed
in the hit-and-run accident.

IT MADE NO sense to Lizzy why Ariel had chosen her
back then. Now she knew that the calculating young
woman had seen a vulnerability in her. She'd seen
someone she could control. She'd come after her and
it hadn't taken long at all before Lizzy found herself
not just under Ariel's spell but her thumb.

"This must have been a horrible shock," the reporter prodded.

"Of course it was a shock."

"But more so for you to realize that your best friend has been dead after all this time."

"Ariel had lots of friends," Lizzy said. "I was just one of many. I'm sure they're all shocked."

"Her mother gave us some photos of Ariel. The one with the two of you has the words *best friends forever* written on it," the reporter said, following Lizzy to the front door of the sheriff's office.

She reiterated what she'd said before about Ariel having many friends.

"Not according to her other friends I've spoken with," the reporter said. "They all say that you were her favorite."

Lizzy cursed silently, knowing only too well who had told the reporter such nonsense. Ashley. She'd seen right away that Ashley had been jealous; Lizzy had been Ariel's pet project from the beginning. Stephanie, Jennifer and Ashley had resented her and made little secret about it.

At one point she'd overheard Stephanie say, *Ariel will tire of her soon and toss her back to the dumpies*, which was what Ariel called Whitney and Kayla.

Having had more than enough of this pushy reporter, Lizzy tried to get to the door of her office. "Ariel had a talent for collecting people. She treated all of her best friends the same." She pitted them against each other, chewed them up and spit them out.

"Everyone I've talked to said you two were inseparable your senior year in high school," the reporter
said, trotting alongside her.

Inseparable was definitely the right word. By senior year, Lizzy no longer had a life of her own without Ariel. They went everywhere together because
Ariel wouldn't take no for an answer. She would pull
up in front of the house and honk until Lizzy came
out. Ariel always insisted on driving. It wasn't until
later that Lizzy realized Ariel wanted to dictate what
time they left and who got to come along as well as
how long they stayed out.

The real trouble began when Lizzy tried to distance
herself from Ariel. Ariel wasn't having it. She would
buy her something, something that she knew Lizzy
wanted. Then Lizzy would feel guilty. All Ariel's other
friends seemed to adore her. They talked about how
thoughtful and generous she was.

Lizzy began to cringe when Ariel would come up
to her in the lunchroom, throw her arm around her and
practically drag her to her table. The more she started
to pull away, the more expensive the gifts Ariel gave
her—always in front of others. If Lizzy saw something
at the mall that she paid even the slightest attention
to, Ariel would surprise her with it.

She begged her to stop since she couldn't afford to
reciprocate. She tried turning down the gifts and only
looked ungrateful and mean. Ariel would act hurt and
confused as if she didn't know what was going on.
But there would be that warning look in her eyes—

The threat was clear. Ariel traded in secrets. If someone didn't want a secret revealed to the world, then do as told or else. If not, things would turn ugly. Ariel began bad-mouthing her behind her back. There were whispered accusations. Lizzy had foolishly pleaded with Ariel to stop.

I miss you, Ariel would pout. *We never talk or hang out anymore. I don't know what's going on with you but I don't want to lose you as a trusted friend.*

The harassment didn't stop. Ariel would post things on social media about her and then deny it.

"You have to stop reacting," her aunt had told her, shoving the book *The Gift of Fear* into her hands. "She won't stop until you do. It's all in this book, under stalkers."

Lizzy had just wanted to graduate and put high school and Ariel behind her. She'd already decided that she was going into criminology. Just a few more weeks, she'd told herself as graduation neared. It was almost over. Then maybe she and Shade...

Now she had to admit guiltily that she'd been relieved when Ariel disappeared right after graduation night. The only time she'd even thought about her over the past ten years was in passing. She'd wondered whom the woman was luring into her web and if Ariel had left a trail of victims through the years.

Lizzy had thought that no one could hate Ariel as much as she did back then. But when she'd looked into that car and had seen the restraints still tied to the steering wheel, she'd been proved wrong. Someone had hated her enough to kill her in a horrible way.

"One more question," the reporter said, having walked backward all the way to the front door of the sheriff's office, the cameraman right beside her.

"That's all I have to say." Lizzy tried to step past her.

Again the woman blocked her way. "Is it true that you and Ariel's boyfriend were cheating behind her back?"

Taken off guard, she answered, "No, it's not."

"You don't deny that you know Shade Sterling, right?"

Lizzy realized the mistake she'd made. She should have stuck with her original statement of not talking. She shoved the camera out of her face as she leaned toward the reporter. "If you push that microphone into my face and block my way into the sheriff's department again," Lizzy said quietly, "I will be forced to have you arrested."

The woman blinked and started to ask another question.

"I wouldn't try me on this unless you want to spend the night in my jail."

With that she shoved her way past the woman and into the building. "Make sure the reporters stay on the sidewalk," she told the deputy coming down the hallway and saw Sid sitting in a chair as if waiting for her. She motioned him into her office and closed the door behind him with a sigh.

"I was in the neighborhood and thought I'd see if you wanted to skip out and grab a bite of lunch. Are you all right?" Sid asked.

Lizzy shook her head as she moved to the chair behind her desk. "I shouldn't have talked to that reporter, huh?"

He shrugged and she noticed that he still hadn't sat down.

"Why do I get the feeling that you're here with more bad news?"

"I saw your live interview on my phone just now," Sid said, making her grimace.

"That bad, was it?"

He chuckled. "Not bad for your first. Best advice I can give, tell them no comment and stick with it. They won't like it, but otherwise…"

"Right, otherwise you dig yourself in deeper, which I did."

"There was a theme to her questions," Sid said. "I happened to see the county attorney earlier. He expressed the same concerns."

She frowned. "That I can't do my job because I went to school with Ariel? Or that it's rumored I was her best friend, which isn't true. She had no real friends."

The former sheriff eyed her. "I believe it's that attitude that has the county attorney worried. What bothers me, though, is that someone put the bee under his bonnet, which leads me to believe that someone wants you off this case."

Lizzy groaned. "Is this political? Or something else?"

Her former mentor shrugged. "If I had to guess? I'd say whoever is spreading the unrest doesn't want you on the case *because* you're so close to it you're going to solve this and unmask a killer."

She hesitated. "They think I might have inside information? That I know too much about Ariel and who had reason to hate her?"

"This is a high-profile case for all the wrong reasons."

"Ariel's father."

"That," Sid said. "And the spoiled rich girl made enemies. Is the sheriff too close to all of it? You know, can you see the forest for the trees?"

"I'm not too close to it." She met his gaze, held it and did her best not to falter. "This is my first case on my first day on the job. I don't want to stand aside. I can do this because I did know Ariel and at least some of her secrets. I also know all of the people who might have wanted to kill her."

He nodded. "And very possibly the person who did. Just don't become part of the story. You have to keep your hands clean. Let everyone else roll around in the mud that's going to get slung."

Lizzy wondered if that was possible. It wouldn't just be other people's secrets that might come out during the investigation. What about her own?

Sid stood. "I have faith in you."

She had to smile as she thanked him. "Maybe lunch some other time?"

He nodded. She considered telling him about some of her worries about the case but changed her mind. She was sheriff. This was up to her to figure things out without Sid's help.

"And watch your back. The one deputy who ran against you?"

She knew at once whom he was referring to. "John 'Ace' Turner."

He nodded. "He just got beat by a woman who he feels is much less deserving than him. That could make him…"

"Angry?" she asked and laughed.

Sid met her gaze. "Dangerous."

CHAPTER FIVE

LIZZY HAD TWO more days in which to try to find out as much as she could about Ariel's murder before the reunion.

The name Progressive made it sound as if their school was an academy for gifted and talented children. Some of the students definitely were. But others needed that smaller, more controlled environment because they'd been in trouble at other schools.

Lizzy had been having a hard time at the end of her junior year. Several of her close friends at the public school had moved away and she'd felt adrift. That's when Gertie had heard about the school and its smaller classes and decided Lizzy should try it.

Gertie had hoped there would be fewer distractions at the small private school. Lizzy could laugh about that now. Ariel had been more than a distraction. Not to mention Shade and her feelings for him her senior year.

The cost of being Ariel's friend had been high, making her wonder what price the others had had to pay for Ariel's brand of friendship.

First, Lizzy had visited Ariel's mother to give her

condolences. Catherine Matheson Warner had remarried after divorcing her imprisoned husband. She'd left town for a while and had only recently returned.

Lizzy had asked about Ariel's personal items that had apparently been boxed up. Catherine had given her several containers that she'd gone through, but Lizzy had found nothing interesting. Certainly nothing about Ariel being pregnant.

Lizzy decided she would start her interviews with those closest to Ariel. Ashley was at the top of her list. The petite, cute, blue-eyed blonde hadn't changed all that much since high school from what Lizzy had seen earlier. With the reunion committee meeting over, she thought she'd pay the woman a visit.

Ashley answered the door in a short romper. Her hair was pulled up in a high ponytail. Lizzy got the impression that Ashley had been expecting someone else. The woman's eyes widened as she looked past Lizzy to the street before giving her a nervous smile. "I wasn't expecting…company."

Uh-huh. "Good, since I'm not company. Are you alone? I need to ask you a few questions about Ariel's death."

Ashley jammed a hand on her slim waist and cocked a hip. "This really isn't a convenient time."

"There really isn't any convenient time with the reunion coming up so quickly," Lizzy said. "We can talk here or maybe you'd like to come down to the sheriff's department to talk. I can have an officer swing by and pick you up."

Ashley's smile evaporated. Her blue eyes narrowed as she straightened. "You've changed since high school."

"I certainly hope so," Lizzy said and stepped forward, forcing Ashley to move aside and let her enter.

"I can't imagine what I could tell you about Ariel that you don't already know," her former classmate said as she led the way into an immaculate living room.

Lizzy wanted to laugh since she was sure that Ariel had something on all of her friends—and vice versa. "Are you telling me you haven't speculated on who might have killed her?" she said as she sat down in one of the chairs and pulled out her notebook and pen.

Ashley shrugged and slowly took a seat, glancing at her cell phone as she did. Lizzy realized that the woman had just sent a short text on her way into the living room. To warn whomever was on their way?

Lizzy glanced around the living room. It looked unlived in. Ashley's husband, Lizzy knew, was a commercial pilot who was seldom home. "Is your husband coming to the reunion?"

Ashley shook her head. "He has overseas flights this week. Just the luck of the draw."

Lizzy got the feeling Ashley wasn't upset that her husband couldn't make it. Not that spouses or significant others were invited the first day of the reunion. Families could come up Sunday for a barbecue and hayride, but since most of the class was still single, they wanted to keep it just the ten of them the first night and day.

"There must be someone you think was capable of murdering Ariel," Lizzy prodded.

Ashley laughed. "You were in our class. None of us were angels or we wouldn't have been at Progressive." She narrowed her eyes and cocked her head in a way that Lizzy had seen Ariel do a thousand times. "What about you, Lizzy? What got you sent there?"

She smiled. "I'm not the one being questioned by the law."

"Maybe you should be."

"Don't worry, the state crime investigators will take care of that part. In the meantime, why don't you tell me why *you* were sent to the school?"

Ashley shrugged. "I thought everyone knew. I broke into the public high school with Christopher and got caught."

Lizzy knew it was more than that. "Why break in?"

"Just for the fun of it."

"Did you vandalize the place?" She'd heard the stories.

"Only Mrs. Brandon thought so because of what we did on her desk." Ashley laughed. "It was harmless."

"You were the only one caught?"

"That time," Ashley said and mugged a face. "Christopher could run faster than me. He tried it again with someone else." Her eyes were bright with spite. "That time he got caught red-handed, so to speak."

"He got caught with Jennifer."

Ashley nodded slowly, eyes narrowing to slits. An old wound that hadn't quite healed.

"Then Christopher ended up at the same school with the two of you—and Ariel," Lizzy said. "I got the feeling that you all had some kind of history."

Ashley shrugged. "Ariel and Christopher, definitely. I always suspected there was more to their animosity toward each other. The two of them were like oil and water."

"You know what they say about opposites. Do you remember seeing Christopher at the party after Ariel left?" Lizzy asked.

"I saw him talking to you."

"That was before Ariel actually drove away."

Ashley shrugged again. "Sorry. I'm afraid I'm not much help."

Lizzy realized that she'd been assuming that whoever killed Ariel left the party at the same time, followed her and had somehow gotten her to turn off into the pond road.

A thought occurred to her. As upset as she'd been, Ariel would have contacted someone because she would have needed to vent. Lizzy had been on the receiving end of those phone calls many times—until Ariel showed up in person or demanded that Lizzy meet her somewhere to talk.

"Did you hear from Ariel after the party?"

"Just one text as she was leaving," Ashley said. "She wanted to meet up and talk."

Lizzy felt a small thrill. Of course, she'd been right.

Who knew Ariel better than her? "She was upset, right?"

Ashley nodded.

"With me."

Another nod, this one slower.

"And Shade."

Ashley looked away. "She was furious, but mostly with you," she added as her gaze came back to Lizzy. "She said you were a traitor and that we weren't to ever speak to you again." She raised an eyebrow, her lips curving into a snide smirk as if proving that even years later, those old insults could still hurt.

None of this came as a surprise though. Much of the sting had been taken out of it by the years and maturity. But that Ariel wielded such power back then and could strike out so easily made Lizzy suspect that Ariel's killer had been on the receiving end of her vindictiveness more than once.

Under the law, Ashley didn't have to speak with her. Lizzy wondered if she knew that. Did the woman just want to get a few jabs in for old times' sake? "Was there anyone else she was angry with?" Lizzy asked.

The eyebrow came down, the lips untwisted from the smirk and that familiar bored look was back. "Brad."

"Brad Davis?"

"He'd parked his car right behind hers and she had to find him to get him to move it."

"There were words exchanged?"

Ashley laughed. "She called him a few names. He

threatened to use some awful photo of her he'd taken at the party in the last school newspaper of the year. The newspaper at Progressive was a joke anyway, like anyone read it, but you know Ariel."

She did know Ariel. The young woman would have been livid.

"So he moved his car." Lizzy realized that other than the killer, Brad might have been the last one to see her alive. Unless, after he'd moved his car, he was so furious that he followed her and killed her.

"Did you see anyone follow her as she left?"

"I didn't see her leave. I just heard the argument with Brad. Her car was parked behind those pine trees beside his house. I heard her rev her engine, make the tires screech as she left before I received the text to meet her."

"Where did Ariel want to meet after the party?"

"At the cemetery."

Lizzy knew it was one of Ariel's favorite places— especially at night. Probably because Ariel knew the rest of them weren't that comfortable there. Ariel liked to sit on the steps of her family's mausoleum like she was holding court.

"So you went there. How long after Ariel's text?" If Ariel had told them to be there, Ashley, Stephanie and Jennifer would have shown up and on time if they knew what was good for them.

"She told me to tell the others and leave right away. I did."

"What time was this?"

"Eleven fifty. I know because I glanced at the time on my phone after I checked the text."

"You told the others?"

She shook her head. "I couldn't find them so I texted them."

"And when did they show up at the cemetery?"

Ashley seemed to give that some thought. "Jennifer was about twenty minutes late, said she didn't get the text right away. Stephanie was closer to forty-five minutes late."

"Do you know where they'd been?"

"At the party. At least that's what they said."

Lizzy studied Ashley. "You didn't believe them. Where did you think they'd been?"

The woman shifted on the couch. "I didn't say I didn't believe them. Maybe they *didn't* get my texts. It was loud at the party."

Or maybe one or both of them was busy tying Ariel to her steering wheel and pushing her SUV into the pond. These women lived with their phones in their hands, constantly checking them as if bored with the people around them. It seemed unlikely that they hadn't gotten the texts right away.

Lizzy chuckled to herself as Ashley proved her point by checking her phone before standing.

"I really have to go."

Lizzy put away her notebook and pen and rose, as well. "Thanks for taking the time to answer my questions."

Ashley shrugged as if to say she had nothing to hide.

"One more thing. How long did you all stay at the cemetery before you realized that Ariel wasn't going to show?"

"Until a little after two."

"That long?" She wondered if one or more of them had known Ariel wasn't going to show, but had to sit there and pretend otherwise. "Were you worried about her?"

Ashley rolled her eyes. "It was Ariel. It would have been just like her to run into someone and change her mind and not bother to tell us."

Ariel would have enjoyed making them wait at the cemetery for her, knowing that they were uncomfortable but that they would do as she asked.

"What did Ariel have on you?" Lizzy asked, making the young woman start.

"I don't know what you're talking about. Ariel and I were friends. You had more reason to want to kill her than I did. But Shade had even more reason. She was having his baby and he wasn't happy about it."

"Did she tell you that?"

"She told me everything." Ashley met her gaze and held it with a hard one of her own. "Shade isn't as innocent as you think." The woman's gaze slid away. "I really have things to do. If we're done here?"

As Lizzy left, she realized two things. Depending on whether or not forensics could establish a time of death, the three friends had given themselves an alibi from after midnight until two in the morning. But before that, their whereabouts were questionable since

Lizzy didn't remember seeing either Jennifer or Stephanie at the party about the time Ariel left.

The second thing that struck her was that Ashley could have lied about the text from Ariel. She could have established her own alibi. Phone companies were required to keep phone records for at least five years for tax purposes. But ten years? Maybe she would get lucky.

She felt a chill as she had a disturbing thought. Even if the text really had been sent from Ariel's phone, it didn't mean that she was the one who'd sent it. By then she could have been in the pond. Which would mean the killer could have sent it. To establish their own alibi?

Lizzy wondered how long it would take to subdue Ariel enough to bind her to the steering wheel and push her car into the lake. She assumed the killer would want to wait until the car sank—just to be safe. Or for more morbid, cruel reasons.

But all of that could have happened within thirty to forty-five minutes. The killer wouldn't even have had to get her hands dirty.

As Lizzy drove away, though, she kept thinking about what Ashley had said about Shade.

I DON'T THINK I ever realized what Ashley was truly like—until now. I knew she was a liar and that she had a daddy complex when it came to men, but I never realized what a mean woman she could be. She actually

rivals me in that department, which makes me won-
der what she was saying about me behind my back.

*Not that I mind her giving the sheriff a hard time.
I would have done the same thing. What's interesting
is that Lizzy is smarter than I thought she was. Better at her job, too. That surprises me. Maybe she can
find my killer before it's too late.*

Or not.

*Let's face it, my killer has gotten away with my
murder for more than ten years. What am I saying? No
one even knew I was dead. That was brilliant, dumping me in the pond. Was I supposed to have been found
sooner than now? Or did my killer just get lucky?*

*It's just a matter of time before the sheriff inter-
views them all. Will she sense which ones have the
most to lose? Which ones have the most to hide? Or
will they all fool her and my killer will still be walking around free while I'm...dead.*

STEPHANIE HAD TO have known that the sheriff would
be stopping by, but she still seemed shocked to see
her. Because of the hour, Lizzy knew she could catch
her at home—and off guard.

Stephanie had married Eric Tanner, the local dentist—a man known for his punctuality. He arrived
at work each morning at the same time, closed his
one-man office every weekday at noon to go home
for lunch, and left a sign on the outer door saying he
would be back at one sharp and he was. He always
left at exactly 4:45 in the afternoon.

Since it was 12:45, Lizzy was pretty certain that she would catch Eric leaving the house for his walk to his office. Stephanie would be cleaning up their lunch dishes.

As she started to ring the doorbell, Eric came out. He was a balding thirtysomething with a slight paunch but a set of perfect, brilliantly white teeth that he flashed when he saw her.

"I'm looking for Stephanie," Lizzy said.

"You definitely came to the right place," Eric said. "She's just inside the kitchen. Go on in."

She did, wandering through the house as she followed the clink of silverware and plates going into the dishwasher.

"Eric told me to come on in," she said at the edge of the kitchen.

Stephanie jumped, dropping one of the glasses. Fortunately, it landed in the dishwasher unbroken.

"Sorry, didn't mean to scare you."

Stephanie continued arranging the dirty dishes in the washer, adding detergent and closing it before she turned around. She was a strawberry blonde with blue eyes. Her hair had darkened some since high school, but her eyes were still that intense blue. The skin around them was lined now as if she'd spent the past ten years staring into the sun.

Leaning against the kitchen counter, Stephanie crossed her arms over her chest. "I'm not sure I want to do this."

"Answer questions about the night of the graduation party?" Lizzy asked.

"On TV they tell you not to say anything to the cops without your lawyer present." She appeared serious.

"That's your choice if you feel you need a lawyer present," Lizzy said. "But if you did, it would make me wonder what you're afraid of me finding out."

"That's just it," the woman cried. "I know nothing about what happened to Ariel."

"Then there shouldn't be a problem. You were at the party. I know that because I saw you there early on. I'm trying to establish where everyone was that night when Ariel left. You can help me by telling me where you were."

Stephanie shook her head. "I didn't see Ariel leave at all."

"You didn't hear the argument she had with Christopher?"

The young woman was either stalling or she'd merely realized that she hadn't started the dishwasher. Turning her back to Lizzy, she hit the button, then moved to the side to pick up a large red metal coffee cup with a lid. She took a sip.

"When did you leave the party, Stephanie?"

"Before ten."

"Where did you go?" Lizzy asked as she stepped to the breakfast bar directly across from the woman.

Stephanie shook her head. "I knew this was a mistake. I don't want to talk to you. I don't have to, do

I?" She put down the coffee container a little too hard. What squirted out the top definitely wasn't coffee. It smelled like vodka. Stephanie gripped the back of one of the stools at the breakfast bar, her knuckles turning white.

"I just need to establish where you were at the time of Ariel's death," Lizzy said evenly. "Establish an alibi—"

"I didn't kill her, and I don't know who did."

"Did you meet Ashley and Jennifer at the cemetery that night?"

The woman's eyes widened. "Is that what they said?"

"I understand you were almost an hour late meeting them."

Stephanie took another drink from her coffee container, her hands visibly shaking.

"If I can verify your alibi, I'll be able to scratch you off my list."

The woman clamped her lips shut in a stubborn, childish pose. Lizzy tried to recall whom Stephanie was dating back then and couldn't remember her having a steady their senior year. She'd met Eric at her dentist's office when he was interning at the end of her senior year. She'd had a crush on him but she hadn't even gone out with him yet. In fact, Lizzy realized that she couldn't remember Stephanie dating more than a couple of times their senior year—and then only at Ariel's insistence when she wanted to double-date.

"You realize that without an alibi, this moves you up my suspect list," Lizzy said.

Still Stephanie kept her lips clamped shut.

"If you have nothing to hide…" Lizzy's words trailed off. Clearly, the woman had something to hide. But murder? Stephanie was the kind of woman who freaked out if she broke a nail.

Lizzy remembered how Stephanie had suggested cancelling the reunion. She'd also been quite vocal as to how she felt about Ariel at the meeting earlier.

"If you change your mind…" Lizzy left her card on the breakfast bar and started to leave but stopped. "One more thing. Did Ariel tell you she was pregnant?"

The shock on Stephanie's face answered that question.

"I guess not. Apparently, you aren't the only one with secrets."

SHADE HAD TAKEN the photos up to the ranch, but he'd felt too antsy to do more than leave them. He told himself that he'd come back early tomorrow and get the slideshow ready to go. He thought about going through the box of prints, but he couldn't get his mind off Ariel's murder—and the sheriff.

So after barely returning to the valley ranch, he wasn't surprised when he looked up to see a patrol SUV headed his way.

"I was wondering when I'd see you again," he said as Lizzy pulled in.

"Do you have some time right now?"

He nodded and smiled. "Come on inside."

Lizzy seemed nervous as they sat down.

"Whatever it is, just ask," he said. "You seem upset."

"You didn't know about the pregnancy until today, right?"

"Right. I told you, the baby wasn't mine."

"Still, you would have been upset if you'd found out that Ariel was pregnant."

Shade sighed. "What are you getting at?"

"I saw you go after her that night as she was leaving the party. Other people saw you, as well."

He sat back. He'd been right. He *was* her number one suspect. He wondered if he needed a lawyer. "Like I told you, I didn't want her driving in the condition she was in."

"No one saw you after that," she said.

"That's because when I started back, I saw you with Christopher and I left."

"Shade, a few days after she disappeared, I saw you. You had scratches down your left cheek."

Nodding slowly, he said, "I told you that Ariel fought me when I tried to take her keys. You know what she was like."

"But I also know that Ariel would have fought her killer. You have to admit that it looks suspicious. You left the party at about the same time she did. You could have been the last person to see her alive."

"This is bullshit and you know it. The last person

who saw her alive is whoever killed her." He raked a hand through his hair. "You can't seriously consider me a suspect. You know me." He met her gaze. She held it for a moment before she looked down at her notebook again. He realized he wasn't dealing with Lizzy, the woman he'd kissed that night. He was dealing with the sheriff.

"Do you have an alibi for the time after you left?" she asked.

"I went for a drive down to Flathead Lake, pulled over and sat for a while, thinking about you and unfortunately Ariel and hoping she wasn't going to continue doing shitty things to try to keep us apart because quite frankly, I wanted to see more of you after our kiss."

He saw Lizzy swallow. "I heard about the fight you had with her a few weeks before graduation," she said.

Shade groaned inwardly. He should have known this would come up now. "I wanted out of the relationship. I had for months, but every time I started to talk to her, she wouldn't listen. That day I made her listen."

"I saw the bruise on her arm where you grabbed her."

He swore. "I grabbed her to keep her from falling off the deck of her house. She was mad and out of control..." He sighed. "When she got like that... Well, that's why I thought she'd ended up in the pond. She would get blind with rage. That day at her house, I told her it was over. She begged me not to tell anyone and spoil graduation. I said that I wouldn't announce it at school but that we were done."

"So why the scene at the graduation party?"

He let out a bark of a laugh. "Because she was Ariel Matheson and she liked to make scenes. She wanted to be the one to break up with me to save face—at least that's what I thought until Ashley told me that Ariel said she was pregnant with my child. We were already broken up so it made no sense to me when she suddenly started screaming and crying and saying it was over between us. But knowing that she might have been pregnant with someone else's baby…"

"You were angry with her. I heard you say that you wanted to wring her neck."

Shade met her gaze and slowly shook his head. "I was sick of her playacting. Everything was drama with her. She'd kept you and me apart for months because she knew I wanted to ask you out." He saw her eyes widen in surprise. "You didn't know how I felt about you?" He let out a soft chuckle that died quickly. "Ariel knew. She was crazy jealous, even though she wanted to break up with me as badly as I did her. Actually, I was pretty sure she'd been seeing someone else for months. If she really was pregnant, then that proves it."

Lizzy wrote something down in her notebook. He wanted to reach over and brush that lock of hair back from her eyes. More than anything, he wanted her to believe him.

"Come on, you know how she was," he said. "Was there anyone who didn't want to wring her neck?"

He wagged his head for a moment before meeting her gaze again. "Is that how she was killed?"

She apparently wasn't going to answer that question. "I'd never seen you as angry as you were with her at the graduation party," Lizzy said.

He sighed. "I'd been dealing with Ariel for months. I was sick of her games, sick of her mean-spirited behavior, just sick of her. I wanted her to leave me the hell alone and like I said, I suspected she was seeing someone else. I just wanted to be free of her so that I would have a chance with you."

"I guess you got your wish."

"Lizzy. You know I didn't kill her. Am I sorry she's gone for good? No. I still wouldn't wish her dead though. What we have to do is figure out who hated her worse than we did."

"Wait a minute—"

"Don't deny it. I saw how she treated you, always talking down to you, running your life. You think I don't know the way you felt about her?"

She flushed. "I didn't kill her."

"Exactly. We both had motive but we know we didn't do it. We just have to figure out who did. Practically everyone in our class had reason to hate her at one time or another. We weren't the only ones she bullied. So let's figure out who went after her that night from the party. There might be surveillance videos." He realized how unlikely that was after ten years and knew he was clutching at straws. "Or someone might remember seeing her leave with one of our classmates."

She held up a hand. "*We* aren't going to do anything. You're still a suspect and I'm still the sheriff."

He held up both hands in surrender. "Sorry. You're right. But I want to help because when this is over…" He looked into her eyes and lost himself. "I want to ask you out."

"This isn't the time to—"

"I know," he said quickly.

"And I can't have you interfering in my investigation, Shade. You need to let me do my job."

He nodded. "I wouldn't dream of keeping you from it, Sheriff." He felt the tension between them lessen. "You know, I haven't been able to think about anything but who might have done this. What if it isn't a student in our class? Remember Miss Cline?"

Lizzy smiled. "I just got a mental image. Tall, skinny, gray-haired, and always brushing cat hair and chalk off her clothing?"

"Ariel got her fired."

"True, but since she wasn't cut out to deal with students like us, she probably was relieved. Also, Shade, she was hospitalized the night of the party and died a week later. I already checked."

"People sneak out of hospitals all the time. Have you forgotten what neighbors always say when they find out they've been living next door to a killer? 'She was such a sweet old woman. Kind, loved cats, gave full-size chocolate bars to the kids on Halloween.'"

To his delight, Lizzy actually laughed. "I really doubt Miss Cline got up out of her deathbed to kill Ariel."

"Just sayin', a killer is oftentimes the person you least expect. Even the most docile can commit murder. It's like someone pushes a hidden killer button in a person, and poof."

"Poof, and Miss Cline suddenly sits up in her bed, says, 'I can't die until I take care of Ariel,' and she becomes a killer."

"Exactly," he said, enjoying this. He loved her smile and the way she would brush back a lock of her long dark hair from her forehead to reveal those deep, clear sable eyes of hers. "The only other teacher-suspect would be Coach."

"Yep, I checked on that, as well. Sorry, but he left the state right after graduation to catch a plane to Hawaii. I remember seeing him on television after his plane had to make that emergency landing. He was standing in Waikiki with palm trees and blue water behind him. Not a bad alibi. Thanks for your suggestions, but I've got this," she said as she put away her notebook and got to her feet.

"I know, Sheriff," he said as he walked her to the door, feeling a little bit better. But there was no doubt. He was still suspect number one.

CHAPTER SIX

LIZZY COULDN'T HELP smiling as she drove away. Shade was incorrigible, she thought, and noticed the time. The day had gotten away from her. She thought about working late since there was a pile of paperwork as well as more suspects to be interviewed. She could feel time running out before the reunion.

But she'd promised her aunt Gertie that she wouldn't miss dinner on her first day on the job. What she hadn't planned was to be thrown into a murder case right off the bat.

If she knew her aunt, she had cooked something special for Lizzy's first day as sheriff. She wasn't about to disappoint her aunt if she could help it. Aunt Gertrude was eighty-two, but she didn't know it, look it or act it. A tiny gray-haired woman with sparkling blue eyes, she loved to stay busy and had more irons in the fire than someone half her age.

"That smells good," Lizzy said as she walked into the kitchen to find Gertie wearing her gingham apron and singing along with the radio.

"Shepherd's pie and salad," her aunt said. "Being

your first day as sheriff, I thought you could use some comfort food."

Lizzy smiled and kissed her on the cheek. Fortunately, Gertie thought anything could be cured with a good hearty meal. Lizzy had lived with her aunt since she was a baby. As an adult, she hadn't moved out. She wanted to be there for Gertie. They looked out for each other, she thought as she set the table, pouring them both a glass of milk. Gertie swore by her glass of milk at meals.

Lizzy's phone rang. She considered not answering it, but her aunt motioned to her that she should. "Could be important."

She stepped out of the room to take the call from Deputy Turner. "There's been a break-in up at the Sterlings' guest ranch," Ace said without preamble. "A hiker saw someone moving around in the lodge."

Lizzy figured it was probably teenagers. Cabin break-ins were often a problem in the area. Usually the teens just drank any alcohol they could find and made a mess. "Have you informed the Sterlings?"

"Not yet. Wanted to check with you and see how you wanted me to handle it."

She glanced toward the kitchen where her aunt was waiting expectantly. Breathing in the wonderful smell of Gertie's shepherd's pie, she told herself that Ace probably couldn't mess this up. It sounded pretty cut-and-dried. "You handle it. Call Shade Sterling and have him meet you up there."

Hanging up, she told herself that delegating authority was also a big part of her job. She had to trust those under her, even Ace.

WHEN THE PHONE RANG, Shade was hoping it would be Lizzy. It was the sheriff's department all right.

"This is Deputy Ace Turner. I'm calling to tell you that there has been a break-in up here at your guest ranch. It was called in by a hiker in the area. He saw someone moving around inside your lodge but didn't see a vehicle. Decided he should take a look."

"A break-in?" Shade was trying to get his head around this. The guest ranch was remote enough that they'd seldom had trouble. A hunter or two had broken into the lodge years ago in a bad storm needing to get to a phone, food and warmth. After that, his father had left the lodge's front door unlocked for just that purpose until some vandals had made a mess and then ever since, began locking it again.

"The hiker apparently scared off the thief, but he said the person got away after making a mess," the deputy was saying.

Shade sighed. "I'll drive right up. We're having our ten-year high school reunion up there." He was thinking about the items he'd already hauled up for the event. "Did the hiker get a look at the intruder?"

"Said he just got a glimpse, couldn't even be sure if it was a man or a woman. Wearing dark clothes, going through some things when the hiker surprised the culprit, who took off out the back door. Didn't see a vehicle anywhere. Must have parked down the road."

"I'm on my way now," Shade said after thanking the deputy. He wondered why Lizzy hadn't made the call. Maybe she hadn't heard. Or maybe she didn't want to talk to him again.

He sighed, hoping she was too busy solving Ariel's murder.

"IS EVERYTHING ALL RIGHT?" Gertie asked when Lizzy came back into the kitchen.

"Nothing that one of my deputies can't handle," she said, hoping it was true.

"So how was your first day on the job?" her aunt asked after they were seated at the table and she'd said the blessing.

"You remember Ariel Matheson?"

Her aunt made a distasteful face before catching herself. Aunt Gertie always said not to say anything if you couldn't say anything nice—and did her best to live by it.

"She was found in the pond just down the road from Sterling Ranch. She'd been murdered."

Gertie's eyes widened. "*Murdered?* My goodness. I would imagine you have a few suspects." That was putting it mildly. "Solving the crime should be a cinch."

Lizzy smiled at her aunt's confidence in her abilities. "Not quite."

"On the TV crime dramas, the killer is always the one you suspect the least," Gertie opined. "That should narrow it down."

Unfortunately, Lizzy wasn't sure who that might be since she suspected everyone at this point. She took a bite of the shepherd's pie. "This is delicious."

"As I've said before, a person's behavior will always give them away." Gertie tapped the side of her nose. "You just have to keep your eyes open. Human nature will sink the culprit every time."

Lizzy had heard it all before. She smiled and nodded. At her age, her aunt had seen all types and could spot trouble a mile away, as she was fond of saying.

"It's all in the eyes," Gertie said.

She thought of Shade's blue eyes, warm and alluring as a tropical sea. She'd been tempted to dive in many times, but never more than she had been today.

Lizzy still couldn't believe he'd said he wanted to help her solve the crime so he could ask her out. She shook her head but smiled at the memory. The man had sand, she'd give him that.

"What's his name?" her aunt said, startling her.

She blinked. "Pardon?"

"I know that smile," Gertie said.

Lizzy chuckled and put thoughts of Shade away to concentrate on enjoying this meal with her aunt. "As a person who has studied the human condition for more than eighty years?"

Her aunt laughed with her. "As a person who's been in love."

"Love?" Lizzy shook her head. "I wouldn't call it love. We haven't even been out on a real date yet."

"What would you call it, then?"

Lizzy gave it a moment's thought. "A small temptation."

"Small, is he?" her aunt asked. "I was imagining tall with broad shoulders."

She chuckled. "Oh, were you now?"

"So did he ask you out?"

Lizzy felt her face flush. "Not yet. But he did mention it."

Her aunt leaned forward with interest. "And what did you say?"

"I told him he's my number one suspect in my murder case."

Gertie's eyes widened. "You can't think for a minute that Shade Sterling killed that girl."

"Wait, how did you know I was talking about Shade?"

"Really, dear. I don't live in a cave."

Lizzy sighed. "Shade was seen going after the murder victim at the graduation party."

Her aunt huffed. "You're just muddying the waters because you're scared to admit that you're interested in this man."

The waters were plenty muddy enough, she thought. "It wouldn't be proper, dating a suspect."

"Just keep telling yourself that. I thought once that girl turned up, the two of you would finally see your way clear to do what comes naturally."

"Is that what you thought?" Sometimes her aunt amazed her. She realized that she must have mentioned Shade over the past ten years. They had crossed paths but one or both of them had been seeing someone else at the time. How odd that Ariel's death had now thrown them together when they were both unencumbered. "It isn't that simple."

"Love never is. Sounds to me like you need to get this case solved as quickly as possible."

Lizzy shook her head, smiling at her aunt. "Shade offered to help me, which is totally inappropriate. I'm the sheriff."

"Yes, you are," Gertie agreed at once. "You'll get it solved in no time and then there will be nothing standing in your way. More shepherd's pie, dear?"

SHADE DROVE UP to the isolated guest ranch high in the mountains overlooking the Flathead Valley for the second time that day. He loved it up here. Since their father died, he and his brothers had divided up the work, with Will running the guest ranch in the summer and Shade and Garrett ranching down in the valley.

He'd been looking forward to having the small reunion at the guest ranch before winter set in. One of the main reasons was that he'd been hoping Lizzy would attend. Now with the murder, there was no doubt that she'd be there.

All of her suspects would be gathered in one place. Unless she solved the murder before this weekend, he thought as he parked in front of the lodge next to the deputy's cruiser and climbed out into the crisp mountain air.

Shade saw that the cruiser was empty. The deputy must be inside waiting for him.

The last of the afternoon's sunlight did little to warm this October day as he took in the place. He'd always been awed by the feeling of peace he felt here.

Sterling's Montana Guest Ranch stood against the mountainside surrounded by towering pines, rocky cliffs and snowcapped peaks. The ranch itself was a large log-and-stone lodge with nine small cabins tucked in the pines off to one side. There was a large new barn after the old one had burned and corrals and a bunkhouse for summer help.

As planned, the reunion would be a three-day event. Everyone would arrive Friday night for a cocktail party and slideshow. He'd brought the boxes of photographs up earlier but had only dropped them off at the lodge and left. He still had to pick up the flat screen for the digital slideshow. He'd forgotten to ask Ashley about the screen she was getting from her folks.

He wondered how much the reunion would change in light of Ariel's murder. The plans had included a Saturday horseback ride, weather permitting, lunch, and then more reminiscing and partying. Sunday was for families to come up in the morning. But since so few of them had spouses and children, they hadn't expected many.

By Sunday afternoon, he would have the cabins and lodge cleaned and everything put away for the upcoming winter months when the guest ranch would be closed.

Now he couldn't see them going on a horseback ride, suspecting that one of their classmates was a killer. Hell, maybe no one would show up for the reunion because of that. No one but him and Lizzy. That would be okay, too, he thought with a smile. He knew Lizzy was hoping to have answers long before the festivities began up here.

He couldn't help thinking of her, worrying about her. But like she said, she was the sheriff. He smiled to himself. She did look damned good in a uniform. He'd been busy living his life over the past ten years and Lizzy had done the same. But he'd think of her occasionally. Or see her in passing. He'd never forgotten her or their kiss graduation night. The timing had just never seemed right. Until now.

As he walked up the steps to the main lodge with its wall of glass and logs and stone, he couldn't stop thinking of her. He'd always compared other women to her. None of them had made him want to settle down. If it hadn't been for Ariel's disappearance hanging over him... But he assured himself that once Ariel's murder was solved, there wouldn't be anything keeping the two of them apart.

On the porch, he could see where a small glass window next to the front door had been broken. Maybe they needed to increase security up here.

Pushing open the door, he stepped in, not sure what he was going to find.

"Hello," he called out, wondering where the deputy had gone. Maybe for a walk around the ranch.

To his surprise, not much seemed to have been disturbed that he could see in the main lounge. He wandered through the dining room and kitchen, checked the refrigerators and freezers. Nothing seemed to be missing from the food supply he'd had brought up for the reunion. Their former guest ranch cook, Buckshot Brewster, would be coming up to do the cooking, so it was going to be very basic.

Shade wandered back into the lodge living room. It was large with worn, comfortable leather furniture gathered before a huge rock fireplace. As he headed back toward the hall where dances were held, he saw that the door to the hall was ajar. He distinctly remembered closing it before he'd left last time because all of the reunion memorabilia was in there on a couple of large tables.

Pushing the door open, he stopped cold. "Deputy?"

The tall, lean officer started and turned. Deputy Ace Turner put down the photograph he'd been studying. Shade was shocked to see that whoever had broken in had apparently gone through the boxes of printed photographs he'd brought up and left here. Photographs were scattered across the table and onto the floor.

Shade stepped in, stopping a few feet into the room to pick up part of a photo that had been torn in half. He stared down at it.

The snapshot had been of him and Ariel at some

kegger down by the river. He could see other classmates in the background. Whoever had torn it had
ripped it right through Ariel's face.

CHAPTER SEVEN

As LIZZY WAS helping her aunt with the dishes, she saw that this time the incoming call was from Shade.

"Go take care of your business," Gertie said, waving her away. "You have a murder to solve."

Lizzy hesitated before she picked up the call on her way to the living room.

"I think you'd better get up here," the cowboy said without preamble. "I'm at the guest ranch. Someone broke into the lodge."

"I heard. One of my deputies notified me. Was there much damage?"

"A broken window that can be fixed easy enough. That's not the problem. It appears whoever broke in went through the memorabilia for the class reunion that I brought up here and destroyed some of the printed photos. They also took the thumb drives, which is no big deal because we can get those photos from everyone again. But I thought you might be able to get a fingerprint off one of the destroyed photos in case our killer might have paid the ranch a visit."

Our killer? She glanced at her watch and sighed. "Where is the deputy?"

"Still here." He lowered his voice. "He was going through the photos when I got here."

"Wearing disposable gloves?"

"Afraid not."

She swore. "Tell him to get his butt back to town. I'm on my way."

THE DRIVE UP to the guest ranch this time of year would have been beautiful with the different types of trees and the variety of colors had it been during daylight. Now in the early darkness, her headlights picked up the deep green of the pines with an occasional flash of color from a stand of aspens.

She hadn't been up here in years and had forgotten how picturesque it was. As she came over a rise, she spotted the rustic lodge and the cabins set against the deep green of the pines in her headlights. She put down her window to breathe in the sweet scent. It was getting late in the season so the air was almost cold.

It had been a long day. Shade's pickup was parked in front of the lodge. As she drove up and parked, he came out on the wide lodge deck. She opened her door, hesitating for a moment as she studied him standing there. His sun-tipped hair was tousled as if he'd been running his hands through it, making the cowboy even more handsome. She had the sudden thought that this was what he would look like when he woke up in the morning.

Shoving that thought down, she climbed out and

started up the steps. Halfway up, she felt a shiver as if someone had just walked over her grave.

"I made a fire," Shade said, thinking she was cold. "The temperature seems to be dropping fast. Come on inside." He stepped aside and she entered, immediately feeling the warmth of the blaze, hearing it popping and crackling in the huge rock fireplace.

The living room looked too cozy. She could imagine Shade's long legs stretched out in one of the leather chairs, his feet up on the large square wooden coffee table, a beer in his hand. Too easily, she could see herself joining him there in the glow of the fire.

"Where are these photos?" she asked, determined to keep this all business.

Shade grinned as if he could see what she was doing and why. "Right back here." He led the way toward the back of the lodge. The doors opened into the dance hall complete with a bandstand. Tables had been set up along one side of the room. On them were photographs, yearbooks and other memorabilia.

"I only picked up one photograph from the floor when I first came in." He pointed to where he'd set it down on a table. "It was on the floor along with the others."

She stared down at the torn photo of Shade and Ariel. Half of Ariel's face was missing. "Did you see the other half of this photo?"

"No, but when I came in, your deputy had a photo in his hand."

"Do you know which one it was?"

"It was one of you. But later, I didn't see it again. He wouldn't have taken it, would he?"

Ace. She swore silently. "He appeared to be going through the photos?"

Shade nodded. "I was surprised."

"What else had he touched?" she wondered aloud.

"I have no idea. I was waiting for you. From what I've seen, though, I'd say whoever broke in was looking for something in particular."

"Why would you say that?" she asked. She pulled on disposable gloves and withdrew an evidence bag from her kit before carefully slipping the torn photograph inside.

"It's clear that the person was going through them. I'd say they were looking for an incriminating photo."

She smiled over at him. "Maybe with him or her holding a length of rope?"

He returned her smile with obvious patience. "Maybe with a clue as to why that person killed Ariel."

"A clue?" She studied the mess on the table. Unfortunately, she had no idea what Ace had touched. Anger rose like heat until she could feel her cheeks burn. She wanted to fire him. To send him packing. No doubt he was butting into this case. She promised herself that she would keep him as far from it as she could from now on.

"And the one that was torn on the floor?" she asked. "What clue should we get from a photo of Ariel with her head severed down the middle?"

"Someone didn't like her?" he suggested with a grin.

Even though he was teasing, she was curious about his take on the break-in. After all, he'd gone to school with these same people. And as much as she resisted his being involved, he was. She said as much to him.

"Say you're looking for one photo that might incriminate you," he said. "You're going through them and you keep seeing Ariel's smiling face and it sets you off. You rip off half her face—something you wanted to do in real life but didn't have the stomach for. Until maybe the night you killed her."

Lizzy agreed that there appeared to be a lot of anger in the person who'd gone through the photographs—and a frenzy, an urgency. But she didn't believe that whoever had done this was the killer. There was still too much uncontrolled rage here. The person who'd murdered Ariel had been more careful since he or she had gotten away with it for ten years. Also, why rip the woman's face in half in a photo after you got to watch her drown?

The reunion would start soon, and this had been the person's last chance to find what they'd been looking for—if Shade's take on the break-in was right. Unfortunately, she had no idea what the person had been looking for or why it was so important. Like he'd said, something incriminating no doubt.

She stooped to retrieve another torn photo from the floor and put it into a separate evidence bag along with others spread around the table before loading the rest into a box. As she put the ones in the evidence bag on top, she stopped to look up at him. "Thanks."

He grinned and shrugged. "I haven't done anything yet."

Suddenly the huge room seemed to shrink. The air between them felt alive with electricity that began to spark. That old chemistry from high school hadn't diminished in the least in the past ten years. If anything, it was stronger than ever and she knew that Shade felt it, too.

She thought about the fact that it was just the two of them up here on the side of the mountain, alone in a guest ranch with a dozen beds. Not that she thought they would ever make it to a bed if they let loose.

As she finished collecting the fallen photos, she got to her feet. She didn't look at him. Couldn't. She had a job to do and she had to stay focused. She couldn't shake the feeling that this wasn't over—whatever it was. It wouldn't be over until the killer was caught.

"Hopefully your intruder didn't wear gloves and I'll be able to lift a print off the destroyed photos," she said, all business, still not looking at him. "At least we'll know then who broke in and hopefully will be able to find out why. I'm going to take these and go through them."

When he didn't answer, she was forced to look at him. She realized at once all he'd wanted was for her to acknowledge the feelings whirling between them. She gave him a small nod, feeling close to tears. She wanted this, too. Her body wanted this. She felt it vibrate with need for him. But not now.

She met his gaze and silently pleaded, *Let me do my job. Please.*

"I'll walk you to your rig," he said, his voice sounding hoarse with emotion as he took the box she'd put the photos in and he carried it out to her vehicle. He shoved the box into the back seat and turned to her. "Have you had dinner? I could make us—"

"Gertie made my favorite, shepherd's pie."

He looked disappointed. "Maybe stay for a drink in front of the fire?"

She thought of the warm, inviting living room and shook her head, knowing as he must that they would end up on that one long leather couch naked. Thrusting the mental picture away, she said, "Thank you, but I need to get these to the lab and start going through the other ones."

"If you're sure. I have cold beer in the fridge. Also it's pitch-black out there. I hate for you to have to drive off this mountain in the dark."

"You're the devil and you know it."

He grinned. "I don't deny it. But being up here alone with you…" He didn't have to finish. She felt the same way.

It was so tempting. "I would love nothing more. The thought of putting my feet up in front of the fire in one of the leather chairs is definitely…"

"Alluring?"

She laughed, glad they were teasing again. Earlier had been too serious, too intimate, too easy to take to the next step—even with him being a suspect and her being sheriff. "Tempting. Very temping to have a beer and stare into the fire after the day I've had." Even more tempting was the cowboy who she'd had a crush on for years. What would it hurt to soak up the warmth of that fire before going back out? But it was the other part, sleeping with a suspect, that she couldn't let herself do.

Shade was right. The night was darker than usual, clouds hung low over the tops of the pines. The days were so short this time of year and she still had so much to do before this day was over.

Lizzy shifted her gaze back to Shade. "Thanks for the offer, but I can't."

"Right, got to find the killer so there will be nothing stopping you from going out with me."

She couldn't help but smile. "Exactly. So I best get on it."

He'd been leaning against her patrol SUV but now stepped away. She saw the change in him. As if he heard something on the breeze. Or saw something lurking in the dark shadows of the pines.

"Lizzy," he said, his voice rough again, only this time with fear rather than desire. "Please be careful." Something in his tone made her stop to look at him with concern. What had he seen, felt, sensed? "Sorry, I just had this strange feeling." His blue gaze locked with hers. "Whoever killed Ariel is dangerous."

"Most murderers are," she said even as his words sent a shiver through her.

"I guess I've just assumed that it was someone who

hated her so much that in a fit of passion, they killed her," Shade said. "A one-time thing. They wouldn't kill anyone else. But just now, I felt…evil and had this sensation that was so strong… Lizzy, this person could kill again."

"If you're trying to scare me—"

He shook his head as if to shake off the feeling. "It's probably just all these years of living in the same house as Dorothea. Her and her intuition about bad vibes." He shrugged uncomfortably. "When I looked at you, I felt such a wave of alarm. It's probably nothing," he said quickly. "Besides, you're the law officer. I'm just a cattle rancher."

She studied him. Shade Sterling was much more than just a cattle rancher. "I'll be careful. Are you staying up here alone?"

He glanced around and shook his head. "I'd thought about it, but no. Everything is ready for the reunion. There is no reason to come back until Friday afternoon."

As she started to open her SUV, he grabbed her hand. She felt the chemical reaction rocket through her as if he'd zapped her with a Taser.

"Promise me that when this is all over…" he began, giving her hand in his large warm one a squeeze before letting go.

She smiled, but as she looked at him, she felt that ominous sensation that had spooked him. "You take care, Shade Sterling," she said.

"You, too, Sheriff."

BACK AT HIS APARTMENT, Deputy Ace Turner studied the photograph he'd pocketed of little Lizzy Conners when she was in high school. Her dark hair had been longer back then and she'd worn it down like a shimmering ebony wave around her slim shoulders.

But it was those dark eyes that captivated him. Sometimes they were a burnt umber but other times there was a fire in them that warmed them to cinnamon. She was a looker, there was no doubt about that. All that, he realized, had probably contributed to her winning the sheriff election.

Too bad the voters hadn't seen Lizzy back in high school with none of that cocky, so-sure-of-herself, so-positive-she-could-do-anything attitude she had now. If they had, he knew she would have lost. This girl looked…vulnerable. This girl hadn't wanted to be a sheriff back then, even though he'd heard that she'd lived next door to Sid from the time she was a baby. No, this teenager in the photograph looked… broken.

So what had happened to her to make her like that back then? Something. A boy who dumped her? Friends who betrayed her? Or something worse?

Ace frowned. What had happened to her parents that she came to live with her aunt as a baby? He thought he'd heard that they were dead. Conners. It shouldn't take much to track down what had happened to them, right?

He fingered the photograph, trying to get inside Lizzy's head. She looked so young. She was still young, twenty-eight and sheriff. There was no justice in the world. He, on the other hand, would be forty-five this year. She was a babe in the woods compared to a man of his maturity. That is unless you talked to his mother or his ex-girlfriend.

Ace pushed those thoughts away. What did they know anyway? What was important here was the high-profile case. Ariel Matheson's murder. Already, the news was bringing up her politician father who was still doing time in the state pen. Solving a case like this would get anyone noticed, but especially some young, green, female sheriff.

If he could just find a way to take over the case, he thought. He looked down into Lizzy's dark eyes in the photo. As he took a straight pin from his desk drawer, he thought that he would do whatever he had to if he got a chance to take over this case.

Driving the sharp end of the pin into her heart, he tacked her up on his bulletin board next to the photo he'd also pocketed of Ariel Matheson.

Tomorrow at work, he'd find out everything he could about Elizabeth "Lizzy" Conners.

LIZZY DROVE THROUGH the darkness down the mountain, pines on each side of the narrow road. Using her hands-free device, she phoned Ariel's mother. "Hello, Mrs. Matheson—I'm sorry, Mrs. Warner." She slowed her patrol SUV to a crawl on the narrow, tree-lined dirt road.

"Please, call me Catherine," the woman said. "After

as many hours as you used to spend in this house, Lizzy… But I should call you Sheriff, shouldn't I? If I didn't mention it earlier when you came by, congratulations on winning the election."

"Thank you."

"Is there anything new in the investigation? Have you caught the person who killed my daughter?"

"Not yet. But I'm working on it. The case is ongoing, Catherine. That's why I'm calling. I need the name of Ariel's doctor."

"Her doctor?" Catherine's voice broke.

Lizzy knew before she asked what the woman would say. "Catherine, was Ariel pregnant?" Lizzy heard what sounded like a sob. "Who was the father of the baby?"

"She wouldn't tell me who—"

From off to her right, headlights suddenly blinded her as a vehicle roared out of the pines from a logging road. She felt the jarring crash against her SUV, heard the blaring crunch of metal against metal, an instant before she was slammed against her side window and the airbags deployed. She hit her brakes as the impact of the other vehicle sent her SUV skidding across the narrow road to crash into the pines. Her vision narrowed before blinking out.

Lizzy came to, probably only seconds later. For a moment, she didn't know what had happened. It had been so fast. She turned and felt a pain in her head, in her neck, in her battered body. Stars danced before her eyes and she thought for a moment that she was going to black out.

Turning her head even though it was excruciating, she could see the vehicle that had hit her. The driver had backed up and left the engine idling only yards away, the headlights still streaming into the patrol SUV blinding her. Had the person backed up to hit her again?

She was fumbling for her radio to call for help when the passenger-side door in the back was flung open. She expected the driver to ask if she was all right. Instead, she realized with shock that the driver was trying to climb into the back seat where the box of photographs was. In the side mirror, she saw gloved hands holding what looked like a length of yellow ski rope as had been used on Ariel.

Unhooking her seat belt, Lizzy fumbled out her gun and tried to turn.

The person must have seen her going for her weapon. The door slammed. She watched the figure dressed in a large black coat with a hood. She couldn't tell by the size whether it was a man or a woman. With the glare of the headlights blinding her, she couldn't make out a face as the person got behind the wheel again. She heard the engine rev.

The driver was going to ram her again. Lizzy braced herself for the impact. But the headlights swung away, and what appeared to be an old sedan left in a cloud of exhaust. She squinted as she tried to read the license plate, but it was too dark.

The person was getting away, she realized, her head foggy. She grabbed her radio and called for help as she watched the sedan roar away. She saw only taillights as the car disappeared over a rise in the road.

CHAPTER EIGHT

SHADE COULDN'T SHAKE his earlier premonition. After watching Lizzy drive away, he felt helpless to do anything about it though. The hiker had scared away the person going through the photos. Had the person found what he or she was looking for? By now they could have destroyed any incriminating photo.

Lizzy had taken the rest of them and planned to go through them. He wished she had let him help. She kept holding him at arm's length in this investigation—as well as personally. He worried that if Ariel's killer wasn't found, he and Lizzy would stay star-crossed lovers forever.

After locking up the lodge as best he could given the broken window, he drove toward the valley ranch. He hadn't gone far when he noticed he had a message on his phone. Before he could check it, he came over the rise and saw Lizzy's wrecked patrol SUV in his headlights.

He slammed on his brakes, getting his pickup stopped just in time. His heart leaped to his throat, his mouth going dry as dust as he threw his truck into Park and jumped out.

As he rushed to her, he could see Lizzy, head back, eyes closed, and felt all the air rush from him. He pounded on the roof of the SUV, terrified that she was dead.

Her eyes flew open and he let himself breathe again, relief washing over him. He tried the passenger-side door but it was smashed in and wouldn't budge. He opened the back seat door. It groaned, but he was able to push the box of photographs aside to reach her. He leaned over the seat and put a hand on her shoulder.

He didn't see any blood, but that didn't mean she didn't have internal injuries. "Are you hurt bad?"

She shook her head and winced.

"Have you called for—" Even as he started to say it, he heard the sound of sirens. "What happened?"

She wet her lips but didn't try to speak as the first EMT vehicle came roaring up. A man and woman in uniform leaped out and rushed to them.

Feeling useless, he slid out of the SUV and let the medics do their job. What had happened? Had she lost control of the SUV and hit not just the trees along one side of the road, but the other, as well? He stared at the smashed-in side of the vehicle in the headlights of his pickup. He saw where a darker brown paint had been left on the patrol SUV and realized what it would take to dent the side of the rig like this.

Someone had hit her broadside and then apparently taken off.

The area was quickly filled with more flashing lights as sheriff's department vehicles began to arrive.

His gaze quickly went to the logging road back up the road a half dozen yards, trying to piece together what must have happened.

She hadn't lost control of the SUV. Someone had purposely hit her. That bad feeling he'd had earlier came back in a wave of nauseating terror. He'd known Lizzy was in danger. He'd felt it up at the guest ranch.

Standing out here in the glow of the flashing lights as Lizzy was put on a stretcher and loaded into the back of the ambulance, he felt that knowing feeling even stronger.

This wasn't over and wouldn't be until Ariel's killer was found.

AFTER BEING TAKEN to the hospital and given a thorough exam, Lizzy had been released. One of her deputies had given her a ride home and brought the box of photographs into the house for her. She'd given him the evidence bags for the lab, ordering that he tell them to put a rush on the fingerprints.

More than ever, she hoped for prints on the torn photos they'd found on the floor. If the person who'd broken into the lodge and gone through the photographs was the same one who'd tried to kill her, she needed to know who they were and quickly.

In the kitchen, she found her aunt cleaning. Gertie always cleaned when she was upset. Hearing her come in, her aunt rushed to her, hugging her, then apologizing for squeezing her too hard.

"I'm not made of glass, I promise," Lizzy said.

She'd called her aunt from the hospital since she didn't want Gertie hearing about the accident from anyone else. "I'm all right."

Her aunt studied her, tears in her eyes. "I worry, you know."

"I know. It was just a car accident. I'm fine."

"Did they feed you a little something at the hospital? I could have brought you down some leftovers if you were hungry, like I told you on the phone."

Lizzy smiled. "There was no need for you to come down. They were running a bunch of tests to make sure that I was fine."

Her aunt nodded. "Well, I made you a plate just in case you get hungry later. It's in the fridge."

She kissed Gertie on the cheek. "Thank you. The rest of the shepherd's pie won't go to waste. You know how much I love your recipe."

"Lately I've been writing down all my recipes for when…you know."

Lizzy stared at the woman in alarm. "Auntie?" she cried.

"I'm not dying," Gertie said with a laugh. "For when you get married and have your own house."

She didn't know what to say. She hadn't thought about what would happen when and if that day ever came. How could she leave her aunt after Gertie had taken care of her all these years? She couldn't.

"I thought we might live here with you," Lizzy said, her voice breaking.

"What? That's ridiculous. You need your own

place, your own life. No, my dear." Her aunt patted her on the arm. "It will be time for you to fly the nest."

Fly the nest? She wasn't flying anywhere. Her aunt didn't give her a chance to say as much.

"I'm going up to bed. I assume you won't stay up long after your ordeal," Gertie said.

"I have some things I have to do and then I'll be up, as well," Lizzy said. Her aunt had already started up the stairs. Lizzy watched her go, telling herself she could never leave Gertie.

SHADE HAD FOLLOWED the ambulance to the hospital and stood around until the doctor came out and told him that Lizzy was being released and that he should go home. "She said she'll talk to you tomorrow."

Relieved that she was all right, he'd done what she asked. But he couldn't get what he'd seen off his mind. He still felt shaken. Lizzy could have been killed.

As he pulled up in front of the large rambling house at the family's valley cattle ranch, he started to get out when he noticed a car he didn't recognize parked next to Dorothea's. She had company? If so, he would make his way directly to his part of the house as quickly as possible.

He heard a woman's voice the moment he stepped inside the house—and froze. Hannah? He hadn't seen Hannah Ames in almost three years, not since they'd run into each other after dating in college, not since—

"Shade, is that you?" Dorothea called.

He took a breath, let it out and stepped on down

the hall to the living room. A brunette was sitting in a chair near the fireplace with her back to him. He saw that she had a cup of coffee next to her. Dorothea was always the good hostess so of course she would have made her guest comfortable.

The woman turned around and his guess was confirmed. The woman hadn't come to see Dorothea. She'd come to see him.

"What are you doing here?" Shade demanded, his gaze on the attractive brunette.

"Shade—"

He spoke over Dorothea's protest at his tone. "What are you doing here?"

Hannah slowly rose to her feet, smoothing the blouse she wore over her jeans. She was rounder than he remembered, her face more full, but that wasn't the only change, he saw. She was wearing a wedding band on her left hand.

"So you married him," Shade said, wondering again what she was doing here.

"Could we talk in private?" Hannah asked.

"I can't see that we have anything to talk about," he said. Dorothea started to excuse herself, but he cut her off. "No, you stay here, Dorothea. Hannah and I can talk in my end of the house." He hadn't taken his gaze off the young woman and now pointed the way to his living quarters situated in a separate wing of the rambling ranch house.

As he started out of the room, he could feel Dorothea's reproachful—and curious—gaze on him. He didn't look at her but he knew she'd grill him later. *What was Hannah doing here after all this time?*

"All right," he said the moment they stepped into his living area. "Let's hear it."

She moved slowly around the room, taking in all of his things before she finally turned to look at him. "You look good," she said.

He shook his head. "Not going back there."

She turned away from him and said over her shoulder, "You're not married. But I remember you saying there was someone you were interested in, back in high school—"

"I'm not talking to you about my love life."

She turned to look at him. "I'm sorry about...about everything."

He shook his head and motioned to the ring on her left hand. "I'm not sure what this is about but aren't you married?" They'd broken up in college because she'd told him there was someone else she was interested in. Then about three years ago they'd crossed paths and hooked up for a night. He'd thought she was single only to find out the next morning that she was engaged.

She nodded and sighed. "It isn't working out."

Shade let out a bitter laugh. "What did he do, cheat on you?" Then he saw that his joke was no joke. "Well, you know what they say, what goes around, comes around."

Hannah turned away from him again. "I knew you would take great joy in that."

"You're wrong. I haven't given you a second thought in more than three years, not since you lied to me."

She turned to him again, her face more sad than angry. "Don't pretend you were heartbroken to find out I was engaged. We both know we didn't have that kind of relationship. Admit it. You didn't love me—" He started to argue the point but she cut him off. "Not the kind of love that would have led to marriage."

Hannah was right. He'd cared about her, loved being with her because she was fun and they were both young and enjoying life. But he hadn't considered marrying her.

"But this other man did marry you," he said pointedly.

She lifted her hand to look at her ring, seeming lost in thought for a moment. "Yes, he married me, but only because I was pregnant."

Pregnant? "You have a child?"

She nodded and smiled sheepishly. "You know how bad I was about forgetting sometimes to take my pill. Such an airhead. That was me, huh?" Her voice broke. "Thomas, my husband, thought the baby was his." She shrugged. "So did I until our daughter was injured and we thought she was going to need blood. Turned out she didn't. She's fine, but that's when it all came out. Thomas couldn't have been the father. Wrong blood type." Her gaze came up to meet his.

"What is this, Hannah?" he said, suddenly wary.

"I'm sorry that I lied to you the last time we saw

each other. It was wrong. But I knew I'd never see you again." She shook her head. "I'd always known there was someone else back home that you were more interested in marrying than me."

He felt a chill race through him. "Hannah? What's going on?"

"She's yours, Shade. Our baby girl, Maisie. She's your daughter."

CHAPTER NINE

EARLY THE NEXT MORNING, feeling bruised and sore, Lizzy went to work continuing to interview her list of suspects. Gertie had wanted her to take the day off, but she couldn't. She had to interview as many as she could before the reunion started tomorrow.

She found Christopher Drysdale out in the driveway of his house filling the back of his SUV with boxes.

"Looks like you're planning a longer trip than just up to the Sterling guest ranch for a weekend reunion," she said behind him.

He whirled around in obvious surprise. "I'm not going. I have a job out of town."

"That's too bad because I really hoped that none of the suspects in Ariel's murder would leave town right now. I hope you don't go any farther than Sterling guest ranch."

Christopher swore. "I'm a suspect? Are you kidding me? Look, this is a really bad time for me. I *have* to take this job."

She pulled out her notebook and pen. "Where's the job? What's the name of your boss?"

Christopher sighed. "Okay, there's no job, but I have to leave. I have no choice."

"Kind of suspicious, you wanting to get out of town so quickly after Ariel's car is found in the pond. I'm sure a judge will agree."

He groaned and rubbed the back of his neck, avoiding her gaze. "You don't understand."

The front door of his house banged open, and a handful of his underwear was thrown out into the grass. It was immediately followed by what appeared to be a bag of his dirty clothes. Lizzy thought she might understand.

"A domestic dispute?"

He hung his head. "You could say that."

"Christopher, I need to ask you some questions about the night Ariel died. Is there somewhere we can do that?"

He glanced toward the house and cringed. With a sigh, he said, "If you want to step into my garage…"

They entered the dimly lit garage. Part of it had been made into a sort of man cave with a television, an old couch and an even older recliner.

Christopher looked embarrassed as he offered her the recliner. She chose the couch, sitting on the edge as he settled on the edge of the recliner, looking nervous and uncomfortable as he glanced toward the door into the house.

"I need to know where you were the night of the graduation party," she said, putting her pen to her notebook.

"I was at the party." He met her gaze. "You saw me there."

She thought about how he had moved in on her after witnessing the kiss between her and Shade. As he'd closed the space between them that night, she'd realized that he'd had a lot to drink. She couldn't remember what he'd said, some throwaway pickup line. She had still been stunned by Shade's kiss and had let Christopher come on a little too strongly before she'd realized what was happening and pushed him away.

He'd gone away easily enough, staggering back toward the house. All of that told her that she could cross him off her list, if he'd really been that intoxicated. The only way he could have killed Ariel was if he'd been faking how drunk he was. After he disappeared into the pines, he could have changed direction and gone to where Ariel was standing around yelling at Brad to move his car. He could have left without anyone noticing.

The killer would have had to use some sort of weapon on Ariel. She wouldn't have willingly let anyone tie her hands to the steering wheel. The killer would have had to bring both the weapon and the rope to the party that night. Unless the rope and weapon were already in Ariel's car, which seemed too coincidental and lucky for the killer.

So this hadn't been a spur-of-the-moment killing. Whoever had killed Ariel had planned it. Lizzy was looking at premeditated murder.

"When did you leave the party?" she asked.

"Not until the next morning. I slept over. Brad didn't want me driving in my...condition."

"Did someone see you there the entire time?"

He looked chagrined and hung his head. "I blacked out at some point, so I have no idea."

"Did you see Ariel leave?"

He started to shake his head but stopped. "I did."

"Was she alone?"

Christopher frowned as if seeing Ariel drive away in his memory. "I thought I saw someone with her..." He shook his head. "It was probably a shadow."

Lizzy felt a chill race up her spine. "Why do you say that?"

"Because they would have been in the back seat, which makes no sense, right?"

She felt goose bumps ripple across her skin. Someone in the back seat?

Christopher's eyes suddenly widened. "Oh hell. Don't tell me that I saw her killer." Tears suddenly filled his eyes and he quickly looked away to wipe at them.

"You think you saw her killer in the back of the car as she was pulling away?"

"I saw someone...a shadow in the back seat for just an instant. Look, I could be wrong. I just got a glimpse of someone. I have no idea if it was a man or a woman. At the time..." His voice broke. "I thought it was one of her friends leaving with her."

Lizzy tried to still her excitement. She'd been convinced that someone had followed Ariel as she'd left the party. But of course it made more sense that the killer was already in Ariel's back seat. As angry and intoxicated as the woman had been, she wouldn't have noticed. Until it was too late.

"Did you have any contact with Ariel during the party?" she asked, hoping he didn't lie. She'd already heard what had happened earlier in the night.

Christopher looked down again as he nervously turned his wedding band. He'd gotten married to Nancy Haggerty right after graduation. By then, his bride had definitely been showing.

"Something happened between you and Ariel at the party," Lizzy prodded.

He let out a long sigh and shook his head as if the last thing he needed right now was to be reminded of something he'd done more than ten years ago. But Lizzy waited as she watched him battle with the past and a realization that still seemed to have him shaken.

When he finally spoke, he spilled it quickly. "I slept with Ariel in Brad's spare room, Nancy walked in and you-know-what hit the fan. Nancy left crying, Ariel was being a bitch, so we got into an argument, which I'm sure everyone within earshot will be happy to tell you about. Ariel stormed off and I proceeded to get drunk. Drunker."

Lizzy had missed the argument, because she'd been outside most of the party. But she'd heard about it later. At the moment Ariel stormed out, Lizzy had been busy kissing Shade back. Ariel had come out of the house and seen them. Perfect timing.

"You didn't go after Ariel following your argument?"

"Are you kidding?" He let out a bark of a laugh. "I'd had more than enough of her for one night, in so many ways." He shook his head. "What was it about her? I couldn't stand her and yet…"

"You slept with her and got caught by your future bride."

Christopher looked up, a sad smile on his face. "Why did we do what Ariel wanted even when it wasn't the best thing for us?"

"She had that kind of power over people—especially kids like we'd been back then. Where were you really going when I drove up just now?" she asked quietly.

He hung his head again. "I don't know. Just away from here. Too much history. Ariel being found… Well, it's stirred up a lot of old pain for not just me but my wife."

"It will blow over," Lizzy said, realizing that wasn't necessarily true. Even when she found the killer, which she would come hell or high water, there'd be the long process of a trial. Ariel Matheson could be in the news for years.

Christopher was shaking his head. "Our marriage has been hanging on by a thread as it is. Ariel…" He let out another laugh. "Even dead, she is screwing with my life."

"Because you slept with her graduation night?" She

couldn't believe that that one incident ten years ago was the problem.

"It's more than that. I was in love with Ariel and I still am." She could see that his confession came hard for him. She heard it in the deep growl of his words. "See what I mean about screwed up? Ariel ruined my life. I hated her and I loved her. And I can't believe she's dead. I always thought she'd come back. I always thought…"

"Christopher, your feelings for her sound like a motive for murder. You sure you didn't drive anywhere that night?"

"Not that I know of," he said.

She knew that he could have made up the person in the back seat to cover the truth. He could have followed her after their fight and killed her without anyone noticing that he'd left or maybe without him even remembering. She'd heard stories about murders being committed during alcohol blackouts. Kind of like killing someone while sleepwalking. People drove long distances, committed murders and drove home again without remembering any of it.

"Before Ariel came to school at Progressive, had you known her?" Lizzy asked.

He nodded. "She was my first. I never got over her and she knew it and used it against me."

Even more motive for murder, she thought. "How about climbing into the back of her vehicle to wait for her?"

He seemed surprised by the question. "I just told you I saw whoever killed her. It wasn't me."

"You've been in the back of her car before, right?" She didn't wait for an answer. She read it on his face. "What is the chance that she had some rope in her car?"

He looked as if she'd slammed her fist into his chest and knocked the air out of him. "Rope? Is that what—?"

"Ski rope. Is there any chance there was some in the back of her car that night?"

"How would I know? Did I ever see ski rope in her car? No." He put his head into his hands, his elbows resting on his knees.

"You carry a pocketknife?"

His head came up slowly. "You don't really believe that I would kill her. I just told you, I loved her."

"You just told me that she used that love against you." Lizzy got to her feet. "I'm serious about you not leaving town. I'd really like you to stay around."

He nodded. "Okay. Maybe Brad will put me up for a while."

"Are you coming to the reunion?" she asked.

"Right. The reunion." His laugh held no humor. "Sure, why not? Where else am I going to go?" He let out a curse. "Everyone will be talking about Ariel nonstop. Who wouldn't enjoy that? But there will be plenty of free booze, though, right?"

OH, CHRISTOPHER, YOU poor fool. Being in love with me is such a waste. Haven't you realized that by now? Or is it guilt you're feeling? You said some terrible things to me that night at the party. Not that most of them weren't true. But we'd just made love.

Or at least that's what you thought it was. You think I didn't know that Nancy would catch us? You really are so naive. I wanted her to find us. I wanted her to know that you would always be mine. But you figured that out, didn't you? Oh, you were so angry. You actually scared me. I'd just ruined your life with Nancy and I think you knew it even back then, even before she lost the baby and couldn't have another one.

Well, that's what you get for sleeping with that cow. Were you trying to make me jealous? Look how that backfired on you.

And yet, you still love me. And hate me. Two emotions so closely aligned that sometimes it's hard to tell them apart. I loved you and hated you, as well. But you're a drunk, Christopher, just like your father and will never amount to anything. I'm sure you know that. My telling you the night of the party probably didn't help matters in retrospect.

But at least you realized that night that you and I were over.

Definitely makes you one of the top suspects in my murder, wouldn't you say? I'm sure the sheriff would.

But nice that you gave her the information about someone hiding in the back of my SUV. Another piece of the puzzle for you, Lizzy. Now all you have to do is find out who it was hiding back there, before holding a knife to my throat and telling me to drive to the pond.

SHADE HAD TOSSED and turned most of the night. This morning, he'd gotten up, showered and dressed, still shaken from everything that had happened yesterday. He called first to check on Lizzy. His call went straight to voice mail.

"Just wanted to be sure you were all right after yesterday," he said. "I know how hardheaded you are, so I figure you're fine. Still..." He hung up, not sure what else there was to say since Hannah had shown up in his life again with a shocking announcement.

He knew that, first thing, he had to find out if it was true. Hannah had lied to him before, but this... This would be a new low even for her if she was lying about something this important.

A daughter. Was it possible he could have a two-year-old daughter he'd never laid eyes on?

He called the number Hannah had left for him. She picked up on the fourth ring. He could hear a child crying in the background.

"I'll call you back," she said, sounding harried, and disconnected.

He stared at his phone, noticing again that he had a message he hadn't checked yesterday. He assumed it was from Hannah, calling from another number, but it wasn't.

When the name Catherine Warner came up, it took him a moment to realize who she was. Ariel's mother who'd remarried.

After Ariel disappeared and her father went to prison, Catherine Matheson had a breakdown. She told friends she'd checked into a spa, but the rumor was that she'd spent some time in a mental rehabilitation ward. Friends packed up any personal items in her house since the government took all assets after her husband, Mark, was sentenced to twelve years for numerous criminal charges.

In the blink of an eye, Catherine had gone from living in the lap of luxury as a prominent, respected wife of a politician to being penniless and a social pariah.

Since then, she'd divorced her felonious husband, remarried and returned to the area about six months ago having reinvented herself. At least that's what he'd heard. He'd kept track of her, hoping that when Ariel turned up, he'd know about it, the mystery of her disappearance would be solved, and he'd be exonerated once and for all.

He listened to the message. "Shade, I found something that Ariel wanted you to have. Can you stop by?" Catherine left her address. "I'm home now if you have the time."

He had no idea when Hannah might call back, so he texted Catherine that he'd missed her message yesterday but that he could come by now. She texted back for him to come on over.

Catherine and her new husband, Bob, a retired software manufacturer, lived in a large house overlooking Whitefish Lake. At Shade's knock, the door was opened by a lithe woman wearing a bright-colored caftan. Catherine's hair, which had been long and dark ten years ago, was now blond and bobbed. Her face had undergone some changes as well, but the blue eyes—so much like her daughter's—were the same.

"Shade," Catherine Warner said and began to cry. She hugged him and led him into the massive living room. "It is so good to see you. Thank you for coming by."

"I was so sorry to hear about Ariel. My condolences, ma'am. It was good to hear from you. How are you holding up?"

"It's been such a shock. I still can't believe it." She dabbed at her eyes with a tissue. "Who would do such a thing to my little girl?"

"I wish I knew. You have no idea either?"

Catherine shook her head. "It makes no sense. Everyone loved her. Our house was always full of her friends…" She met his gaze. "I thought at first that she did this on purpose because of her father, you know, that she'd killed herself." With a sigh, she added, "Then I was told that she'd been *murdered*." Her eyes filled with tears again. "What would make someone do that to her?"

He'd wondered the same thing. "I want to find out who did this as much as you do," he said and Catherine smiled through her tears.

"That's why I asked you to stop by," she said. "Ariel loved you. She told me that you'd asked her to marry you."

That wasn't true, but Ariel had never let the truth stop her. He waited, saying nothing. "You said she left something for me?"

"I wasn't around when everything was packed up at the house," Catherine said, avoiding his gaze. "I didn't go through her things that had been boxed up. I just assumed she would come back one day and…" Her voice broke. "But after she was found, I went down to the storage room. I thought there might be something in her things… I saw one of the boxes had been marked for you. It's in Ariel's handwriting. I have no idea what's inside, but clearly she wanted you to have it. She must have put your name on it and taped up the package before the graduation party. That's odd, isn't it?"

Not, he thought, if Catherine knew that he and Ariel had broken up. He feared what his former girlfriend might have put in the package. Definitely not anything good given her mood the night of the party.

"It's in the storage room downstairs. I left it down there because I wasn't sure when you'd be able to come by for it."

He followed her down carpeted steps to a daylight basement. Through a door in the wall, the storage room was a huge space under the garage. It didn't take Catherine long to find the boxes marked ARIEL. On the outside of each was a notation about what was inside from CLOTHES to SHOES to STUFFED ANIMALS.

"The sheriff took a lot of the boxes," Catherine was saying. "I hadn't found this one at the time. Not that I would have given it to her. Ariel wanted you to have this so I would have saved it for you."

She picked up a four-inch-thick package about ten by fourteen. She held it for a moment, before handing it over. "I wish…" She faltered. "I wouldn't have minded having you for a son-in-law and now…" She shook her head as tears filled her eyes again. "But what if there is something in there that will help find her killer? You're friends with Elizabeth Conners, the new sheriff?"

He nodded, sorry that Ariel had lied to her mother. He'd always liked Catherine and thought she deserved better treatment than she got from her husband and her daughter. "And don't worry. If anyone can find out who did this to your daughter, it's Lizzy. If there is anything in here that might help," he said, holding up the package, "I'll make sure she sees it."

She nodded and patted his shoulder. "Thank you." She walked him out to the front porch and stood hugging herself as he drove away.

Shade knew he should call Lizzy and let her know about the package. But he had to know what Ariel had left him first. He'd already been blindsided by Hannah's announcement. He couldn't even imagine what a vindictive Ariel Matheson could have left him.

He thought about those last few months with Ariel. They'd been pure hell. The more he'd pulled away, the more needy and demanding she'd been. He hadn't wanted to hurt her so he'd let her manipulate him through guilt. Why had she told her mother that they were going to get married? Because she really was pregnant? He assumed it was a lie, certainly not something he'd put past her.

It had been her idea not to announce their breakup until after the graduation party. He should have known she would make a scene at the party and break it off with him to save face. Or to embarrass him? Not that it mattered. He'd actually been fine with it. Let her have it her way. As long as he was free to date Lizzy, he hadn't cared. Now, though, he realized it might have been much more complicated—if Ariel really was pregnant.

But then Ariel had disappeared, leaving a dark cloud hanging over his head all these years.

So when had she wrapped up this package for him? When had she been planning to give it to him? After their graduation party, apparently.

Shade looked over at the package on the passenger seat. He didn't expect it to blow up exactly. But he had no doubt that whatever was inside was explosive.

CHAPTER TEN

*I HAD FORGOTTEN all about the package I'd left with
Shade's name on it. Oh well. I'd planned to give it
to him myself a few days after the party. Kind of like
my breakup gift to him. I hadn't planned on getting
murdered.*

*More disturbing was seeing my mother. Catherine
looked...happy. I had forgotten what happy looked like
on my mother after what my father did to her. Maybe it
was being underwater for ten long years and turning
to little more than bones, but I wish I could remember
being happy. I wish I hadn't spent so much of my life
being angry. And yet I'm still angry. Not even death
can bring me peace.*

*I try to remember happy moments. Like the day my
father brought home my cute baby blue SUV. But even
that felt bittersweet since I knew he was only trying to
buy my silence. I knew what was going on with him.
My mother didn't know the whole story. But she knew
enough to be angry with him.*

*I called Lizzy to go riding with me to get out of
the house because my parents had been screaming at
each other. Did my friends know how troubled things*

*were at my house? I hope not. I never wanted anyone
to know what went on in that huge, beautiful, too-
expensive house in my pretend picture-perfect life.*

*But at least my mother is happy now. My father?
Well, he has more years in prison. My daddy. In
prison. It still breaks my heart. I wonder if prison
could have changed him for the better. Would I have
been able to repair my relationship with him, had I
lived?*

*I still hate to think of the horrible fight we had
graduation night before I left for the party. I'd been
so angry with him. Not for lying and cheating, but for
getting caught and humiliating me and my mother. I
said such hateful things. I wish I could take them back.*

I wish I could take a lot of things back.

BACK IN HER OFFICE, Lizzy spread the photographs out
and began to go through them. Last night, after a few
hours, her head aching along with her neck, she'd decided that whatever might be in the photographs, she
wasn't up to finding it. She'd given up and gone to
bed, exhausted.

Today wasn't much better. Her head ached from
her car accident. Not an accident, she reminded herself. Had the person driving really planned to kill her?

She tried to focus. She'd promised the doctor she
would rest, but she had to at least try to find out why
someone had wanted these photographs so badly. Was
the answer to Ariel's murder in these somewhere?

Lizzy tried to concentrate on the prints, telling herself that she had her deputies looking into the accident along with DCI. She picked up one photo of her and Ariel. Ariel had her arm around her and wasn't looking at the camera but at her. The look made her shiver.

There were two dozen photos of all of them. Most of them Ariel had made because she had a photo printer and she liked sharing them. They'd had such a small class, such an unusual school, so they spent a lot of time on field trips visiting museums and landmarks. There were photos on buses, photos near rivers and lakes, photos in Glacier Park with a carved wood grizzly at the center.

She found one of Ariel and Jennifer. It made her pause for a moment. Jennifer was looking at her friend with such love in her eyes. Ariel was smiling back at her in a way that told Lizzy she'd known how devoted Jennifer was to her.

Flipping through the rest, of high school kids mugging faces at the camera and being silly, she couldn't imagine why anyone had gone to the trouble of breaking into the ranch for these. Not that she knew what she was looking for. She wasn't even sure there was anything to find.

Given the torn photo of Ariel, it was a pretty good guess that the burglar was one of their classmates. No one else would have known the photos were at the guest ranch.

Her phone rang. She picked up, glad for the interruption. Even more glad when she heard that the lab had found fingerprints on the photographs that had been damaged and thrown on the floor.

"That quickly?" She didn't know if she was more surprised by how fast they'd gotten a hit or the fact that whoever had broken into the Sterlings' lodge had been so careless as to leave their fingerprints.

"Her prints were all over the photos, making it apparent that she was the last person to touch them."

"Her?"

"There were numerous prints, but the ones on the top of the other prints—other than Deputy Turner's—belong to a woman named Stephanie Curtis."

Her name before she married Eric Tanner. "Her prints were on file?" Lizzy asked in surprise.

"A driving-under-the-influence arrest."

"When was that?" she asked.

"Just over ten years ago." He read off the date.

The night of the graduation party? That was why it hadn't been in the newspaper—Stephanie had been underage at the time of her arrest.

The night Ariel was murdered. Was this why Stephanie had been late getting to the cemetery to meet Ashley and Jennifer? It could explain why she hadn't wanted to give Lizzy her alibi. Especially if Stephanie hadn't been alone.

"Was anyone else involved?" she asked.

"Mark Matheson was in the car with her. It wasn't clear who was driving, according to the officer's report. Both refused Breathalyzer tests. Both were clearly intoxicated. Matheson called his lawyer and swore Stephanie was driving the car."

She'd bet he'd let her take the rap, knowing she was underage and it would get buried. What was Stephanie doing with Ariel's dad at that time of night with them both being legally drunk?

Lizzy's head was swimming. Stephanie's fingerprints were on the photos. Why would Stephanie break into the lodge and go through the snapshots? Could it have something to do with why she was with Ariel's father the night of the graduation party?

Maybe more baffling, why would she rip up photos of Ariel? Clearly, even the woman's besties hadn't been such good friends after all. Stephanie had been friends with Ariel from as far back as Lizzy could remember. The girl had practically lived at Ariel's house—which could explain what she was doing with Mark Matheson that night.

Lizzy thought about the person who'd killed Ariel. Had it been building up until graduation party night when the person couldn't take it any longer? Had the person been planning Ariel's death for days, weeks, even months?

As she left her office on her way to her favorite judge's home, she tried to imagine the petite blonde smashing the window at the lodge to reach in and open the door. Stephanie was at the reunion meeting so she would have known that Shade had taken the photos up to the lodge.

Had she been looking for one particular photo as

Shade had suggested? It seemed like a good theory given that Stephanie had gone to the trouble of driving up there, breaking in and searching through the photographs—until she was almost caught. But was she also the person who'd crashed into Lizzy that evening on the mountain road?

Lizzy felt at least some of the pieces coming together. Stephanie had admitted leaving the graduation party early and refused to tell her where she'd been. Also according to Ashley, when Ariel had texted about meeting at the cemetery, Stephanie had arrived forty-five minutes late and hadn't provided an explanation.

Now the question was, had she found whatever she'd been looking for when she broke into the lodge? And was it so incriminating that it would put her behind bars for Ariel's murder? Or was it merely to hide both her DUI and her relationship with Mark Matheson, the father of her good friend?

Lizzy swung by the judge's house, knowing he wouldn't have left for the office yet. She needed a search warrant before she visited Stephanie with what she did know.

STEPHANIE, STEPHANIE. YOU had to know that the truth was going to come out. It was only a matter of time. Some secrets just can't stay buried. I suspected where you'd gone the night of the graduation party. I couldn't believe, though, that you wouldn't take my threat seriously.

I told you that if you ever saw my father again, I

*would expose you and not just to my mother. I would
tell everyone—especially that dental student you had
a crush on.*

*But you didn't listen, did you? Well, my father fi-
nally proved what kind of man he was that night, didn't
he? He let you take the fall for driving drunk with the
promise of his lawyer smoothing it all over since you
were underage. That's my daddy for you.*

*Why would you though? Because he said he was in
enough trouble without being caught driving drunk
with his teenage lover?*

*Did you really think he would leave my mother
for you? Guess you didn't know he would be going
to prison for twelve years. Decided not to wait for
him? That was probably the smartest decision you
ever made, but you seem a little bitter about it. Not
that I blame you. But you didn't have to marry that
boring dentist. That was your choice.*

*Don't feel bad. I'm living—so to speak—with my
bad choices, too. At least you're still breathing. For
the moment.*

Once back at the ranch, Shade took the package from
Ariel into the kitchen. His brothers must have been out
working somewhere on the ranch. Dorothea had her
knitting group this afternoon, followed by a date with
her fiancé, former sheriff Sid Anderson. The house
was peacefully quiet.

Shade was glad to be alone. He wanted to see what
Ariel had left him without anyone looking over his

shoulder. He couldn't imagine what might be inside. Something bad? Or maybe she just wanted to return presents he'd given her while they'd been going out.

But with Ariel, he expected the worst.

He was anxious to talk to Hannah again and just wanted to get whatever this was from Ariel over with as quickly as possible.

Taking a sharp knife, he cut the tape on the package and then carefully dumped the contents onto the kitchen counter. There'd been no rattle of anything inside. He realized that was because she'd wrapped the contents in his favorite T-shirt that she'd taken when they'd first started dating.

The T-shirt had been shredded. No surprise there. As he lifted it by what was left of one sleeve, a disk fell out. He stared at it in confusion. There was no label, no hint as to what might be on it.

He looked through the rest of the package but found nothing else. His destroyed T-shirt and an unlabeled disk.

"I SAID EVERYTHING I had to say the last time you were here," Stephanie said when she opened her front door to find the sheriff standing on her doorstep. "I'm not saying another word until my lawyer is present."

"Then I suggest you call your lawyer," Lizzy said, holding up her badge and the warrant. "We can talk here or I can have you taken down to the sheriff's office. Your choice. But right now I have a warrant to search the premises."

Stephanie looked past her to the two deputies standing outside and began to fish out her cell phone. Within minutes, her attorney arrived at the house. He read the warrant and then spoke with his client for a moment before waving Lizzy and the deputies inside. She noticed that Stephanie's face was the color of bone as her attorney took her hand and the two sat down on the couch to watch her house being ransacked.

Within minutes, they'd located an unregistered gun, some old rope the same color as that used to tie Ariel to the steering wheel and photos taken from the lodge break-in.

"I've never seen that rope before in my life," Stephanie cried when she saw one of the deputies bagging it as evidence. "Where did you find that? It's not mine. And the gun—" Her attorney stopped her from saying any more.

"Stephanie Curtis Tanner," Lizzy began, "you are under arrest for the burglary of Sterling's Montana Guest Ranch. You have the right to remain silent. Anything you—"

"I broke into the lodge," Stephanie cried as her lawyer tried again to get her to be quiet. "But I didn't kill Ariel. I'm telling you the truth. I can prove it."

"You're not being charged with murder," her attorney said as he fought to get her attention. "You really shouldn't say anything more."

"I can prove I was nowhere near that pond the night she died," Stephanie cried as she was helped to her feet and handcuffed.

"Your lawyer is right. You're being arrested for breaking and entering, robbery, and trespassing." Lizzy watched the woman's face as she continued to read her her Miranda rights and then led her out to the patrol SUV.

SHADE WAS ABOUT to put the disk into his computer, when his cell phone rang. He cursed and checked to see who was calling. Hannah. He glanced at the disk as his phone rang again. He took the call. What were a few more hours in the big scope of things?

"Hello?"

"Do you want to see your daughter?"

"Hannah, if you're lying—"

"I'm not. We're staying at a motel on the edge of town." She gave him the name and address. "There's a café across the street. We'll be waiting there for you. Can you come now before I change my mind?"

He disconnected and headed for his pickup for the drive into Kalispell. He couldn't believe how nervous he was. What if this really was his daughter? The thought blew his mind. He always knew he'd get married someday, but kids? Those were so far down the road he hadn't even imagined them yet.

Shade knew what his brothers and Dorothea would probably say about it. That he wasn't ready for that kind of responsibility. He was too young. He was still sowing his oats. He hadn't even thought about settling down—until Ariel's body was found and he'd thought that finally there was nothing standing in his way of dating Lizzy.

He tried not to think too far ahead. Until he knew for certain…

Swinging into a parking spot in front of the café, he looked into the front windows. He couldn't see anyone because of the glare. Taking a breath and letting it out slowly, he climbed out of his truck.

He didn't see Hannah at first as he stepped in the door of the café. But when he did, his gaze flew to the little girl standing on the booth seat next to her.

"May I help you?" a woman holding a stack of menus inquired.

Shade barely heard her. Maisie. She had his blue eyes and the sandy blond hair he'd had at that age. She looked like photos he'd seen of himself before his first haircut.

She saw him and her big blue gaze locked with his. He found himself walking toward the little girl, pulled like metal to a magnet.

CHAPTER ELEVEN

WHEN SHE RETURNED to her office, Lizzy took a better look at the two photographs that had been in Stephanie's purse. They appeared to be random shots taken at a party. At Brad's house? She thought so. Brad had lived with his father, a long-haul trucker who spent most of his time on the road.

Lizzy recognized the few people dancing or standing around drinking in the living room. Everyone appeared to be there except for her and Kayla. Past the dancers on the left side of the photo, she could see into the kitchen where two people were barely recognizable.

Pulling out the magnifying glass from her drawer, she examined the photo. Ariel and Shade appeared to be having a heated conversation. Seeing the two of them gave her heart a little bump of jealousy, even though she knew this photo must have been taken before graduation—the two were clearly close to over, if they hadn't been already.

She searched the rest of the photograph but didn't see Stephanie. Picking up a similar photo, she studied it, as well. It appeared to have been taken at a slightly different angle. Shade and Ariel were still arguing in the kitchen, but in this shot, Lizzy could see through the front window out into the yard.

Two figures stood near a tree, both barely more than shadows.

She put the magnifying glass on them. The woman was definitely Stephanie, and she was with a man. They were embracing. Lizzy picked up the first photo again. She hadn't noticed the people outside in the first one, but she could see them now that she knew where to look.

As she put the magnifying glass on them, she realized why Stephanie had stolen the photos and what she'd hoped to hide. The man with his arms around her was Mark Matheson.

After all this time, Stephanie was still determined to keep this secret? Lizzy realized that she must have never told her husband about her former lover. Who else knew about this secret? Ariel.

Lizzy thought about the rope and gun they'd found at her house, then called the office to verify something.

Hanging up, she made the calculations. Stephanie had been released after her DUI arrest in plenty of time to return to the party, climb into the back of Ariel's car, and kill her before meeting Ashley and Jennifer at the cemetery.

CHAPTER TWELVE

HANNAH HAD TEARS in her eyes and a half smile on her lips as Shade approached the table in the café. She looked as nervous as he felt. Could he have misjudged her? He reminded himself that she hadn't been honest with him three years ago. That didn't make her reliable.

But as his gaze went back to the little girl, he felt his heart inflate to near bursting. He slid into the booth across from them. Maisie had a spoon and was trying to pound it on the table. Hannah was having none of it and took the spoon. Before the little girl could protest, Hannah handed her a packet of sugar, shook it. Maisie's sweet face went from a scowl and near tears to lit up in a heart-stealing smile instantly.

Hannah must have seen the way he was staring at the girl. "She looks like you in the pictures I've seen of you at this age."

He recalled her going through the photo albums the Christmas he'd brought her home to the ranch. Dorothea had been shocked that he'd brought a girl home. She'd thought it was serious—until she was around them for a few days.

"She's not the right one for you," Dorothea had said, as if he didn't know that.

"We're friends. That's all," he'd told her. "She didn't have anywhere to go over the holidays so I brought her to the ranch. Sorry you read too much into it."

"She's more serious than you are."

He'd laughed and shaken his head. "We're just having fun. She knows that."

But Dorothea had given him that knowing look of hers. "Be careful or you'll find yourself married before you know it."

"Me? Married?" That was a laugh.

He certainly hadn't been ready for marriage at that age. Only recently had he even thought of settling down and only because of Lizzy.

Maisie began to sing softly. He didn't catch all the words, but he could tell it was a song she was making up on the spot. He caught enough of it, though, to hear her cute little lisp. It clutched at his heart.

When she saw him watching her, she smiled and said, "It's juth a thong I made up." She shook her head. "I don't know real thongs. I'm only two and a hav."

With a thud, he fell in love with this little girl. If Hannah was wrong and Maisie wasn't his... "I'm going to have to see some kind of blood test or DNA test," he said as he swallowed the lump in his throat.

Hannah nodded. "I figured you'd say that. I made an appointment for us to have the test done here in town at a lab this afternoon at three." She slid a card across the table to him with the name and address of the lab.

"Wow." His head spun. Everything was moving way too fast for him and he said as much.

"I thought you'd want to know as quickly as possible," she said in her defense.

He studied her for a long moment, suspecting there was more going on here. What was he missing? "Fine." He looked again at Maisie. She was singing softly and shaking the sugar packet in time to music in her head. He didn't think any little girl could be more adorable. He felt his heart swell at even the thought that she could be his.

The waitress came over to take their orders. He shook his head. He didn't think he could get down a bite or drink a thing. "I need to go, but let me buy the two of you lunch." He pulled out his wallet.

"We aren't after your money, Shade." Hannah sounded offended.

He froze for a moment, but then took out a twenty and laid it on the table. "It's just lunch, Hannah. I'll see the two of you at three."

LIZZY FINALLY HAD a chance to check her voice mail. She saw that Shade had called to see how she was feeling. As she listened to the message, she noticed she was smiling. The realization didn't make her happy. Too much was riding on her solving Ariel's killer to let Shade Sterling distract her. And what a distraction the cowboy was. She smiled again despite herself. Too bad it had taken ten years and Ariel's death to free them from the past.

Pocketing her phone, she headed for the door. She wanted to talk to Stephanie. But at the jail, she had to wait for the woman's lawyer and then Stephanie refused to say anything. Lizzy was sure that she had her killer, but she needed more proof.

Anxious to talk to more of her classmates before the reunion, she found Brad Davis at his newspaper's office in downtown Whitefish. It was a hole-in-the-wall kind of place since actual printing of the paper was done elsewhere.

She walked past two women working in the front. One started to speak, but Lizzy waved her off and kept going until she reached the back of the building where Brad had his feet up on his desk, his chair leaned back and a phone pressed against his ear.

He sat up quickly, his shoes hitting the floor with a thunk when he saw her. "Let me call you back," he said into the phone and got to his feet. "Sheriff, to what do I owe this pleasure?"

Lizzy closed the door to his office. "I want to ask you about Ariel."

"Ask me what?" He seemed to shake himself. "You can't seriously think that I…" He laughed. "Why would I kill Ariel?"

"You tell me. What were some of the names she called you?"

His smile turned into a scowl. "That was high

school. There were bullies and there were nerds. I was a nerd who liked to read and write. Ariel was…" His gaze narrowed. "I don't have to tell you what Ariel was. You had firsthand knowledge. And before we go any further, I think you should know…" He hesitated. "After what I saw at the scene of the murder, I had a thought. I looked in my family's garage."

"You found the rope."

He nodded. "It was old, stuffed back under a bunch of junk. My father's a hoarder. The rope had been cut. I left it right where it was, knowing I'd be seeing you and could tell you where you could find it. Now does that sound like I was the one who killed her?"

Lizzy slid into a chair across from his desk and pulled out her notebook and pen. "Tell me about the night of our graduation party."

He groaned and took his chair again. "Let's make this quick. I have work to do. Yes, I saw Ariel. She came storming over to me, demanded I move my car because it was blocking her in."

She frowned. "Why was your car parked behind hers?"

"She'd arrived before I got back with more ice, so I pulled in behind her. By then, it was the only place to park."

Lizzy nodded and encouraged him to continue.

"I told her to hold her horses. She got abusive. No surprise there. So I took my time moving my car and she cursed at me the entire time."

"What did you do after you moved your car?"

"I parked it again and came back to the party. You can ask anyone who was there. I didn't leave. I didn't follow her out to the pond."

"Was she alone in her car?"

He shrugged. "As far as I know."

"Who saw you after she left?"

He sighed. "I don't know. I saw you talking to Christopher. You looked upset. I saw Shade leave not long after Ariel. I was looking around for Stephanie but I couldn't find her."

"Why were you looking for Stephanie?"

"I wanted to give her shit for something she wrote in my yearbook, okay?"

"But you didn't see her?"

He shook his head.

"Did you see anyone nearby when you went to move your car?"

"You mean like someone hiding in the bushes?"

She didn't bother to answer.

"No. But it was really dark that night. The wind had come up. I was parked behind Ariel's SUV in the pines." He shrugged and looked at his phone. "If that's all, I have a newspaper to put out if you don't mind."

"You saw Ariel leave."

"Tore out like a bat out of hell and didn't bother to look back."

Lizzy nodded and got to her feet. "You'll be at the reunion at the guest ranch?"

"Wouldn't miss it for the world. Now how about giving me some information on the investigation?"

She walked toward the door, then stopped to turn back. "How was it that you ended up at Progressive?"

The question seemed to catch him flat-footed. "I didn't fit in at the regular high school. The jocks took offense that I breathed the same air they did. I got tired of having my head stuffed in toilets. It's an old story."

She wondered if that was all there was to it.

"There was one other thing," he said as if he'd been saving it. "At the time, it didn't seem important. My mother complained that one of her knives was missing from the kitchen. Now I'm thinking the killer might have taken it to cut the ski rope in my garage and maybe use it to get Ariel to drive to the pond?"

She studied him. He'd been holding on to this information from the moment he heard about Ariel's body being found. Or maybe longer.

"But you didn't see anyone in or around her car but Ariel."

"I'm telling you everything I know." He held up his hands. "I'm doing my best to help you. How about reciprocating and telling me something I can print about the murder investigation?"

"It's continuing," she said over her shoulder as she left. "I'll have one of my deputies pick up the yellow water ski rope from your garage."

Walking toward her patrol SUV, she saw something fluttering on her windshield. The piece of paper had been stuck under the wiper blade on the driver's side.

Touching as little of it as possible, she pulled the torn piece of paper out and read:

Don't act like you're above all this. You were no better than Ariel. I'd watch your back if I was you or you'll end up in that same pond.

CHAPTER THIRTEEN

HIS EMOTIONS ALL over the place, Shade returned to the ranch. Right now he welcomed any distraction from the thought of the DNA appointment that afternoon. He had no idea what he would do if it turned out that Maisie wasn't his. Or if Maisie *was* his, he thought. What would he do? What had Hannah come here looking for? Marriage?

He shook his head. He wouldn't marry a woman he didn't love even for his own adorable daughter. Though, just the thought of Maisie made him realize that there wasn't much he wouldn't do for her—if she was his daughter.

All he knew for sure was that he'd never be the same. If Maisie was his, he didn't know what kind of relationship they could have or what kind of connection Hannah would be comfortable with. But surely she wouldn't have come here to tell him this news unless she wanted him to have a relationship with his daughter, right?

What if Hannah didn't know who Maisie's father was and had come here trying to solve the riddle?

That thought rattled him. Maybe she'd had other lovers around the same time he'd been with her.

Desperately needing a distraction, he headed straight to his area of the house, glad that he hadn't encountered any of his family or Dorothea on the way. As he entered the living area, he saw the disk next to the computer, right where he'd left it. He picked it up and pushed it into the drive. Was he ready for this on top of everything else? Bracing himself, he hit Play. His computer screen flickered and went dark. Nothing happened for a few moments.

He was asking himself why Ariel would have left him a blank disk when the screen flickered again and he heard grunting before he saw what appeared to be a man's bare back filling the screen. His heart slammed against his ribs. It was dark in the room, but he didn't need to see to know where this had been recorded or what was happening.

It was Ariel's bedroom. The camera must have been set up in her closet. He didn't recognize the man nor could he see the woman in the dim light. But he could see the edge of the bed and what appeared to be the lower half of a woman's dress discarded there. He'd seen that fabric before. It was Lizzy's favorite dress. His heart thundered in his chest. He listened to the man's labored grunts as he finished and reached down to pull up his pants.

Shade saw the tattoo on his forearm an instant before the screen went black.

Shade watched until there was nothing more. He

ejected the disk, sick to his stomach. He'd recognized the tattoo. He knew that man.

LIZZY COULDN'T HELP being a little spooked after finding the typed note and recalling what had happened not quite twenty-four hours ago up on the mountain. Her head and neck still ached from being rammed by the old-model sedan. She didn't need another threat.

Lizzy looked around the parking area but didn't see anyone lurking nearby. She felt a shudder as she climbed into her patrol SUV, even though she knew this kind of thing often went with the job. She had deputies trying to track down the car that had T-boned her, but so far nothing.

After arresting Stephanie Curtis Tanner, Lizzy expected the deputies would find something that implicated the blonde. It seemed too much of a coincidence that Stephanie had broken into the lodge and taken photographs and not been the person who'd wrecked Lizzy's SUV later that evening.

But at the same time, the threat to kill her the same way Ariel had died didn't seem to go with whoever had T-boned her on the road from the guest ranch. Whoever had crashed into her had been serious. No warning at all.

She had read the description of how Ariel had probably died from the coroner. She couldn't imagine what the young woman had gone through her last minutes in that sinking car. She wondered if the killer had enjoyed watching her die.

Back at her office, she had the note checked for fingerprints and wasn't surprised when there weren't any. Unlike Stephanie with the photos, this person had known not to leave any evidence behind.

Why leave the threat on her windshield? They had to know she wasn't going to stop her investigation. All she could think was that someone was worried about what she would discover.

"Ace," she said as the deputy walked past her office. She hadn't wanted him involved in this case. But they were short staffed and she didn't want to put this off. Plus it was something she thought he could handle. "I need you to check on something for me."

He stepped in, clearly reluctant, clearly belligerent. She wanted to tell him to knock it off, but decided the best way to handle this was to pretend nothing was wrong. She was the sheriff. Period.

"What do you need, *Lizzy*?"

Okay. "First off, I'm Sheriff Conners. Second, I need you to check all the surveillance cameras around the local newspaper office. See if my car is on any of them in the last couple hours. Specifically, I'm looking for the person who left a note on my windshield."

Ace smirked. "Got a nasty note about you being sheriff?"

"No, I received a death threat from a possible killer."

He blinked. "Ariel Matheson's killer?"

"Please get right on this. Thank you." She looked at the papers on her desk until he left. She'd known he was going to be a problem since he ran against her for the election—and it was clear he didn't like working for a woman. He might as well adjust to it because the world was changing and quickly. Women were coming into their own across the country. Maybe Ace hadn't heard.

She had more important things to worry about than the deputy though. She saw she had a message from Catherine Warner with Ariel's doctor's name and a note saying Catherine had told the doctor to provide whatever information Lizzy needed.

Lizzy picked up the phone and made the call. To her surprise she was put right through to Dr. Henry Dodd, the same doctor who'd delivered Lizzy.

"I'm pretty sure I know why you're calling," Dr. Dodd said after a few moments of chitchat.

"Was Ariel pregnant?"

"Six weeks along."

So definitely not Shade's. "She didn't mention the father, did she?"

"I'm afraid not."

"One more question. Did she seem happy about the pregnancy?"

"Not at all. She was quite upset and quickly got on her phone to someone."

"I'm guessing you overheard the conversation."

Silence, then a sigh. "It's been ten years so I don't remember exactly. But she said something like, 'This is all your fault. Watch it, or I might just keep this baby. You know what that would mean...' I'm sorry

I don't know anything else. I only saw her that one time about the pregnancy."

Lizzy thanked him and disconnected. Ariel had been pregnant with someone's child. A man who'd wanted to remain a secret. What if she'd threatened to keep it, something she clearly knew the father of the baby didn't want? Another motive for murder. But who was the baby's father? Who feared the truth would come out?

Her first thought was Christopher. She called the cell phone number he'd given her. "Did you know Ariel was pregnant when she died?"

"What?"

"Was it your baby?" she asked.

Silence, then a low laugh followed by a curse. "No, it wasn't mine."

"What would you have done if it had been?" Lizzy asked.

No hesitation this time. "I would have married her."

She disconnected and sat for a moment, thinking. There had always been too many secrets, her own included. Ariel traded in secrets, cashing in as needed. Step out of line and she just might slip and tell someone what she knew.

Lizzy feared this was only the beginning of the secrets that would be revealed before she was finished with this murder case. She sighed. Ariel was gone but definitely not forgotten. The young woman had been malicious to so many people. No wonder Lizzy felt a little overwhelmed when she even thought about who might have wanted the woman dead.

She leaned back in her office chair. She had a pretty good idea what had happened that night. The killer had been in the back of Ariel's SUV waiting for her. It was so dark that night that she wouldn't have noticed even if she hadn't been drunk and blind with anger. She hadn't been in any shape to notice anything. Lizzy knew for a fact that Ariel never locked her car. She'd always joked that someone would have to be a fool to steal the car of the state attorney general's daughter.

Lizzy had seen Ariel storming away from the party toward the pines where her car was parked, with Shade chasing after her. They'd argued and Shade said that he'd left. Ariel must have then realized that Brad's car was blocking her in and gone to get him to move it. Brad had said that he didn't see anyone else when he'd moved his car.

He'd said that once he did, she'd taken off like a bat out of hell, as he'd put it. The killer had to already be in the back of her car without her noticing. That night the wind was whipping the tops of the pines, a thunderstorm looming. The night had been dark and Ariel had been in a state. And she'd parked in the trees where it had been even darker. Ariel would have left and headed toward home, which meant she would have driven in the direction of the Sterling Ranch—and the pond.

All the killer had to do was wait until the perfect

moment. Before Ariel reached the turnoff to the sub-division where she lived back in the hills, the killer would have popped up, threatened her with the knife from Brad's kitchen and instructed her to keep going the half mile up the road to the pond.

The killer had the rope and must have already planned to tie Ariel's wrists to the steering wheel.

Lizzy thought of Stephanie locked up in jail. If Stephanie was the killer, Ariel would have thought she was joking. At first. How would Stephanie have been able to tie Ariel's wrists to the steering wheel without putting down the knife? She could have used a drug on her. A roofie or something like it.

But if true, then Stephanie had planned the murder and brought the drug with her to the party. Lizzy's head ached. She had too many questions and few answers.

The police would have taken Stephanie home—and not back to the party after her DUI arrest. Mark Matheson wouldn't have been driving after the close call with the DUI either. Stephanie could have still come back to the party. Her parents were always out of town so they wouldn't have known about the arrest.

At the party, she could have climbed into the back of Ariel's car. But then how did she get to the cemetery later that night? From the pond, it would have been a short walk. If she kept to the trees, she wouldn't have been seen. So she could have pulled it off.

Lizzy called Ashley. "How did Stephanie get to the cemetery to meet you and Jennifer that night?"

It took the woman a moment. "I'm trying to remember. I think she said she had someone drop her off after she got the text."

CHAPTER FOURTEEN

SHADE WATCHED THE recording again, this time with the sound off. He had to be sure of what he'd seen. When it ended, he popped out the disk and picked up his phone. Lizzy's phone went straight to voice mail.

"Ariel left me something. Her mother gave it to me. We need to talk." He disconnected and, putting the disk and T-shirt back into their box, headed out the door. He couldn't sit around waiting for her call. He had time to do a few things before his three o'clock appointment and he knew he'd go crazy if he didn't keep busy.

Also the reunion would begin tomorrow at the guest ranch. He had to be ready no matter what was going on in his personal life. Dorothea had hired two young women to take care of getting the cabins ready. The kitchen had been stocked. Buckshot's leg had healed after he'd broken it last spring and he had been more than ready to come back to work for the weekend.

Basically, everything was ready. Shade needed to pick up the portable screen for the digital slideshow and double-check with Ashley about the awards she wanted given out, and talk to Christopher about the beverage order. He'd said he could get the liquor at cost from a friend's bar.

Shade pulled up to Ashley's, hid the box under his jean jacket on the passenger seat and hopped out of his truck. He knocked at the front door of her place and then tried the knob. Last time he'd talked to her, she'd said to swing by today. He hoped she hadn't forgotten. When the door swung open and he stepped in, he assumed she'd left it unlocked for him. Perhaps the portable screen and awards were just inside.

He froze at the sound of laughter. A female's laughter followed by a male's. Ashley had made a point of telling him that her husband had international flights all week and wouldn't be at the reunion. Maybe his piloting schedule had gotten changed.

Then he heard a voice he recognized. Not her husband's. And from the sound of it, the speaker was headed his way. Shade swore under his breath. He really didn't need this today.

LIZZY COULD FEEL time slipping away. Worse, she was no closer to proving that Stephanie had killed Ariel. What she had so far felt too thin. She needed someone to put Stephanie back at the party when Ariel left. Christopher had seen a shadow in the back of Ariel's SUV. Lizzy needed more than that.

Kayla Harrison lived with her invalid mother down by the river outside of Columbia Falls. Fifteen minutes later, Lizzy pulled up in her drive. The house was surrounded by thick vegetation that gave it an eerie, haunted look. It was clear that the place had been neglected since Kayla's father died.

Her parents had been in their late forties when they adopted Kayla. Her father had died when Kayla was eleven and now Lizzy had heard that her mother wasn't doing well.

Climbing out, she walked down a rock path to the front door, feeling like Gretel without her Hansel. That made her think of Shade. She felt a stirring at the thought of seeing him this weekend. All weekend. But knowing she'd be on a mountainside with a possible killer in the mix did take some of the romance out of it.

Her knock was answered almost immediately. Kayla must have heard her drive up. She'd also probably been expecting her.

"Lizzy," the dark-haired woman said on a ragged breath. "I just put my mother down for her nap. Come in." She stepped aside to let her enter.

The house was cool and dark but neater than Lizzy had expected with Kayla being a full-time caregiver for her mother.

"Would you like something to drink? I have tea."

She shook her head. "Thanks, but I'm fine."

Kayla offered her a chair in the kitchen. "It's more comfortable in here than the living room. I don't want to wake Mom."

"How is she doing?"

"She has good days and bad. This is one of the bad."

"I'm sorry."

Kayla picked at a loose thread in the tablecloth. "Do you know who killed Ariel?"

"No, but I'm trying to find out. You were at the party graduation night," Lizzy said. She remembered seeing her planted on the couch watching everyone like a fly on the wall. In so many ways, Kayla had been like that at school, as well. She was small, quiet and nondescript, a shy girl who barely spoke their senior year. Kayla moved through her classes like a dark ghost, but she was always watching, missing little.

"Did you see Ariel leave that night?" Lizzy asked.

Kayla shook her head. "I was in the house."

"But you must have heard the commotion outside."

"Ariel yelling at Brad." The woman nodded.

"Who was in the house during that time?"

Kayla seemed to think about that for a moment before shaking her head. "No one. I think everyone had gone outside. Brad had set up the beer keg in the garage along with the stereo."

"Who did you see outside?"

Kayla shrugged. "Jennifer and Ashley. I think Josh and Christopher were already in the garage by then."

"Did you see Stephanie?"

"No. I saw her earlier arguing with Ariel. And later I saw Ariel arguing with Jennifer. Ariel was fighting with everyone that night."

"What were they arguing about?"

She shrugged. "I don't know. I only heard bits and pieces. They were trying to keep their voices down."

"Who did you see after Ariel left?"

"I went home. I thought I heard thunder. My mom has always hated to be alone in a bad storm."

Lizzy considered what Kayla had told her. Ariel and Stephanie had been arguing at the party, but also Ariel and Jennifer. Stephanie was getting arrested for a DUI that night so she couldn't have climbed into the back of Ariel's car. Had anyone seen Jennifer after Ariel left? That's what she needed to know. Jennifer could have climbed into the back of Ariel's car to hide while everyone else was distracted by the argument with Brad.

"Did you notice anyone in the kitchen before that?" Lizzy asked, remembering what Brad had said about his mother's missing knife.

Kayla shrugged. "They were all in and out because there's no bathroom in the garage. I saw Ariel mostly going into the kitchen to argue with people so I couldn't hear from where I was sitting on the couch. But like I said, all of them were in the kitchen at one point or another."

"I'm curious," Lizzy said. "How did you end up at Progressive?"

The woman looked away for a moment, her normally pale face suddenly flushed red. "I had problems in public school. I didn't fit in." She smiled. "My mother thought I'd be happier at Progressive because it was smaller."

When Kayla finally looked up and their gazes met,

Lizzy could see that Kayla found humor in that because she hadn't been happier there.

SHADE FROZE AS their former classmate Tyler Brent walked into the room wearing nothing but a white bath towel wrapped around his waist. His dark hair was wet and even from a distance, Shade could smell a cedar blend of bath gel.

Tyler stopped at the sight of Shade standing just inside the door and laughed. "Honey, I think we have a visitor!" his former classmate called back down the hall.

"What are you talking about?" Ashley sounded irritated. She came out wrapping a bright floral print robe around her. Like Tyler, her hair was wet from the shower. She stopped the moment she saw Shade.

"The screen for the slideshow," he said by way of explanation. "You also said something about awards?"

Heat rushed to her face. "I forgot. I—" She glanced at Tyler and her mouth opened. Shade half expected her to say, "This isn't what you think it is." But what would be the point?

"The screen is still in my SUV parked out front," she said. "I'll bring the awards when I come up to the reunion."

He nodded, realizing that Tyler's vehicle must be hidden in the garage. "Sorry to have…" He didn't bother to finish as he turned and went out the door. He was loading the screen from Ashley's car into the passenger side of his pickup when he heard her come out of the house.

Turning, he found Ashley standing barefoot behind him, nervously tying and retying her robe sash. He closed the truck door. "You really don't have to say anything," he told her.

"I feel like I do."

"I'm not going to tell anyone," Shade said. "It's your personal business."

She let out a bitter laugh. "As if anyone can keep a secret in a town this size. I lied. Lance isn't here because of his flight schedule. He fell for one of his flight attendants. He left me but no one knows yet." Her face twisted into a grimace. "Clichéd, huh? Except the flight attendant is older and nowhere near as pretty as me." She threw out the last words on a sob. "Why does that hurt even worse?"

"I'm sorry," he said, wishing he'd thought to call before coming over. He didn't want to know any of this.

"Tyler is…" She laughed. "I have no idea what he is. Temporary, that much I know." Her gaze met his. "I'm sorry I forgot you were coming over."

"Me, too." He'd had enough sexual intrigue for one day. Tipping his Stetson, he went around to the driver's side, slid behind the wheel and started his pickup's engine. Ashley was still standing in the driveway, looking lost, as he drove away.

WHEN SHE RETURNED to her office, Lizzy found the report from DCI in her email inbox. She quickly opened it and printed it off, anxious to have a hard copy to take with her to study. She saw that she had a message from Shade. She promised herself that she'd call him once she looked at the report.

She didn't expect that there would be much in Ariel's car that would help her find the killer. As it came out of the printer, she scanned the report, hoping for at least a thread that she could follow.

Ariel had been tied to the steering wheel with yellow ski rope made of polypropylene, half inch in diameter, which she'd seen for herself at the crime scene.

She dropped down the page. *Probable cause of death.* Drowning.

Farther down the page, she read on. *Decomposition of body.* Due to the tepid temperature of the water in a pond fed by a natural warm spring, the body could have decomposed within days. After ten years, the body had been almost completely skeletonized.

Feeling sick to her stomach, Lizzy let her gaze go to the other information the lab had sent. Little had been found in the car. Most of the clothing had decomposed except for some of the denim and buttons on her jeans and jacket. Her purse and its contents were still intact.

She scanned down the list.

Wallet with eighty-two dollars and forty-seven cents.

Nail clipper.

Small mirror.

She stopped on the line for a small bottle of Juicy perfume.

Instantly, she could smell the scent as if Ariel had walked into the room. It was the woman's signature perfume. None of her friends were allowed to wear it. The scent made Lizzy's already weak stomach roil.

She continued down the list, stopping at the word *lighter* followed by *packet of cigarettes*. Ariel smoked? Lizzy couldn't have been more shocked, until she checked the brand. She remembered who smoked those. With a start, she realized that the cigarettes weren't for Ariel. She'd had Christopher's.

Lizzy already knew that they had been together that night at the party. But why did Ariel have the cigarettes and lighter? Had she planned to meet up with him later? If so, Christopher must not have known or had failed to mention it.

Down the list, Lizzy found something else that stopped her.

Bottle of prescription medicine.

Ariel was taking antianxiety drugs? But then Lizzy saw that the prescription was in Ariel's mother's name.

Then something else caught her eye.

USB flash drive, inoperable.

There probably wasn't anything of interest on the drive anyway. Ariel had often put her homework on a flash drive that she brought to school.

Lizzy reached the bottom of the list and realized something was missing. Ariel's cell phone. She pushed the report aside. Was it possible it had been lost before she'd drowned in the vehicle?

Another thought struck her. What if the killer had

taken it to monitor Ariel's calls? Or to send a text to her friends? The text that got them all to the cemetery that night.

SHADE COULDN'T BELIEVE he was about to get a paternity test as he walked into the lab just before three in the afternoon. He found Hannah sitting in a chair reading a magazine. Maisie was playing in an area filled with toys.

When Hannah saw him, she put down the magazine and said, "We've already had ours done."

The receptionist told him to come right in. As he stepped through the door, he glanced back at Maisie before the door closed. Her blond head was bent over a doll as she attempted to take off the baby's clothing.

It all took only a few minutes including the buccal swab of his mouth. He was told it usually took from two to three days before the results came back, but because of the circumstances, they would put a rush on them.

"We should have results within the next twenty-four hours," he was told. "Do you want to come back in for them or—?"

"The circumstances?" he asked, but the technician was busy writing something down.

When she looked up, she smiled and said, "Or shall we call you with the results?"

"Call." He gave her his cell number, feeling as if caught in a whirlwind.

"Is there anything else we can do for you?" the technician asked, making it clear she was busy.

He shook his head. Feeling as if he was sleepwalking, he returned to the waiting room. He saw that Maisie had climbed up on her mother's lap. Those big blue eyes couldn't seem to stay open. Hannah had her arms around her. With surprise, he saw that Hannah was crying softly.

When she saw him, she hurriedly wiped her eyes and tried to rise. But Maisie's weight seemed too much for her.

He rushed to help, taking the little girl in his arms. He thought she'd put up a fuss, but instead, she cuddled against him and closed her eyes. She felt warm and soft and smelled sweet in his arms. Past Maisie, he saw the expression on Hannah's face.

"What's really going on here?" he asked quietly.

She motioned to the door and he followed her outside where she stopped at the curb and turned back to him. "I'm so sorry to hit you with all of this. First Maisie got hurt and then I found out she was yours and…" Her voice broke. "I never wanted you to know."

"You were never going to tell me that I had a daughter?"

She swallowed. "Thomas had raised her for two years. I thought…" Her voice broke again. "Please, this is hard enough for me. There's more. I wasn't going to tell you this until we got the results, but I already know what they will be—and I think you do, too. Maisie is yours and she needs her father now more than ever—"

"Excuse me, but where does your husband fit into all of this?" he interrupted.

"Thomas doesn't. He wants nothing to do with me or Maisie since learning the truth about her paternity."

Shade blinked. "But he raised her for two years, surely—"

"He and Maisie were never close. I think he suspected she wasn't his since she looked nothing like him, nor does she have his temperament. He was also very disappointed she wasn't a boy. He had his heart set on a son."

Bastard, he thought as he held the sleeping child closer. How could any man have this child for two years and not be the father she needed even if they weren't blood related? "I'm trying to get my head around all of this, but what I can't understand is why you're here now, especially if you planned to keep all of this from me. You do realize how wrong that would have been, don't you?"

She looked away as if trying to get her emotions under control.

"I can see that finding out the truth has been like dropping a bomb into your life. I'm sorry," he continued. "But if Maisie really is mine, what is it you want from me, Hannah?"

Tears filled her eyes again. "I realized that you had the right to know."

He nodded, remembering what the lab tech had said. "You asked for a rush on the DNA tests and they agreed because of the *special circumstances*?"

Hannah looked away for a moment and then wet her lips before she turned back to him. "I'm dying, Shade."

CHAPTER FIFTEEN

SHADE HAD THOUGHT his head was already spinning.
Then Hannah had dropped even more shocking news
on him. *She's dying?* He was having trouble taking
it all in as he left Hannah and Maisie at their motel.
Struggling with his own emotions over everything
he'd learned, he'd actually forgotten all about the video
until he got the call from Lizzy saying she'd gotten his
message. He'd been too upset to think about anything
but what Hannah had told him and what it meant. Before long, Maisie would be without a mother.

"You said Ariel left you something?" Lizzy asked
over the phone. "Shade?"

He'd been in a shocked haze since leaving Hannah and Maisie. He'd carried Maisie to their motel
room and put her on the bed, shaken by the news. If
Maisie hadn't fallen and punctured a hole in her thigh,
they might never had found out that she wasn't Hannah's husband's child. Shade would never have known
Maisie was his. That was if the DNA test came back
positive, of course.

He cleared his throat, thinking how much his life
had changed in a matter of hours and how much more

it could change depending on that DNA test. "It's good to hear your voice," he said, realizing how true it was.

"Shade." She thought he was flirting with her.

"I'm serious. I needed to hear your voice." He could tell that she was busy and didn't want to keep her. But he worried that the video might be important to the case, although he couldn't see how.

"So what did she leave you?"

"A disk. What's on it is…disturbing. I think you might want to take a look at it."

"I'm on my way."

He'd been shaken by the video at first. Now, he was merely angry. When he'd seen the fabric of the dress on the edge of the bed, he'd had one heart-stopping moment where he'd thought it was Lizzy because of her dress. But then he remembered seeing Ariel in that dress and even Jennifer. The girls had all shared their clothes. In that split second, he'd known that the woman in the video wasn't Lizzy.

By the time he'd seen the tattoo on the man, he'd known better. So if Ariel had wanted to put doubt into his mind for longer than a second, she hadn't succeeded.

If Ariel had given the video to him and not died, would he have called Lizzy and insisted she watch the video and assure him it wasn't her? She would have been insulted and probably never spoken to him again—once she got over her initial shock about who was on the video and what it meant.

What disturbed him even more was that Ariel had

recorded this scene. Were there other videos around? Had she used them to blackmail the participants? Or had they known they were being recorded?

If Ariel had been the woman in the bed, had the video been a cry for help? Was it possible that Coach was the father of her baby?

Even if Ariel had lived and given Shade the package, he wouldn't have believed that the girl was Lizzy. But he would have shown it to Lizzy and the truth would have come out. Or had Ariel been so sure that he would believe it and wouldn't show the video to Lizzy that she'd gambled on it?

He realized he was driving himself crazy with these thoughts. He'd never been able to understand Ariel when she was alive. Now that she was dead and gone and had left a twisted mess for them to unravel, it was worse.

However, thinking about Ariel and the video kept him from stressing about the DNA test and Hannah and Maisie. He tried hard not to let himself worry about anything past the paternity test. Once he knew if Maisie was his...he'd deal with it.

He paced the front porch until he saw Lizzy's replacement patrol SUV coming up the road to the ranch house. He'd found the video more than unsettling— just as he knew Ariel had meant it to be.

Lizzy pulled in and got out. He saw her expression change when she saw how upset he was. "Is the video that bad?"

"It is, but there's a lot more going on right now," he

said, knowing this wasn't the time to get into it with her. What would she think if it was true and Maisie was his daughter? More important, what would she think if suddenly he was a single father raising his daughter alone?

"I thought you'd want to see it." He opened the door and led the way down the hall to his living quarters. Living on the ranch with his brothers had worked out all these years because they had added living areas of their own. The ranch house had taken on separate wings so he and his brothers and Dorothea all had plenty of space to themselves.

With the guest ranch and the house his brother Will and his wife, Poppy, shared up on the mountain during the warmer months, there was no reason for them to build another house in the valley. His brother Garrett and his wife, Joslyn, were planning to build their own home next spring near the main valley ranch house. Now with Dorothea getting married soon and moving out, Shade realized it wouldn't be that long before he, too, would be ready to move on. Maybe much sooner than he'd thought. With Lizzy? Now things seemed so up in the air, he didn't know what he could hope for.

He pushed open the door to his living area and handed her the remote. "I'll leave you to it." He thought about telling her to watch out for the part where the woman's dress hem was in view—as well as the man's tattoo—but he knew she'd catch it, just as he had.

Restless, he wandered back outside to sprawl into

one of the chairs on the front porch. Looking out across the land, he tried to concentrate on anything but the woman watching the video inside the house and Maisie's sweet sleeping face as he'd set her on the motel bed earlier.

At the sound of the front door opening sometime later, he sat up and turned to look at her.

"The woman in that video isn't me," she said.

"I recognized the dress, just as Ariel hoped I would."

"It was mine. But I wasn't wearing it the day that video was made because I wasn't the woman on the bed. Ariel borrowed the dress and never returned it, no doubt because she knew it was my favorite. But she wasn't the only one who ended up wearing it. Ashley, Stephanie, Jennifer..." She shrugged. "So the woman in the video could be any one of them."

He'd had time to think about it. "It's Ariel's bedroom and her video so she knew who it was."

Lizzy nodded. "I wouldn't be surprised if it was her in the video. I'm sure she was hoping you'd recognize the dress and think it was me." She made a sound under her breath. "So Ariel left this for you?"

"I doubt she knew she was going to die."

"No, I'm sure she didn't." She sat down in the chair next to him and leaned back to close her eyes as if to take a moment to enjoy the late-afternoon sun. "It was her payback for you breaking up with her. She thought it would be her word against mine. No one ever said she played fair."

"She made it to hurt me and keep the two of us apart," he said, studying her beautiful face in the sunlight. He felt scared that the two of them might never get their chance after all.

Lizzy stirred, opened her eyes and sat up as if ready to go back to work. "Whether she meant to or not, that video proves that someone in Ariel's tight circle of friends was sleeping with our history teacher, Coach Nick Rice. If not Ariel herself."

"Coach," Shade said under his breath. The man had only taught history at Progressive, but apparently he'd coached football at his last school. He liked the nickname and often wore a jacket with *coach* printed on the back.

Lizzy turned to look at him. "You were right. Ariel was six weeks pregnant."

So WHO WAS the mystery woman in the video? I'm not telling. Too bad it didn't work out quite like I'd planned it. I'd hoped the video would come as a shock to Shade and sour his feelings for Lizzy.

But he saw right through my ruse even before Lizzy confirmed that it wasn't her doing the nasty with Coach. Maybe if I'd lived, I could have convinced him otherwise and changed his mind about breaking up with me.

But I hadn't planned on being murdered and dumped into a pond for years. So to say things didn't go so well is putting it mildly.

Given my murder, of course I knew he would show

the video to the sheriff and she would tell him it wasn't her and the two of them could then speculate. Did it have anything to do with my murder? My pregnancy? Let them wonder.

Once Lizzy talks to Coach, he'll set her straight. Or maybe he'll lie. That would certainly make things more interesting. Is he that smart? He might not be, given that he didn't know he was being recorded in my bedroom with a minor.

I do hate that my dirty laundry will be hanging out for everyone to see before this is over. Why didn't I take more of it to my grave?

You reap what you sow. *Isn't that what my grandmother told me when she caught me being my bad self? Grandmother's long dead and I don't need the reminder now. I can clearly see what being vindictive and malicious and conniving has gotten me. A watery grave at the ripe old age of seventeen—and my most buried secrets about to be exposed.*

Worse, the video has only pushed Shade and Lizzy closer. Now they both feel sorry for me. Admittedly, it was pretty pathetic recording Coach that way, but I'd hoped that the video might come in handy...

But Shade and Lizzy aren't out of the woods yet, are they? It appears that I'm not the only one throwing a monkey wrench into their budding relationship.

Shade's former college romance is doing that. So at least I'm enjoying that.

LIZZY FOUND HERSELF deep in thought as she drove back toward town with the video as evidence.

But evidence of what? Maybe all it proved was that Ariel was a very warped young woman, something they'd known for some time now.

She tracked down their former history teacher, Coach Nick Rice. He was teaching at a small private school back east. She called his office number and left a message for him to call. It was time to find out who the woman was in the video.

As she hung up, her concern turned to Shade. He'd acted strangely earlier. On the phone, she'd thought he was flirting with her, joking around like he often did. She'd wondered at the time if he ever took anything seriously.

But sitting on his porch with him, she'd seen a different side of him. Something had been bothering him and she didn't think it was the video. Surely he didn't think that the woman on it had been her.

No, something else was worrying him. The upcoming reunion? The murder investigation? Or something even more serious?

She reminded herself that she didn't have time to worry about Shade Sterling. Glancing at the clock, she realized she might be able to catch Jennifer as she was leaving work. But when she stopped by the café where Jennifer waitressed, she was told that she'd been fired.

Lizzy had seen Jennifer only a few times since high school. She'd always seemed down on her luck. Looking up her residence, Lizzy swung by the apartment complex. Jennifer's older-model sedan was parked in apartment nineteen's slot.

Parking on the street, Lizzy headed for number nineteen. Jennifer answered on the second knock. She was still wearing her uniform from the café. Lizzy caught the faint scent of grease.

"Sheriff," Jennifer said, smiling. "I heard you would be stopping by." She stepped back. "Please come in. Can I offer you a beer? I was just having one myself."

She declined the beer but took a seat in the living room and pulled out her pen and notebook as Jennifer disappeared into the kitchen, returning with a bottle. The woman took a seat. She seemed excited to have company. Lizzy could imagine that she'd had a rough day and was trying to forget it. Even talking about her friend's murder must have seemed better than how the rest of her day had gone.

"So are you getting closer to catching the killer?" Jennifer asked and took a long drink.

"It's still under investigation."

The woman chuckled. "You sound just like the law on TV. I love it."

"I need to ask you about graduation night—in particular, the party."

"Sure, what do you want to know?"

"I understand you had an argument with Ariel earlier in the evening."

Jennifer laughed. "Let me guess. Kayla. Of course she would tell you. That little eavesdropper." She leaned forward, making Lizzy aware that this beer wasn't her first. "What did she tell you?"

"I'd prefer to hear it from you."

Jennifer waved it off. "It was just Ariel being Ariel. You know how she was. She was in a bad mood and taking it out on me."

"Did you see Stephanie before you left?"

Jennifer shook her head. "I don't remember seeing her at all. I'm sure she was there, probably out with the guys."

"When did you leave the party?"

"Before Ariel left. I was tired of all the arguing. A storm was coming in and I wanted to get home before that."

Lizzy frowned, trying to remember if she'd seen Jennifer's car at the party. "Did you drive your car home?"

Jennifer looked surprised. She took a sip of her beer. "No, I ran into this guy I knew. He had a motorcycle. He took me for a ride. Then I got this text from Ashley to meet at the cemetery. I wasn't going to go. I'd really had enough for one night, but I eventually had him drop me by there. I figured one of them would give me a ride to my car."

"Where had you left it?"

"At that convenience mart near Brad's. That's where I saw Snake filling up his bike."

"Snake? What's his real name?"

She shrugged. "I have no idea. He said he used to ride with some biker gang out of California. That's all I know. But I loved riding on the back of his bike and that night I really needed it. I'd just graduated and

I didn't have a clue what I was going to do with my life." She met Lizzy's gaze. "Unlike the rest of you all headed off for college or marriage or whatever."

"What was Stephanie's relationship with Ariel?"

Jennifer looked away for a moment. "It's all going to come out anyway because of Ariel's murder."

"I'm not sure I'm following."

"Her diaries. I'm sure Ariel wrote it all down in them, didn't she?" Jennifer frowned. "You really didn't know? Stephanie told me that Ariel said she had it all in her diary. She said it was all lies but that she couldn't get Ariel to tear out the page. I just assumed you'd read them."

Diaries? Lizzy had gone through what Ariel's mother had given her, but there hadn't been any diaries. Avoiding the question, she said, "What had Ariel written about her that was a lie?"

"I have no idea. I never saw the diaries. I didn't even realize Ariel kept a diary, let alone that she wrote down things about us. When Stephanie told me, I was surprised. But it was just Ariel's take on things. I didn't understand why Steph was so upset. Are you sure I can't get you a beer?" Jennifer asked as she got to her feet to take her empty into the kitchen and presumably get another.

Lizzy rose and put her pen and notebook away. "No, I'm fine. One more thing. Did you see anyone around Ariel's car or anyone possibly following her as she left?"

"Like I said, I left before she did. I saw Shade go

after her, but he came right back. She was arguing with Brad about moving his car before I left."

"Did anyone see you leave?"

Jennifer shrugged. "I think everyone was busy watching Ariel. She always was the center of attention."

"Thanks for taking the time to answer my questions."

Jennifer had stopped in the middle of the room still holding the empty beer bottle. "Who do you think killed her?"

Lizzy avoided the question by saying, "Hard to say with so many people having motives."

"Me included," Jennifer said with a laugh. "I hated her and wasn't sorry to hear she was dead." She must have realized what she'd said and colored. "You know what I mean."

Lizzy did.

SHADE TOLD HIMSELF that he wasn't going to say anything to anyone about Hannah and Maisie until he knew for certain. But the next morning as he was getting packed up to head to the guest ranch to get everything ready for the reunion, Dorothea tapped on his door.

"Want to talk about it?" she asked as she plopped down on the end of his bed.

He smiled, remembering all the times growing up that she'd done the same thing. After their mother had died, Dorothea had become like a mother to them. She might not be a witch and have psychic powers like she claimed, but she definitely seemed to know when he needed to talk.

"Hannah," he said. "Did she say anything to you?"

"About why she was in town, why she wanted to see you?" Dorothea shook her head. "But it upset you, her being here."

He joined her on the end of the bed and without looking at her said, "We dated in college. She broke up with me. Then we met again about three years ago, went out, spent the night together."

"Oh. So she was here trying to get back together again?"

Shade laughed. "Not exactly. She married the guy she broke up with me for and had a kid. Turns out three years ago, she was engaged to him when we met up. But recently she found out, she said, that the kid wasn't her husband's." He glanced over at Dorothea.

Her eyes widened as she looked at him. "This child—"

"Might be mine. I saw the little girl yesterday. Maisie is the spitting image of me at that age."

Dorothea let out a breath. "I see."

"The DNA test results should be back anytime. I'm waiting for the call."

"Does Hannah know you're in love with someone else?" she asked.

He swallowed the lump in this throat. "That's not the problem. Hannah's husband wants nothing to do with Maisie since he found out she isn't his and Hannah is… She's dying."

This time Dorothea let out a whoosh of breath. "Oh my. That poor woman. That poor child." She looked over at him. "Shade, what are you going to do?"

CHAPTER SIXTEEN

LIZZY GOT THE email from the phone company early the next morning. She'd been packing for the reunion when her phone sent the notification. She loaded her car and headed for her office, anxious to see who'd contacted Ariel the night she died—and vice versa.

At the office, she printed out the information and began to go through it, surprised the phone company was able to give her information from ten years before. Her instincts had told her that Ashley might not have been telling the truth about the text from Ariel's phone—but there it was, 11:50 p.m. on the night of the graduation party, minutes after she was seen leaving the party.

What was odd was that Ariel had made a call only minutes after the text. It was the last call made from her phone. Lizzy didn't recognize the number. When she looked it up, she was even more surprised. Why would Ariel call Kayla Harrison, the wallflower back at the party?

And if Kayla got the call, why wouldn't she have mentioned that Ariel called her possibly minutes before she was murdered?

Lizzy would make a point of asking Kayla at the reunion. It surprised her that Ariel even had her number. She looked to see if Ariel had made any other calls to Kayla. She couldn't find any from that date.

The call nagged at her. She tried Kayla's number. No answer. She didn't leave a message. She would see her soon enough.

Realizing there were two classmates she hadn't interviewed yet and that she might still have time to catch them before the reunion, she put Kayla out of her mind temporarily. She didn't know why she'd left Josh and Tyler for last. Maybe because she suspected them the least?

She smiled to herself as she thought about what her aunt had said about the killer being the one you overlooked.

Tyler Brent lived in one of the mansion-like homes on Whitefish Lake. He used to brag that he'd been kicked out of every expensive school in the country before ending up at Progressive. He always dressed preppy, and being a loner, had managed to stay above the fray their last year in high school—the only year he attended.

Ariel called him stuck-up and often tried to bait him, but he'd never risen to it. He'd always stayed aloof as if she didn't bother him. That should have driven Ariel crazy, but for some reason, she left him alone most of the time. Lizzy had always suspected that Ariel envied Tyler because he came from old money.

But it still didn't explain the apparent treaty they'd had between them.

When Tyler opened the door to her, he was dressed in khakis, loafers and a button-down shirt under a cashmere sweater. His hair was a little longer than it had been in high school, but he looked the same. He'd moved back in with his parents after getting kicked out of a number of Ivy League colleges.

"Good morning, Sheriff. I thought you'd forgotten about me."

Lizzy smiled. "Not at all. Do you have a few minutes?"

With a sweep of his arm, he invited her into the huge living room that opened to an even larger kitchen and sunroom. The view of the lake and the mountains was incredible. This morning a light mist hung over the crystal clear water making the surface sparkle. Like a lot of Montana fall days, there wasn't a cloud in the sky. Once the mist burned off the lake, it would be a picture-perfect day, the kind that made people say they wouldn't live anywhere else.

That was until winter set in and many of them turned into snowbirds and headed south. Tyler's parents had already flown the coop for warmer climes, she'd heard.

"I won't take much of your time," Lizzy said. "Are you planning to come to the reunion?"

She expected him to decline and was surprised when he said, "Wouldn't miss it."

"Really? I don't recall seeing you at our graduation party."

He chuckled as he took a chair across from her and crossed his legs, exposing argyle socks. "You're going to want to know my whereabouts. Okay. Here at home. Alone. But you know how I was. I never did play well with others."

"But you're coming to the reunion at the guest ranch?"

His smile broadened. "Only out of curiosity. I want to see how they react when thrown together after what happened to Ariel. They might tear each other apart."

Lizzy certainly hoped not. "Did you kill Ariel?"

"That was blunt enough," he said, looking nonplussed. "Why would I?"

"She wasn't very nice to you."

He laughed. "She was brutal to most everyone. I was lucky that she was only not very nice to me. Also if I killed everyone who wasn't nice to me…" Tyler shook his head. "Ariel didn't bother me. She was a spoiled brat. I probably understood her better than anyone."

"You didn't answer my question."

Grinning, he leaned toward her. "You don't really expect to get the truth when you ask a question like that, do you? Of course I didn't kill her. How's that? But I have some theories on who did."

"I'd love to hear them."

He leaned back. "Maybe I'll share them at the reunion. Until then, I should get packed." He rose to see her out. "Unless you have more questions."

SHADE HAD BEEN doing little other than asking himself what he was going to do about Maisie. Now sitting on the end of his bed talking to Dorothea, he shook his head. "If that little girl is mine…"

"Do you really need the DNA test to confirm what you already know?" Dorothea asked.

Shade pushed to his feet and raked a hand through his hair. "Am I ready to be a father? Hell's bells, until recently, I would have told you I wasn't ready to settle down and be a *husband*. I thought kids were so far into the future I never gave them a thought. But when I saw Maisie…"

"She's already stolen a piece of your heart."

He turned to look at her. "She has and I don't want her to. What if she isn't mine? What if Hannah is lying about everything? What if I make a terrible father and Maisie ends up hating me?"

"You're that afraid of getting your heart broken? No wonder you've never had any relationships longer than a few months," Dorothea said, getting to her feet. "A child is a lifetime relationship. So you'll have time to figure out fatherhood, trust me. You think I knew what to do with you boys when your mother died? I had to wing it and have faith. Since I already loved the lot of you…"

He smiled at her. "You've done a great job."

She scoffed at that. "That's my point. You don't

have to do a great job. You just have to do your best
out of love. Have you told Lizzy yet?"

He swore. "We haven't even been on a date. Don't
you think it's a little early to be dumping this on her?"

"Have a little faith in her. If Lizzy is the right
woman for you, then she can handle it. It will come
as a shock—just as it has for you—but it sounds to me
like you and Maisie are going to be a package deal."

His cell phone rang, making him jump. Checking
it, he saw that the call was from the lab. He let it ring
a second time as he braced himself and picked up.
"Yes, this is Shade Sterling. Yes, I'd prefer to get the
results now over the phone, please."

He listened, then disconnected before turning to
stare at the woman he'd trusted his secrets to since he
was a boy. "I'm a father of a two-year-old."

She smiled and nodded, tears in her eyes as she
clasped her hands as if in prayer. "I can't wait."

JOSH ADAMS LIVED as differently from Tyler Brent as
night and day. Lizzy drove to the trailer park where
Josh had lived in high school with his mother. While
his mother still lived in the court, Josh had bought a
trailer a few rows away.

Lizzy parked in front of the double-wide next to
Josh's highway patrol car. She'd heard that he'd married and divorced not long after high school. What had
surprised her was that he'd gone into law enforcement.

Behind a chicken-wire fence, a mongrel dog began
to bark as she climbed out. Before she could reach the

gate, Josh stuck his head out the door. He squinted at the patrol SUV and then at her.

"Max doesn't like cops," he said and laughed at his joke before turning to the dog. "Shut up, Max!"

The dog slunk off as Josh turned back to her and said, "Come on in, Sheriff. I've been expecting you."

The inside of the trailer looked as if a bachelor lived there. He cleaned a pile of clothes off the couch to make room for her to sit. The air smelled of laundry detergent with only a little undertone of dog. She took a seat on the couch as Josh dropped into a well-worn recliner, his dark gaze narrowed as she pulled out her notebook and pen.

"How about I confess and you take me to jail," he said before she could ask her first question. "I could use the rest and I'm sure the food's better than what I cook."

"*Did* you kill her?"

He sucked at his teeth for a moment. "Someone needed to."

Like Tyler, Josh had been a loner in high school. Moody, bored and generally obnoxious. He'd been the one who always sat in the back of the class with his feet up on the chair in front of him, his arms crossed, his eyes closed. He'd put in his time at school like punishment.

But now he smiled and she realized with a start that he wasn't bad-looking. "Sorry, I know this is serious. Ask your questions."

"What was your relationship with Ariel?"

He looked aghast. "*Relationship?* I ignored her and she didn't abuse me quite so badly."

"Are you coming to the reunion?"

Josh shook his head. "No. I think it could be a bloodbath." He held up his hands quickly. "Just kidding. Kinda."

"I don't remember you attending the graduation party at Brad's."

"Because I didn't."

"Where were you that night?"

"It was my mother's birthday. We threw a party for her. I stayed late and helped her clean up. She'll swear to it on my old man's grave." He grinned. "But then again, she hated his guts." He laughed, then sobered.

"Look, I don't know who snuffed Ariel. Maybe she didn't deserve it." He shrugged. "I doubt she's been missed. Do I think anyone in our class could have killed her? Absolutely. I don't have to tell you what she was like. Me, I didn't let her get to me." He shook his head and sighed. "But she did a number on some of the others. They say you never get over high school." He shrugged again and laughed. "I didn't have any trouble getting over it."

Lizzy shut her notebook and put it and her pen away. "I was surprised when you went into law enforcement."

He nodded. "You and a lot of other people."

She studied him for a moment, realizing how different he was from high school. The past ten years had changed him. Or she hadn't really known him.

Wasn't that her fear? That she hadn't known any of the students she went to school with?

"If you had to pick the one person who hated Ariel the most, who would it be?"

He chuckled, leaning back in the chair as he gave it some thought. "That one blonde. Definitely that one blonde." He grinned.

"Are you saying it was one of her best friends or all of them?"

"Take your pick. They're all capable of murder, trust me."

AFTER GETTING THE news from the lab, Shade told Dorothea he needed to take a walk. He headed out across the ranch, stretching his long legs and breathing in the fall morning as if short of oxygen.

When he finally stopped, he pulled out his phone and called Lizzy. "I need to talk to you."

"Sounds serious."

"Any chance you could get to the guest ranch a little early so we could have some time together? It's important."

"I'm all packed. I could probably leave now." She sounded hesitant.

"This isn't me just trying to get you alone to charm you," he said.

"That's good to hear because you aren't all that charming."

He chuckled. "We both know that isn't true. Seriously," he said. "It's important. There's something I need to tell you."

"You don't want to give me a hint?"

"I'd rather not get into it on the phone."

She sighed. "You do realize what you're suggesting. That I meet my number one suspect at an isolated guest ranch before anyone else arrives. Sounds dangerous."

"Come on, we both know you aren't afraid of anything, especially me."

Lizzy laughed, sounding almost nervous. "Just shows that you don't know me."

"You'll be safe."

He heard her chuckle. "I'm not so sure about that," she said.

"This time, I promise."

She made a worried sound. "Is everything all right, Shade?"

"Yes and no and maybe so. We'll talk when I see you."

"Okay, then I'll see you soon."

He disconnected and headed back to the ranch house. Dorothea gave him an encouraging nod when he found her in the kitchen and told her about his meeting with Lizzy, but he couldn't help feeling scared. What if he told her and that was it? What woman would be interested in taking on a man like him— and a two-year-old? That he and Lizzy might not get their chance made his heart ache. Seeing her again had made him realize that he'd wanted this for a long time.

The timing had never been right since high school. Now it might be fatherhood, something he was terrified about, but at the same time excited.

He stepped out of the kitchen to call Hannah.

She answered on the first ring. "You heard from the lab?"

"I did. But I knew yesterday when I saw Maisie. I need to ask you something—"

"I have maybe a few months."

"That wasn't what I was going to ask you. This weekend is my class reunion. Ten year. It's a long story. But it's being held up at the family guest ranch. I have to go."

"Dorothea told me."

"But maybe you and Maisie would like to come up Sunday. That's family day."

She was quiet so long he feared he'd lost her. Then he heard her sniff. "That would be nice."

"Great. It's Sterling's Montana Guest Ranch. Google doesn't work real well in this part of the country."

"Don't worry, I'll find it."

He cleared his throat. "How's Maisie?"

"She's good. She said she likes your whiskers. She doesn't understand designer stubble."

Shade laughed. "Tell her that I like her blue eyes. I'll see the two of you Sunday." He disconnected and swallowed the lump in his throat. He was doing this.

Lizzy had just loaded her bag in her SUV when she got the call from Ace.

"Sorry, no video surveillance that I could find on your car the day you were parked in front of the newspaper office," the deputy said.

She'd known it was a long shot. "Thanks. You know I'll be up at the Sterling guest ranch today through the weekend. There's no cell service up there but the dispatcher has the main lodge number if I'm needed."

"I'm sure we can hold down the fort, Sheriff."

She wished she were sure about that. She disconnected, only to get another call as she slid behind the wheel. Their former history teacher, Coach Nick Rice, had heard about Ariel's murder and sounded shocked.

She asked, "Did you know she was pregnant?"

"No."

"Were you the father?"

"She was pregnant?"

"Nick, I have a video of you making love in Ariel's room."

"What? Are you kidding? A video? You're sure it's me?"

She sighed. "It's you. I need to know who you were making love to."

He swore. "I should have known. Ariel made a video? Of course she did." He groaned.

"Was she blackmailing you?" She feared for a moment that he'd hung up.

"Oh man," he said. She could hear how rattled he was. "Look, I had nothing to do with her murder. I wasn't even in town. I was on a plane that almost crashed."

"You haven't answered my question. The video is now part of my investigation. I need to know who the woman was and if Ariel was blackmailing you."

"With the kind of money a teacher makes? Why would a rich girl blackmail me?"

"Why were you making love in her bedroom?"

He swore again. "Okay, it happened once. Just once. I'd had too much to drink. I wasn't thinking clearly. It was hard to find a place to meet so we used Ariel's room. She wasn't supposed to be home, let alone recording us."

"Who's *us*?"

"Ashley. She wasn't underage. She'd turned eighteen by then."

"You were her *teacher*."

"I'm not suggesting it is right, but she was legal…"

"I know Ariel. She wouldn't have made that video unless she used it against you in some way."

He sighed heavily. "She wanted a better grade in history so I gave it to her. That was it. She could have turned me in to the school board but she didn't. That was the end of it. Honestly I didn't even believe it when she said she made a video of Ashley and me. I just changed her grade. That was it."

"You're telling me you never slept with Ariel?"

"Never."

"Is there anyone who might have wanted to kill Ariel?"

He laughed bitterly. "Everyone who knew her."

"Anyone in our class."

"It would be harder to come up with a name of someone who didn't. Sorry."

She got off the phone feeling as if she needed to wash her hands. Ashley and Coach? She shuddered. All Lizzy could think was that Ariel had put her up to it.

That alone gave Ashley motive for wanting to kill Ariel—especially after she heard about the video.

Lizzy recalled what Jennifer had told her last night about Ariel's diaries. She called Ariel's mother. "I hate to bother you again, Catherine."

"No, please, anything I can do, you know I will. Are you all right? I heard about your car crash."

"I'm fine. A little sore but fine. Did Ariel keep a diary?"

"If she did, I wasn't aware of it. But she was very private and out of respect, I never went into her room unless she was there. I didn't want to be the kind of mother who snooped around looking for trouble. Now I wish I had. Maybe I'd know what was going on with her before…" Her voice broke.

"I went through everything that you gave me," Lizzy said. "If you run across any diaries, you'll let me know?"

"Of course. I'll take another look and call if I find anything."

Lizzy had barely disconnected when she got the call from the lab. The yellow ski rope that had been found cut in Brad's garage matched both the rope found at the crime scene—and at Stephanie Curtis Tanner's house.

Had Lizzy found her killer? She had the rope along with circumstantial evidence. Was it enough? She called only to find out that Stephanie had made bail. Would she come up to the reunion? Or would she run? All Lizzy knew was that she didn't have enough evidence to arrest her again. Not yet.

It was nearly two by the time Lizzy headed up the mountain to the guest ranch. Her head hurt and her body still ached from her wreck. Worse, she still didn't know who'd killed Ariel. She thought about Stephanie and the look on her face when the deputy had come out of the garage with the piece of ski rope. The woman had been more than shocked; she'd been furious. What if she was being framed?

As she drove, Lizzy mulled it all over, trying to keep her mind off why Shade needed to talk to her. She thought that Ariel might have simply told Jennifer she kept a diary and wrote down everything just to scare her. Or maybe whoever killed Ariel had gone to her house that night and taken the diaries. All of them had come and gone at Ariel's house through a side door at all hours of the day and night. Her parents stayed on the opposite side of the house and apparently let her do as she liked.

But assuming the killer wasn't someone who came and went all the time at Ariel's house, how would they have been able to get in and take the missing diaries?

Lizzy had a thought. She made a call. "Question—were the keys in the SUV when it was found in the pond?"

"Sorry, that should have been in the report. The key was in the ignition."

"Just one key?"

"Just one. No key ring."

She disconnected. So the rest of Ariel's keys and phone could be at the bottom of the pond. Or the killer could have taken them. Lizzy felt a sliver of excitement. Why take the keys unless the killer was headed for the house? That meant that the killer was comfortable going to the house but still thought they might need a key to get in? Or was there a key on the ring that opened a special compartment where the diaries were kept hidden?

Find the diaries and you'll find your killer. Except now she was on her way up the mountain to the reunion. She couldn't imagine anything worse than getting all the suspects together at an isolated guest ranch high in the mountains—but especially if one of them was the killer, which she suspected more than ever.

But didn't that mean that one of them had the diaries? Had maybe already read them?

She'd thought the reunion would be the perfect time to unmask the killer. But now all Lizzy could think was that whoever had murdered Ariel might think it the perfect time to settle more old scores.

She thought of the note she found on her windshield. Digging into the past was turning up dirt that someone obviously didn't want unearthed.

Lizzy passed the spot where her patrol SUV had been rammed and felt a shudder. She was lucky she hadn't been killed. She just hoped her luck held.

MY PRECIOUS DIARIES. I hate to think of all the secrets I wrote in them, believing that no one would ever read them. It isn't like I thought someone might kill me because of those secrets and the diaries would come to light.

Except now they're missing and Lizzy is looking for them. As if I don't know who has them. My killer trotted right up there to my house that night. Knew about the key to the box I kept hidden. Knew about the side door. Not even my mother knew about the diaries. I hate being impressed by my killer, but I can't help it. Who would have known that while I was busy learning things about my classmates, some of them were busy learning all about me?

Now what? I really doubt the diaries have ended up in a bonfire and every last page destroyed. Too many pages worth reading for that to happen. What would I do, if the shoe were on the other foot? No contest. I would use them to my advantage, letting secrets out like small bombs that would go off. Surprise!

But that's just me. Remember, I'm the hateful one, the vengeful one.

Because if there was one thing Ariel Matheson was good at, it was learning other people's secrets and using that knowledge against them as needed. Oh, this could make the reunion even more entertaining.

Except now everyone will know even more about me and just how low I would go, won't they? My grandmother must be rolling over in her grave.

CHAPTER SEVENTEEN

As Lizzy came over the rise, she saw the lights on in the lodge. The warm glow drew her, but not as much as the thought of seeing Shade again. As much as she tried to fight it, she was excited about the idea of the two of them going on a date. Nothing might come of it. She knew Shade's reputation.

But there had been something to that kiss so long ago. Not to mention the sparks that flew when she was around him. Her heart beat faster and she felt something low in her belly that she recognized as a desire like none she'd ever felt for any man other than him.

She quickly reminded herself how he'd sounded earlier on the phone. That gave her pause. Shade had never sounded so serious. He had something he wanted to talk to her about.

A shiver ran the length of her spine as she pulled up and parked next to his pickup. It appeared that it was just the two of them. The work on the barn must have been completed because she saw no workmen around. Shade had said to come early so they would be all alone.

She felt another shiver, this one of desire. Both

were dangerous. She didn't believe she could ever be afraid of Shade, no matter what it was he had to tell her. In her heart, she knew he'd had nothing to do with Ariel's murder. But she couldn't help being concerned by what she'd heard in his tone earlier. She got out of her SUV and started up the steps to the lodge.

She hadn't gone far when he appeared on the porch above her. She stopped to look up at him and felt that jolt she always did. He was so handsome, so masculine, so confident. Except right now, the cowboy looked nervous.

"You made it," he said and looked past her to the road as if to see that they really were alone. The reunion committee had decided to hire a party bus to bring everyone up so there wouldn't be any classmates drinking and driving. The bus could take anyone back who had to leave early. Also they wouldn't have ten cars to worry about parking.

But the bus wasn't supposed to arrive for at least another half hour or more. Lizzy slowly mounted the steps. "You said it was important that we talked before the others arrived."

"Come in. I'll take you to your cabin and help you with your bags later." He stepped aside to let her enter the lodge. A blaze crackled in the huge rock fireplace.

She moved toward its golden warmth, too aware of the cowboy behind her as he closed the door. Standing in front of the fire, she warmed her hands, surprised at the chill she felt as he joined her. She watched him out of the corner of her eye. She'd never seen him this nervous. Whatever he had to tell her, he was worried she would…would what?

"I can't believe I waited ten years to ask you out," he said and shook his head. "I feel like a fool now."

"I'm sure the women you dated were glad you kept busy those years," she said, trying to lighten the mood.

He chuckled. "None of them were you."

She could feel his gaze on her. Had she been wrong about why he'd gotten her here early? Maybe it wasn't about anything more serious than seduction. But when she met those amazing blue eyes, she felt her heart stutter in her chest.

"What is it you need to tell me?" she asked, her voice a hoarse whisper.

He sobered at once. She saw him swallow before he said, "I found out something that could change everything between us."

She stared at him. "About Ariel's murder?"

Shade quickly shook his head. "No," he assured her. "No, it's more complicated than that. There's this woman I knew in college and—" At the sound of the front door opening, they both turned.

Lizzy hadn't heard a vehicle drive up over the pounding of her heart. There was this woman he knew in college?

But then Brad Davis came in, his boots thumping on the hardwood floor, his rolling suitcase squeaking as he let the door close behind him.

"Hey!" Brad called out. "The temperature is really dropping out there." Like a blustery gust of cold air, he blew in, quickly joining them at the fire. "Glad to have some heat. Hope there's heat in the cabins."

Shade looked pointedly at the clock on the wall. "You're early. Why didn't you take the party bus?"

Brad shook his head. "Thought you might need some help. I also wanted to have a look around the place before everyone got here, maybe take some photos." He glanced at Lizzy before returning his gaze to Shade. "Had a feeling the two of you might already be here. Ready for the excitement to begin?"

"I'm not sure how exciting it's going to be," Lizzy said, hoping it was true as she tried to get her footing under her again. What was it Shade was going to tell her? Something he hadn't wanted to, which was why he hadn't just blurted it out and gotten it over with. She felt sick to her stomach and realized she had really been looking forward to going out with Shade— and where it might lead given the chemistry between them. He'd said that whatever he had to tell her might change everything. It was that serious?

Brad laughed as he looked around. "Oh, I think anything could happen up here during the reunion. Actually, I'm counting on it," he said. "So no one else is here yet? You think they'll all come? I mean, if you were the killer, you wouldn't want to miss this, right? You've gotten away with murder for ten years. You'd be cocky, thinking you're smarter than everyone. You wouldn't want to miss the speculation while everyone tries to figure out which of us did it." He grinned. "We should have a contest. Throw some money in and the person who guesses right gets the pot."

"Or gets killed," Shade said.

Brad chuckled. "There is always that."

Lizzy turned to study the man. "You certainly have figured out what the killer is thinking. Don't forget that you're a suspect and right now, you've just moved up my list."

Brad beamed. "I think that's the nicest thing you've ever said to me. I'm honored."

"Let me show you to your cabin," Shade said to him. Turning to her, he added, "I'll be right back."

"Why don't I tag along and you can show me to mine?" She needed to get him alone to find out what he was going to tell her. It would haunt her the entire reunion if she couldn't find out what else he was going to say.

Or maybe it was better not to know, she told herself. As they all left the lodge, the sound of a vehicle engine could be heard coming up the road.

SHADE GROANED INWARDLY. He could see how this whole weekend was going to go. Why had he thought any of this was a good idea? All he wanted was to get Lizzy alone and tell her about Maisie. Why hadn't he let this go for now? Lizzy had enough on her mind. Why hit her with this?

He mentally kicked himself. He'd wanted to get it over with. No, what he'd wanted was to find out if this changed everything—his greatest fear. Dorothea seemed to think that he was underestimating Lizzy if he thought it would be a deal breaker.

He should have known Ariel—if nothing else—would have all of their classmates anxious to get here, to find out what was going on with everyone else. No one wanted to miss anything with all the murder intrigue. And he agreed with Brad. The killer would come to the reunion.

The cabins were all stuck back in the pines and some distance apart. "You're in cabin nine," he told Brad. It was the last one and the farthest from the lodge. "Go on down. I'll join you in a minute." He turned to Lizzy. "Here, let me help you with that."

She shook her head, insisting on carrying her own overnight bag. "What cabin am I in?"

"One. It's the closest." His gaze met hers.

Brad grumbled as he headed off down the trail toward the last cabin in the distance.

As Shade and Lizzy started up the side of the mountain toward her cabin, he said, "I'm sorry we were interrupted."

"Me, too. You were saying something about an old girlfriend from college."

He glanced over at her. He didn't remember saying anything about Hannah being an old girlfriend. "Hannah and I dated, she broke up with me, but we ran into each other three years ago. I didn't know it but she was engaged at the time." They reached the cabin. He stopped and turned to her.

"Shade, please."

He looked into her dark eyes and just as impulsively as he had the night of their graduation party, he reached for her. Cupping the back of her neck, he pulled her into a kiss. It was something he'd wanted to do for so long that he couldn't help himself.

At first she was too surprised to respond, but then he felt her lean into him, lean into the kiss. Time seemed to stop. The world seemed to withdraw around them until it was the two of them alone on their own island.

Then Brad yelled something from down by his cabin and the moment was lost. Shade let go of Lizzy. Her face was still turned up to him. "I can't tell you how long I've wanted to do that."

She nodded, evidently still as stunned by the kiss as he'd been. "Shade—"

"Hannah ended up marrying the guy and having a child. That was over two years ago. She came to see me yesterday because she's dying and she's worried about what will happen with her little girl…" His voice broke. "Maisie."

Lizzy's eyes widened. "She wants you to take her? What about the girl's father?"

He held her gaze and blurted it out. "I'm her father."

LIZZY STARED AT him speechless. Ten years hadn't dulled that rocket-fueled chemistry between them. Heat had rushed from her lips to the toes of her boots. That old, unfulfilled ache had shot to her center. What was it about this cowboy?

Her head swam. From that sudden amazing kiss. To this news. "Did you—?"

"I had no idea. Not a clue. We were together just that one night about three years ago. I didn't know at the time that she was engaged." He shook his head. "I got the DNA results today confirming it, but I knew yesterday, the moment I saw her, that she was mine."

She swallowed the lump in her throat. He'd known since yesterday?

"Maisie looks exactly like I did at that age, blond with big blue eyes."

"Maisie?"

"I'm as shocked as you are. I know this is a lot to lay on you right now since we haven't even gone on a date, but I had to tell you because…" He stepped to her and took her shoulders in his big hands.

She felt a surge of electricity followed by a warmth that made her want to lean into him, into his strength, to nestle against him and breathe in his scent. For a moment, she thought he would kiss her again.

"Because I want us to have a chance. You and me and now I'm afraid—"

The sound of the bus pulling up was followed by "Hey! Let the party begin!" Christopher stumbled out of the bus with a large duffel bag, dragging a cooler with wheels. "Which cabin's mine?"

Shade let go of Lizzy and stepped back to call, "Seven!" without looking at the man. "Your names are on the doors." He kept his gaze on Lizzy as if afraid that she might...what? Run away? "Tell me this isn't a deal breaker," he whispered.

She cleared her throat, her head spinning. "Your daughter—"

"She's two. Lizzy?"

"Shade," she said and let out a breath. "I don't know what you want me to say. You and I—"

"I know we haven't even begun. Just tell me that you haven't given up on me. That you won't."

She looked into his blue eyes and felt her heart lurch before she smiled. "I haven't given up on you. I can't."

He started to reach for her again, but Christopher appeared next to them.

"Hey, you two," he said, grinning.

"Cabin seven," Shade repeated.

"Right." Christopher stood for a moment, still grinning, and then lumbered off with his load of belongings toward his cabin.

Others began tumbling out of the bus with their bags.

"We'll talk later?" Shade said.

She nodded, feeling as if she'd been dropped into the center of a tornado. Shade was the father of a two-year-old girl he would be raising soon. She knew he must feel even more thrown than she was. The cowboy had been busy sowing his oats all this time. To become an instant father...

"Maisie," she said to herself. Shade had said the little girl looked just like he had at two. Lizzy wanted to see her. To meet her. She wondered how long the mother had and what would happen next. She had no idea. Shade was a father. She felt her heart warm as she realized he would be a great one. But she'd thought it would be with their children—when she'd dared dream that far ahead.

She stepped into her cabin, shaken by the news. Shaken by the kiss and being in his arms again. She hugged herself, smiling like a fool as the tip of her tongue touched her top lip. She could still taste him. Outside, she could hear people hollering and loud music. She closed her eyes, wishing it was just the two of them up here on the mountain. She couldn't wait for this reunion to be over.

As she began to unpack her overnight bag, she reminded herself that she couldn't think about anything but her job now. While she wasn't wearing her uniform, she wore her gun in her ankle holster beneath her jeans. She was still the sheriff. And she still had a killer to catch.

CHAPTER EIGHTEEN

SHADE HUNG ON to Lizzy's words, telling himself there was hope. But right now, he had to shift gears, become the host of a reunion and get everyone settled in their cabins, when all he wanted to do was curl up in cabin one with Lizzy.

But as he saw her come out and walk down to where everyone was gathering, he reminded himself that she was working, as well. He thought about the car that had hit her on the road out of the ranch. Ariel's killer was still out there.

No, he thought, Ariel's killer was probably now on this mountain.

In the large lodge kitchen, he found Buckshot. The cowboy cook was busy at the stove. Buckshot had cooked at the guest ranch for years—until earlier this year when he'd broken his leg and Will had hired a caterer. That caterer, Poppy Carmichael, had turned out to be an amazing cook who'd stolen his brother's heart. The two were now married and Buckshot was healed and back cooking at the ranch—at least temporarily.

Next summer, Will and Poppy planned to run the guest ranch together. Her food had been such a hit that word had gotten out and they were already booked solid.

"How are things going?" Shade asked the rugged old cook. Buckshot grunted and pulled a large cast-iron pot from the oven filled with shredded beef for the burritos. He had a pot of beans on the stove and a variety of other ingredients for burritos. He put the beef back into the oven and turned it off.

Taking off his apron, Buckshot announced, "I'm leaving. You're all set. The rest of the meals just require you putting them into the oven."

"You're not having dinner with us?" Shade asked, though not surprised. The old cowboy cook had never been what you'd call social.

Buckshot snorted. "Not with this bunch of yahoos." With that he left to return to the valley.

"Can I help?" Lizzy asked as she came into the kitchen shortly after the cook retreated.

Shade chuckled. "It's all ready. I told everyone that the cuisine was going to be basic."

"They didn't come up here for the cuisine," she said.

"Why did they come?" he asked in all seriousness.

She shook her head. "I was just asking myself the same thing."

He could hear the guests entering the lodge and heading for the bar.

"Are you ready for this?" he asked and for a moment she wasn't sure if he meant the reunion or what might be ahead for the two of them.

"I am if you are." She smiled. Their gazes met and held.

He returned her smile and pulled her to him into a blistering kiss. She came willingly, pressing against him as he deepened the kiss and pulled her even closer. He swore he could feel the pounding of his heart in sync with hers.

"Lizzy," he whispered against her lips.

Someone cleared her throat behind them.

Shade didn't want to let Lizzy go. He knew she didn't want to let go either, as if both of them had wanted this for so long.

LIZZY STEPPED FROM Shade's arms and turned to find Ashley standing behind them, her arms crossed and a knowing look that went with the smirk on her face.

"You're just the person I wanted to see," Lizzy said and instantly wiped the amused look off Ashley's face. "I need to ask you something."

Clearly, her classmate had forgotten that Lizzy was the sheriff and still investigating Ariel's murder. "I've already told you everything that I—"

"You were closest to Ariel." Lizzy stepped closer and lowered her voice. "Did she keep a diary?"

Something flickered in Ashley's eyes for just an instant. "I have no idea. A diary?"

If Jennifer knew, then Ashley probably would have, as well. "I thought you'd know since the two of you were so…tight."

Ashley shook her head and frowned as she avoided

eye contact. "You might ask the others." The woman looked past her to where Shade was checking something on the stove. "What smells so good? I'm starved. I forgot to eat lunch and that drink Christopher just made me really went to my head. I think he's trying to get us all as drunk as him."

Lizzy could hear the others in the lounge, Christopher's voice carrying over the clink of glasses and ice. She left Shade and Ashley and went in to see who else had gathered. There was Kayla, Brad, Josh and Tyler. Josh was at the bar getting himself a beer. Apparently he'd changed his mind about coming to the reunion. Tyler stood back from everyone, appearing to just be watching—much as he had in high school.

A roar came up as Lizzy stepped into the room, but none of them were looking at her. Instead, everyone was cheering Jennifer who'd just come in the front door carrying a box with more booze.

This is going to get interesting, Lizzy thought. Behind her, Shade came out of the kitchen to stand next to her.

"Did everyone find their cabins all right?" he asked, seemingly not surprised to see Josh and Tyler. Everyone must have already been drinking because some of them seemed to be having trouble finding their cabins earlier, despite the blackboards with names on each door.

"Once you've all had a drink and are settled in," Shade said, "we'll have dinner." Then he whispered to her, "Is it just me or is all of this small talk very weird?"

Lizzy nodded even though all of them being together again wasn't just weird. She could feel something in the air like heat lightning. It made the hair at the back of her neck quill and her skin prickle. It made her think of a book she'd loved when she was younger... *Something wicked this way comes.* When she looked over at Shade, she saw that he was feeling it, too.

This time when the door flew open, it was Stephanie. There was straw in her hair, her blouse was torn and her face was streaked with mascara where she'd been crying. Her gaze took in everyone in the room before she made a beeline for Ashley.

Lizzy intercepted her. "What's going on?" she demanded, noticing that the woman's fist was balled up around something that crackled in her hand like dried leaves. "Stephanie?" She was still surprised that the woman had shown up for the reunion. She hoped it had nothing to do with settling old grudges, especially if she had killed Ariel. So why did Lizzy get the feeling that wasn't why Stephanie had come?

Tears pooled in her blue eyes before spilling down her cheeks.

"Stephanie?" Lizzy repeated.

The woman pulled her glare away from Ashley. Her gaze softened. She swallowed and whispered, "Not in front of everyone."

"You can take her upstairs," Shade said, suddenly at her side. "First door on the right."

THE LOUNGE FELL into a deathly quiet as Lizzy and Stephanie made their way upstairs. Shade could feel the tension.

"If that's what she looks like when she wakes up in the morning…" Tyler quipped, no doubt hoping to lighten the mood.

Shade wondered what had happened to Stephanie. He quickly narrowed down the places where she could have gotten straw in her hair. "Have any of you been in the barn?"

When no one spoke up, he considered everyone's shoes, his gaze coming to rest on Tyler's. "What's that on *your* shoes?"

His former classmate looked down at his expensive loafers and swore as he saw something along the edge of his sole that definitely wasn't mud.

"There are only a couple of places you could have picked up manure," Shade said.

Tyler looked indignant. "I checked out your horses before I came up to the lodge. If you're insinuating that I would go in the barn with Stephanie…" He headed for the door to find something to clean off his shoes, no doubt.

Josh laughed. "You going to check my shoes, too?"

"Oh, knock the chip off your shoulder," Ashley said, sounding as if she'd had plenty to drink already, though the reunion had just started. Then again, Christopher was making the drinks and she'd said he was making them strong.

"Tyler's already a suspect. I'm next if things go the way they did in high school," Josh said.

"We aren't in high school anymore," Christopher said, putting his arm around Josh's shoulder for a moment. "Have another beer and chill."

Shade tried to remember anything in school that Josh might be referring to. He'd never heard anything about either him or Tyler when it came to trouble. Christopher was another story.

LIZZY HANDED STEPHANIE a warm washcloth and picked the rest of the straw from her hair. The two sat down on chairs next to each other in the living area of the large upstairs suite.

Lizzy had never been close to Stephanie. Or Ashley and Jennifer for that matter. They'd all seemed to resent her when Ariel had befriended her, calling Lizzy her best friend.

It didn't help that Lizzy had recently arrested Stephanie.

She noticed that whatever Stephanie'd had clutched in her fist earlier, it was no longer there. "Tell me what happened."

Stephanie shook her head and swallowed. "It was nothing. I was just upset. One of the horses in the barn got out of its stall and knocked me down."

Lizzy considered her for a moment. "When you

came in, you were furious and headed for Ashley. I can't help if you don't tell me the truth."

"There's nothing to help."

"Stephanie, you already don't have an alibi for the night Ariel was killed and you just got out of jail for breaking and entering. You should also know that the rope found in your garage matched the rope used to kill Ariel."

The woman let out a groan as if in pain.

"Can you please stop lying to me and tell me what's going on?"

For a moment, Lizzy thought Stephanie would weaken. "I'm fine now," she said and handed back the washcloth as she rose.

But before she could reach the door, Lizzy said, "What was the paper you had balled up in your hand earlier?"

Stephanie froze just inches from the door. "It was nothing."

"Then I'd like to see it."

"I'm sure you would." The woman turned slowly, her eyes narrowing with anger. "I heard you went up to Ariel's house and took everything she left behind." Lizzy had a feeling she knew where this was headed. "So why don't you guess what it was?"

"A page from one of her diaries."

Stephanie's eyes widened in alarm. "It was *you* in the barn?" She reached for the doorknob when Lizzy stopped her again.

"You were attacked in the barn but not by a horse and certainly not by me. Let me see the page."

"You already know what's on it." Stephanie sounded close to tears. "I hate all of this. No one understands, but my husband…" She met Lizzy's gaze, hers hardening. "He can't find out about any of this old shit. I won't let that happen, no matter what I have to do. It's bad enough what I've already done."

What she'd already done? "Did you leave the note on my windshield?" Lizzy saw the answer in Stephanie's face and held out her hand. "Give me the diary page."

"Someone is trying to frame me for Ariel's murder."

Lizzy said nothing, still waiting. The woman slowly reached in her pocket and pulled out the balled-up diary page. With obvious distaste, Stephanie dropped it into her palm.

Lizzy flattened it as best as she could and attempted to read what was written. Her heart began to pound. "Is any of this true?"

CHAPTER NINETEEN

EVERYONE HAD BEEN quiet as they sat around the fireplace waiting for Lizzy and Stephanie to return. It was as if they were all trying to hear what was happening upstairs. Not that they could.

For Shade, it was more like waiting for the other shoe to drop.

"Well, we'd planned to have a digital slideshow of all the photographs we took during high school," Ashley said with a sigh. "I suppose we could watch some of them before dinner."

"It isn't like we need the reminders," Josh said. "We were all there." He glanced at Kayla. "You need photographs to remember high school?"

She seemed to realize he was talking to her and shook her head before dropping her gaze to stare at her hands.

This reunion wasn't going well, Shade thought even before Lizzy and Stephanie came down the stairs. Stephanie looked much better, but Lizzy appeared pale and upset.

"Why don't we have dinner?" he said, getting to his feet. At this point, he just wanted to get everyone fed. He'd thought they would all go to their cabins before dinner, but everyone seemed hesitant to leave the lodge. It had already gotten dark out. The reunion committee had planned for the slideshow tonight and then music and possibly dancing if it was too cold outside. Otherwise they would have a campfire.

He'd had this crazy idea that they would all get up here and it would be clear who the killer was, he thought as he went into the kitchen. The plan had been for Buckshot to make some dishes ahead and then everyone would help with serving and dishwashing. He was relieved when Ashley and Josh came in to help, followed by the others.

They set the meal up buffet-style, everyone joking and helping. It wasn't until they were all finally seated that Ashley said, "I think we should go around the table and say something about Ariel in memoriam."

Tyler burst out laughing. "Seriously? And spoil everyone's appetite?"

"I'll go first," Kayla said, surprising Shade and apparently everyone else at the table. She cleared her throat. "I know she made fun of me, but there was this one time when I tore my pants in between third and fourth period and my underwear showed. I was in the bathroom close to tears because I had nothing else to wear and I couldn't go home to change because I had a test the next period…"

She looked around the table for a moment. "Ariel thought it was funny—until I burst into tears. She said, 'Oh, stop being such a baby' and took off her sweater and tied it around me. 'I want that sweater back and don't get anything icky on it. Never mind, now that I think about it, I don't want it back after you've worn it. It's yours.'"

Josh laughed the hardest at the story. "That was too touching. You're going to make me cry."

"Her story shows that there was another side to Ariel," Ashley snapped. "That she wasn't all bad." There were groans at the table. "Give her a break. She's dead! She died at seventeen while the rest of us got to go on living."

"Don't you think it was her own fault that she died so young?" Stephanie demanded. "She treated most of us outrageously bad. But I still don't think we should talk this way about her." As if realizing that everyone was looking at her, she added, "I'm not saying she didn't deserve that kind of retribution, but to die so young—"

"Oh, come on. Ariel asked for it," Tyler said, putting down his fork after eating very little. "She thought that she could just treat people any way she wanted and there would be no consequences. I would have loved to have seen her face when the pigeons came home to roost."

"Didn't you see her expression right before she died?" Brad asked. Tyler merely glared at him. "Seriously, someone at this table did see her at the end— the person who killed her."

"What makes you think it was one of us?" Jennifer asked.

"Because the people at this table had motive and opportunity," Brad said.

"*You're* at this table, Brad," Josh pointed out. "Let's hear what you have to say about Ariel. Seriously," he said, leaning in where he could see Brad better from down the table. "I really want to hear one of your memories of her."

Brad sighed. "I didn't have much contact with Ariel, sorry."

"Oh, come on, Brad," Josh said, not letting it go. "I saw you and Ariel at the back of a classroom one day. Not sure what you were talking about, but it was definitely a heated conversation. I saw her slap you and when you grabbed her, I thought for sure you were going to strangle her, but instead, you kissed her and she didn't seem to mind it."

Brad's face reddened as Ashley said, "We all know that Ariel dumped you after a short fling and we all know that you didn't take it well."

"I guess there are no secrets at this table," he said and turned his attention to his plate and the half-eaten burrito on it.

"Since this was your bad idea, Ashley, I believe it's your turn," Stephanie said pointedly.

Shade could feel the animosity between them. He looked at Lizzy incredulously, but she seemed lost in thought.

Ashley turned her nose up and said, "Ariel was my friend. I'm not saying it was easy being her friend. She was…difficult. Demanding, hurtful, self-centered.

But she was young, we all were, and if she was mean sometimes—"

"Oh, please," Stephanie interrupted. "Mean sometimes? She ripped other people to shreds and if you even mentioned anything about her, like that she had a pimple, she was horrified and hurt and made you feel like shit that you could be so mean to her. I'm sorry, but she deserved everything she got and more."

"I think drowning like that was probably more," Jennifer said.

"Why are you defending her?" Stephanie demanded. "You hated her as much or more than we did. It wasn't just me she fat-shamed, Ashley. Look at how little is on your plate even now. It's as if you think she's here watching, still judging you. And you, Jennifer—"

"It must be my turn," Josh said. "I liked Ariel. You didn't have to try to read her. It was all out there for anyone to see. She was a mess, probably had to do with her family. She struck out because she was hurting, not that I gave a damn. I still found her to be a bitch."

"That is quite insightful," Brad said. "Fortunately, I was invisible to Ariel except on occasion when she had no one else to pick on. But it was good for me in a lot of ways. Her death made me realize that neither she nor anyone else was ever going to tell me how to live my life ever again. It freed me."

"Killing her might have even been more freeing," Tyler said and held up his hands. "Just sayin'."

"Christopher hasn't said anything yet," Stephanie pointed out.

He looked up from his plate as if his mind had been elsewhere. "I think you've all said it quite well."

"Oh, no you don't," Josh said. "You aren't going to get off that easily."

Christopher looked around the table for a moment. "I loved Ariel. She broke my heart numerous times and made my life miserable, but even at the end, I still loved her."

The room went silent for a long time before Ashley turned to Lizzy. "We haven't heard from you, Sheriff. How did you feel about your best friend?"

Lizzy, PULLED FROM her thoughts, looked up. "Yes, I knew Ariel. She used to say I was her best friend but we all know the only reason she said that was to hurt Ashley, Jennifer and Stephanie, who'd been her friends for a lot longer. If anything, her death has made it obvious that Ariel had few friends because she didn't know how to be one."

Christopher swore. "Yes, Ariel was often cruel, but none of us were saints. Look at Josh. Big highway patrolman now. But in high school…"

"You're drunk," Josh said.

"True enough. I'm an alcoholic, but everyone in this room had a flaw that Ariel used against them," Christopher said. "Why not share? She's gone. She can't hurt any of you ever again."

Josh shook his head. "No big secret. I might have smoked a little pot."

"And sold some on the side?" Christopher said with a laugh. "But mum's the word now that you're the law." He turned to Jennifer. "We all know your secret, Sticky Fingers."

Jennifer blanched. "Shut up! It's not true. Ariel put that scarf in my purse. It was Ariel."

"Maybe the first time, but what about the other times after that? Hey, don't be insulted," he said. "There are far worse secrets in this room. Isn't that right, Tyler?"

"Jennifer's right. You should shut up," Tyler said and gave him a threatening look.

"Okay. How about you, Kayla? Why don't you roll up those long black sleeves and show everyone how you relieved your stress in high school?" He looked up at the others. "What? You didn't know that Kayla cut herself?"

"That's enough, Christopher," Stephanie said. "You're an obnoxious drunk and always have been, just like your father."

"Ouch. At least I don't sleep with other people's fathers," he snapped.

"Let's not do this," Ashley said. "This is exactly what Ariel would have wanted to happen—all of us turning on each other."

"Ashley's right," Christopher said. "See, being anorexic all those years didn't turn her mind to mush." He pretended to put his finger down his throat but then laughed, spilling his drink. "Maybe it was all that... coaching you got."

Lizzy could see that all of this was making Shade as uncomfortable as it was her. No good could come of it.

"I think we should all just eat," Shade said.

Christopher looked around the table. "You're all willing to talk about Ariel and how bad she was. But you don't like having the spotlight on us. Like Brad," he said, turning to look down the table at the newsman. "He's got no problem writing about other people, but Brad never took a test he didn't know the answers to, isn't that right? Because they were written on his cheat sheet."

"Christopher, that's enough," Shade said.

"Oh, it's all right to air all of *our* dirty laundry," Stephanie said. "But don't touch you or Lizzy or Tyler for that matter?"

"Christopher, I'd like to know how you happened to know everyone's secrets," Lizzy said.

He shrugged. "I read some of Ariel's diaries."

"And where are they now?" she asked.

Christopher shook his head. "I thought you probably had them. I sure would hate for them to turn up." He grinned around the table. "I think there are a lot more secrets to come out. What do you think, gang?"

"After we finish eating, I thought we'd have a campfire down by the barn," Shade said, clearly trying to change the subject.

"I brought everything for s'mores," Kayla said.

"Great," Christopher said. "We're all freaks." He raised his glass. "To us. The graduating class of Progressive! And to Ariel. Let's face it. If it wasn't for her, we wouldn't all be here." He drained his glass.

Lizzy felt some of the tension evaporate around the table. Would the revealing of secrets defuse the situation? Or make it worse? The shameful things that had seemed so overwhelming in high school might be nothing now that they were adults. They'd all made mistakes, they'd all had things that they hadn't wanted others to know. Ariel had used those painful things against them.

If only they had all known back then how easy it would have been to neutralize her with the simple truth. But it was high school, a painful time in so many ways, she thought—especially for this small, isolated group.

She noticed that Jennifer had made a point of not sitting by Ashley or Stephanie. She'd wondered if the three had remained friends after high school. Ashley had married a pilot after college. Stephanie had married a dentist. Jennifer's marriage to a bar owner had ended in divorce. Now she worked as a waitress and likely didn't have as much free time or funds as the other two friends. Lizzy wondered what else played into the loss of those friendships.

She looked down the table at Kayla. She'd pushed back one of her long black sleeves. Lizzy could see the faint lines where she'd cut herself repeatedly. It made her flinch inside, her heart going out to the awkward, shy girl Kayla had been and the awkward, lonely woman she must be now.

As she glanced around the table, she saw what a sad bunch they all were. Lizzy questioned if any of them would have crossed paths if they hadn't been thrown together in the small private school.

She thought of the diary page Stephanie had given her. There were still some secrets that hadn't surfaced. Not yet anyway, if what Ariel had written in her diary was true. Either way, Lizzy was more convinced than ever that there was still a murderer among them here at the reunion.

The missing knife from Brad's mother's kitchen, the ski rope from the garage… Whoever had climbed into the back of Ariel's car was at the party that night in plain sight. One of her classmates was a killer, Lizzy thought. Stephanie? Or was someone setting her up? Someone at this table who'd attacked her in the barn and left the diary page.

The gun and the rope found at Stephanie's house seemed damning. But what about the missing knife from Brad's mother's house? Was that what was used that night to threaten Ariel and not a gun at all? It was almost as if the killer was trying to confuse her, Lizzy thought.

As if also contemplating who might be a killer at the table, Josh said, "That was all very enlightening, Christopher, but you left out the most important question. Which of us killed her?" He looked around the table. "Who hated her the most?"

"I know what we should do," Brad said. "We should all write down whether or not we killed her on a slip of paper, put it in a hat anonymously and see for sure if the killer is in this room. Let's do it," he said, with some of the others agreeing.

"As if the killer would be truthful since the sheriff here would just run the fingerprints on the slip of paper admitting the murder and compare our handwriting," Tyler said with a shake of his head. "What I want to know is the killer's motive."

"I thought we pretty well covered that," Josh said.

"No, it was one thing to hate her," Brad said. "It was a whole different ball game to kill her."

"Not just kill her but plan it," Christopher said. "I've given this a lot of thought. You all knew Ariel. The killer had to have a weapon. A knife. A gun. A Taser. Otherwise, Ariel would have fought like the beast she was."

"Maybe she did," Ashley said.

"But wait," Jennifer said. "How did they get to her to begin with?"

"They could have texted her to meet them at the pond," Kayla said.

Lizzy realized that they'd all given this a lot of thought.

"No, I can't see that happening," Josh said. "The night of the graduation party the wind was howling. Ariel would have had to have a very good reason to agree to that. The pond?" He shook his head. "Unless it was to buy drugs maybe."

"She didn't buy drugs," Ashley snapped. "You should know that since that's more up your alley. Or used to be."

"Josh is right," Jennifer said, speaking up. "She wouldn't have driven out to the pond for any of us."

"Also, Ariel texted me as she was leaving the party," Ashley said. "She wanted me, Jennifer and Stephanie to meet her and it wasn't at the pond."

"So the killer either followed her…" Tyler let out a curse as if it just came to him. "Or was already in the back of her car when she left the party."

Brad looked down the table at Lizzy, but didn't tell what he already knew about the rope and the missing knife. For now, apparently, it would be their secret.

"Maybe she picked up someone after she left," Kayla suggested.

"What? Like a hitchhiker?" Stephanie said. "And at that hour?"

"She could have planned to meet someone we didn't know about," Jennifer said.

Brad was shaking his head. "I agree with Tyler. It makes a lot more sense that the killer was already in the back of her car, hiding."

"Wouldn't she have noticed?" Jennifer said. "I suppose a man could hide in the back of an SUV like the one she drove."

"Who says it was a man?" Brad said.

"Ariel always kept that blanket in the back," Stephanie said. "If the person was hiding under it…"

"And in the mood she was in when she left, I doubt

she would have looked in the back seat to see if someone was hiding there," Brad said.

"But how did the killer force her to go to the pond?" Kayla asked.

"Ariel would have had to be persuaded, that's for sure," Josh said with a laugh. "That's why the killer would have had a weapon, which means premeditation."

Brad nodded in Josh's direction. "Exactly. Ariel was *tied* to the steering wheel," he said, as if that answered everything. "She didn't have old ski rope lying around in her car or tie herself to the wheel and she would have put up one hell of a fight if anyone else had tried."

Lizzy groaned inwardly as she listened to all the details come out. But she had to admit, it was interesting hearing them try to figure out how it could have happened when one of them knew the truth. She could only hope that person would give him or herself away.

"At that point, Ariel had to be knocked out. Or at least dazed enough that she couldn't fight back," Jennifer said. "The killer must have hit her or—"

"Immobilized her with something like a Taser," Josh said.

"This is so much better than a silly slideshow," Stephanie said and shuddered. "What a coldhearted bunch you all are."

Everyone seemed to ignore her.

"You know what? The killer could have given her a drug. Maybe a roofie," Tyler said, also clearly getting into this. "She would have been watching it all happening but wouldn't be able to do a thing about it." He seemed to relish the thought of Ariel even more helpless than being tied to the steering wheel as she drowned.

"Or just coldcocked her," Brad said.

The room had gone quiet for a moment. Lizzy felt the change even before Josh spoke.

"Ariel wasn't the first person to die from our class," he said. "Have you all forgotten about Whitney?"

"It's not the same thing," Ashley said quickly and rubbed her bare arms as if feeling the chill. "Whitney's was an accident."

"Was it?" Josh asked and shrugged. "Ariel hated her from the moment she laid eyes on her. Whitney was prettier, richer, had a bigger house, a better car. Ariel would have driven her out of Progressive—if Whitney hadn't died first."

The room had gone deathly quiet again. Lizzy held her breath, thinking again of what she'd read on the diary page she'd taken from Stephanie. She glanced down the table toward the woman. Stephanie had her head down, looking at her plate, her face pale, her lower lip quivering.

"We're lucky that even half of us are still alive," Josh said. "It isn't like we were the cream of the crop. Hell, it's amazing that by our ten-year reunion some of us aren't in prison."

"I don't think that's funny," Ashley said.

"But true," Tyler agreed. "Once Lizzy finds the

killer—zip, off to prison, another member of one of Progressive's graduates gone. That's if we survive this weekend. You don't really think that Ariel was the only one who made enemies in our class, do you?" He laughed. "I look around this table and I—"

"I've had enough of this," Ashley said as she shoved back her chair and rose from the table. "This was supposed to be fun."

"Fun?" several people cried.

"Ariel was *murdered*," Christopher snapped. "That's why we're all here. Would you have really come to this if it wasn't for Ariel's body being found? None of us have anything in common except that we were in the same class at a private school."

"That's right," Tyler said. "You and Josh were there on scholarships."

"Tyler—" Ashley looked appalled.

Christopher laughed. "And Ariel never let me forget it."

"I was fine with it," Josh said. "How else would I have had the honor of meeting all of you?"

Silence fell over the room for a moment.

"I think we're all here because we're afraid," Kayla said in a small voice. "We're all scared that whoever killed Ariel isn't finished."

"Most killers don't wait ten years to strike again," Josh said.

"They do if they think they're about to be caught," Jennifer said and looked around the table, her gaze slowing on both Ashley and Stephanie.

"Or if they still have grudges," Tyler said.

"He's right," Christopher said. "This reunion has brought it all back, all the pain and suffering and not just at Ariel's hands. So why not kill again? What's one more in the grand scheme of things, right? Ariel died a horrible death. You're all so busy figuring out how it happened that you seem to have forgotten that."

"You're just trying to scare us," Ashley said with disgust.

Lizzy felt her stomach turn. They were getting very close to the truth of what had actually happened to Ariel the night she died. She felt a shiver as she reminded herself that someone in this room knew *exactly* what had happened and was now having way too much fun playing along.

Ah, togetherness. Here they all are, all having fun at my expense. Well, at least one person at that table knows exactly how I died. But the rest are getting very close. Too bad they can't figure out who at that table they can trust—and who they can't.

That has always been a problem. Even in high school. It was hard for me to tell who was really my friend and who would stab me in the back. That's why I don't feel sorry for any of them. Ashley, Jennifer and Stephanie have proved what kind of friends they were. And then there's Lizzy.

I'd almost feel sorry for the new sheriff—if Lizzy hadn't betrayed me by wanting Shade. Wanting Shade and getting him are two different things though. I've managed to keep the two of them apart without even trying. Now I don't see that they have much of a chance for happiness.

Sorry, but I agree that my killer isn't finished just yet. I suspect that more of my classmates will be joining me before this night is over. I feel it. Strange to have that kind of knowledge now when it does me no good at all.

I suddenly have the oddest feeling that once my killer is caught this will be all over for me, as well. The thought terrifies me. Then I really will be dead and gone. It really will be over.

Fortunately, it appears that Lizzy has no clue who at that table is not just capable of murder but quite good at it. So good that the killer can't stop.

CHAPTER TWENTY

"I DON'T KNOW about the rest of you," Christopher said, getting to his feet. "I could use a drink and, Shade, didn't you say something about a bonfire?"

"We were going to roast marshmallows and tell ghost stories," Ashley said and groaned. "But I feel like that's what we've already been doing."

"S'mores and ghost stories," Tyler mocked with a laugh. "Well, I'd much rather do that than this."

"I agree," Jennifer said, also getting to her feet. "Let's get this all cleaned up and go outside. It's a nice night and we might not have too many more of them before winter." Everyone began to rise and help clear away the dishes.

Shade cornered Lizzy. "Are you all right?"

"Fine." It came out too quick and he knew it.

"You looked upset earlier when you came downstairs with Stephanie. And I don't know about you, but that discussion at dinner made me nervous."

"Me, too. It really brought it home, didn't it?" She met his gaze and he felt his heart ache. He reached over to brush her hair back. He felt a shiver move through him as his fingertips brushed her warm skin.

Being this close to her up here on the mountain… It was pure hell not being able to hold her with all these people around.

"I need to go out and start the bonfire so the fools don't burn down the new barn, but I don't like leaving you alone," he said.

Lizzy smiled, clearly seeing how hard this was on him. "I'm not alone. I'll be fine." She glanced toward the kitchen now full of people loading the dishwasher. "Everyone's pitching in—as per plan."

"Come out to the fire when you can?"

She nodded and touched his hand as if needing the human contact right now as much as he did.

He grabbed her fingers, squeezing them for a moment as he held her gaze. "Don't be long, okay?" He let go with reluctance and went to get his coat from the hook by the door before heading out to the firepit. The ranch provided warm coats on the hooks by the door; nights were often cold up here, even in the summer.

He saw that Christopher was already gathering up some kindling for the fire.

"Looked like there were enough of them in the kitchen to handle cleanup," the man said. "I thought I'd help out here." He looked toward the lodge. "I couldn't take any more of that in there. We're all a bunch of hypocrites. Do you think they were right about what happened to Ariel?"

Shade shook his head. "I have no idea. It's all speculation."

Christopher held his gaze. "Is it?" He let out a huff.

"Or is the killer in there laughing at the rest of us for being such fools?"

"It makes me uneasy, too," Shade admitted.

"I don't know what I'm doing here," Christopher said. "I guess I'm like the rest of them and wanted to see what would happen when all the suspects were in one place together after ten years. I should have known it would be ugly."

"You didn't help matters."

Christopher laughed and Shade saw that he wasn't as drunk as he'd been pretending. "I thought maybe if all the secrets were out…" He shook his head. "How could I make any of this worse, really?"

Shade was thinking the same thing as he put newspaper under the kindling and then added some split logs on top before lighting the fire. Flames leaped as the newspaper licked at the dry kindling. "And nothing may be resolved when this reunion is over."

"I think that's my greatest fear," Christopher said. "I want Ariel's killer to pay. If I knew who it was…"

Shade didn't like the sound of the threat. He'd been all for having the reunion, getting old friends together, not necessarily finding out who Ariel's killer was. But now he couldn't shake the unsettling feeling that it all really had been a bad idea. There were too many old resentments, too many remembered slights, too much animosity. They could unite in their feelings for Ariel, but there were also old grievances among them, as well.

He recalled the look on Stephanie's face when she'd

barreled into the lodge, looking as if she wanted to murder Ashley. He wondered what that was about. He suspected Lizzy knew and it was bad. That's why she'd been so pale and upset when she'd come down the stairs earlier. He regretted again telling her about Hannah and Maisie. She had enough to worry about.

Worse, now he had no idea where they stood for the long run. Maybe Lizzy didn't even know how she felt about what he'd told her. He'd certainly been knocked off his boots by the revelation. He could see where Lizzy might want to reconsider a relationship with him, especially since they hadn't even had their first date yet. The chemistry was there. They'd both felt it, he was sure of that. But would it be enough?

He realized he hadn't been listening. "I'm sorry, what did you say?"

Christopher tossed a chunk of wood on the fire and stared into the flames for a few moments. "I'm serious. If we find out who killed Ariel this weekend… and I have my way, that person will never get out of these mountains alive."

Shade stared at him, thinking of Lizzy. The sheriff would never let Christopher take the law into his own hands. Not if she could stop him.

LIZZY FELT AS if she was in over her head and not just with the investigation of Ariel's murder. She'd been sheriff for only a matter of days. Did she really think she could solve this murder quickly—especially since she was so close to the suspects herself? What she'd learned was that she'd never really known these people or what they were capable of just because they'd shared the high school experience so intimately at Progressive.

Look at Josh. No one had expected him to become a highway patrolman. He was the one they all thought would be behind bars by now. And now it would seem that one of them was a murderer.

If that wasn't enough to throw her, there was Shade's news. She'd known he had a past. She had one, too, only much more limited if the stories about him were true. But to find out that he had a two-year-old daughter whom he would soon be raising? That had come out of left field. She hadn't even had time to consider how she felt about any of it.

The only thing she knew was how she felt about him. She still wanted that date. Just as she'd wanted the kisses and more. She wanted to get closer to him, she realized as she went into the kitchen to find that the work was done. The dishwasher whirred and the mood was lighter as everyone got ready to go out to the campfire. She watched them help themselves to the warm heavy coats on the hooks by the front door—compliments of the guest ranch—since the October weather was cold at night.

As Stephanie passed her, the woman grabbed her arm and held her back from the rest. "What are you going to do?"

Lizzy didn't have to ask what she was referring to. She was still stunned by what had been written on that diary page. "I don't know yet. But you don't have to worry about it."

Stephanie gave her an incredulous look. "Ashley told Ariel that I was driving the car that hit Whitney."

"Were you?"

The woman's eyes widened in horror. "*No!* Why would Ashley do that unless…?"

"Unless she was covering for someone else. I will definitely look into it after this weekend is over. I promise. In the meantime, let's all try to get along. There is enough going on without adding more." Without adding yet another murder to the mix.

Stephanie shook her head, her face pinched in anger. "One of them is trying to frame me. I thought we were all friends."

That, Lizzy thought, could be the theme of the entire weekend. Some high school friendships lasted for a lifetime. A lot of them were superficial and ended with graduation. Some had never been real, as if everyone had been wearing a mask.

But now the masks were coming off and she wasn't sure any of them were ready for what was underneath.

SHADE LOOKED UP as Lizzy and Stephanie joined the rest of them around the large campfire. Lizzy's face in the firelight was so beautiful that he felt his heart do a slow, painful somersault. He wanted her, like nothing he'd ever wanted before. He moved to her, tempted to whisk her away, forget about everything but the two of them—just for a little while.

He saw her shiver as she looked around at the others standing around the warm fire. The temperature had dropped. He knew he shouldn't have been surprised when he saw the first snowflake come lazily spiraling down to disappear into the flames.

Christopher had pulled a cooler full of beer over against the barn. He was handing out beer, his earlier mood replaced with a let's-party one.

Kayla went to her cabin to grab a throw blanket and get the s'more ingredients from the lodge kitchen. Shade told Tyler where the metal skewers for roasting could be found right inside the barn and several others went with him to get them.

Shade threw more logs on the fire and went again to stand by Lizzy. "How are you doing?" he whispered.

She smiled in answer and he put his arm around her and pulled her close for a moment. He could feel everyone around the fire watching them and could well imagine the speculation.

Josh had brought his guitar and began to play, singing as the group with the skewers returned from the barn. "Join in!" he cried as he reached the chorus and some of them did with varying vocal abilities.

Shade looked around the campfire. Everyone seemed to be enjoying this. Someone who didn't know them and their history would believe that they were all friends. Right now, studying their faces, he couldn't imagine any of them drowning anyone. He saw Christopher move toward the cooler in the shadow of the barn to get more beers.

Tyler called to him that he'd take one but that he had to pee first. As he disappeared around the side of the barn, the first firecracker went off.

It exploded in a string of loud pops that spewed hot burning embers all over them and sent them all scurrying back from the flames and into the darkness beyond it.

Shade swore, immediately realizing what had happened. Some fool had thrown firecrackers into the campfire. "That was a dumb-ass thing to do," he said as he ground out embers that had flown as far as the dried fall grass. Others joined him in putting out the embers before the grass went up in a blaze.

"Anyone want to take credit for that?" he asked as he looked around the group, angry with the culprit and suspecting Christopher, the usual troublemaker.

Shade didn't have time to realize who was missing from the group before a scream pierced the cold night air.

CHAPTER TWENTY-ONE

THE BLOODCURDLING SCREAM brought them all up short. Lizzy ran with Shade in the direction of the scream, and another shriek filled the night air. As they rounded the corner of the barn, they saw Kayla standing with her hand over her mouth staring down at the ground at her feet.

Next to her was the bag of s'more fixings that she'd dropped beside the body on the ground. She was clutching the blanket she'd brought from her cabin, her mouth open in a silent scream.

Lizzy stepped toward the dark mound of clothing on the ground and knew at once that all her fears had come true. "Stand back," she said to Kayla. She crouched close to the body, careful not to disturb anything, and checked for a pulse. To her relief, it was strong.

Rising, she saw that others had come running, as well. "Please go back to the fire. All of you, please."

"Who is it?" Ashley asked, trying to see into the darkness next to the barn.

"Oh, my God, it's Tyler," Jennifer cried. "He and Kayla left the fire at the same time."

"But they went in different directions," Josh pointed out. "At least for a while," he added.

Shade put an arm around Kayla, who was crying uncontrollably now, and drew her back away from Tyler's inert body. Everyone was moving in closer, trying to get a better look.

"You heard the sheriff," Josh said in a loud voice. "Back to the fire." He moved in front of them and began herding them back. "Let her do her job."

She'd never been more grateful for Josh than at that moment. Shade had his hands full with Kayla. Lizzy could see that he was wondering the same thing she was. What was Kayla doing out here beside the barn? How was it that she'd found Tyler?

Squatting down next to Tyler, Lizzy pulled out her cell phone, useless up here without cell service except for the flashlight. She hadn't seen any blood when she'd checked his pulse but he was wearing a heavy coat and his body was curled away from her. As she knelt over Tyler and held the flashlight higher, she saw the head wound. It appeared he'd been hit in the temple with a blunt object.

She shined the light around nearby and saw a brick lying next to the barn. There was a dark spot on it that looked like blood.

"We need to call for an ambulance," Lizzy said.

"He's alive?" Kayla sounded as shocked as Shade looked.

Lizzy pressed one of her gloves against the wound.

"I'm going to need help getting him up to the lodge. He can't stay out here in the cold."

As Shade moved to her side, she could hear the rest of her classmates around the fire speculating. The conversation about Ariel's death in the dining room had sounded almost like a game they were all playing. Now, though, they all sounded scared. Except for Josh. He seemed to be handling things.

Tyler groaned and tried to sit up.

"Don't try to move just yet," she said to him.

"What happened?" He sounded as if in pain. His hand went to his head and came away stained with blood. His eyes widened in alarm.

"You seem to have been struck in the head," Lizzy told him. "Just lie still for a moment." But even as she tried to keep him down, he pushed himself up to a sitting position. "Do you think you can make it up to the lodge if we help you? Here, keep this pressed to the side of your head." She saw that Kayla had gone around the corner to the fire. Everyone was asking her what had happened. Lizzy couldn't hear her reply.

She took a couple of deep breaths as she pocketed her phone. As a deputy she'd seen car accidents, a couple of murder victims and definitely some bloody messes with domestic arguments. But it never got easier, especially the initial shock.

"Did you see who hit you?" she asked Tyler.

"No. It was dark. I just remember finishing peeing when the lights went out." Which would explain why no one had heard anything. Except maybe Kayla.

As she and Shade got on each side of him, Lizzy noticed that Tyler had a piece of paper sticking out of his coat pocket. She reached over and pulled out a page from Ariel's diary. Carefully, she slipped it into her pocket as they neared the lodge. Tyler seemed to be getting stronger, more able to walk on his own as they climbed the steps to the lodge.

The snow was picking up now. Large lacy flakes drifted down from the dark heavens and whirled around in the breeze. As she glanced back, the campfire sparked and popped softly. She reminded herself that everyone around that fire was a suspect, including Josh.

Someone had thrown firecrackers into the blaze to distract them long enough to go around the side of the barn to attack Tyler? Had the plan been to kill him? She felt relieved that she didn't have another murder on her hands.

With the snow falling harder, she couldn't keep them around the campfire for long. It was already beginning to stick to their clothing. She also needed to go back for the brick before the snow washed away any evidence that might be on it.

Leaving Tyler on the couch by the fire in Shade's capable hands, she ran back down to the side of the barn to retrieve the brick. It was gone.

Any one of them could have picked up the brick. With a start, she realized Kayla had been standing there, as well. She hadn't noticed when Kayla had moved away to go back to the fire. She could have picked up the brick.

In fact, she'd been standing nearby when Lizzy had shined the flashlight beam on the brick. If she hadn't been sure what weapon had been used on Tyler, she was now.

As soon as Shade had Tyler settled comfortably on the couch, he went to the phone to call for an ambulance. He had no idea how badly the man might be hurt. But he was conscious and didn't seem to be in very much pain.

"I'll get the first aid kit out in a minute," Shade told him. His mind was whirling. Who had done this and why? After the fireworks incident, Shade couldn't be sure who had left the fire. They'd all been bundled up, having helped themselves to the extra coats hanging by the door up in the lodge. Anyone could have stepped away from the fire, attacked Tyler on the side of the barn and returned to the fire without being noticed.

Lizzy came in as he was hanging up the phone. She must have seen his expression. She moved to him quickly. "Shade, what's wrong?"

"I couldn't get through to your office or the coroner," he said, keeping his voice as calm and quiet as possible. "The phone's dead."

Her eyes widened for a moment, then she nodded. She wasn't one to panic. "I have Josh taking care of the others for the moment but I can't leave them all out there. It's snowing much harder than earlier." She turned. "How is Tyler?"

"Better, I think. I can't tell if he has a concussion or not." He looked past her to where Kayla had come in the door. She stood just inside, looking scared.

"I need to question Kayla," Lizzy said. "I thought I'd make her some tea."

"I'll do what I can for Tyler," he said. He stepped into his office and brought out the first aid kit. He went to work cleaning the wound. It wasn't as bad as all the blood had made it appear. He'd just finished when he heard the teakettle begin to whistle.

In the dining room, he found Lizzy and Kayla sitting at one of the tables. He stepped into the kitchen to pull the teakettle off the fire. "I'll bring you both a cup of hot tea in just a minute." Kayla appeared to be in a trance.

"I need you to tell me what you saw," Lizzy said quietly as Shade made two cups of tea.

Kayla shook her head. "I didn't see anything."

"Why did you go to the side of the barn instead of coming back to the fire?"

The young woman looked confused for a moment. "I heard someone call my name."

"A man or a woman?"

She shook her head. "I don't know. When I went around the corner of the barn, I just saw someone lying there and screamed. I thought he was dead."

Shade flinched, the tea sloshing a little. He met

Lizzy's gaze. "I can drive Tyler down to the hospital. I can also call your office from there."

She seemed to consider that, looking longingly at the steam coming off the hot water. "It wouldn't do any good to get a forensics person up here. Just take Tyler to the hospital. I wouldn't be surprised if some of the others want to leave, as well."

He hadn't thought about that. "Maybe it would be for the best."

Lizzy didn't argue the point.

"I know this must come as a shock," Lizzy said to Kayla as Shade moved back into the kitchen. From there, he could still see that Kayla's hands shook as she picked up the cup of tea he'd put in front of her. "Do you remember seeing anyone nearby?"

Kayla shook her head.

After checking to make sure that Tyler was resting comfortably, Shade took one of the flashlights from his office and headed for the large area used for dances behind the main lounge. He exited through the back door into the dark snowy night. Flakes swirled around him. The weatherman had called for possible snow in the mountains, but the forecast hadn't looked bad. Now he feared a heavy snowstorm might make a bad situation even worse.

He moved along the edge of the lodge, fearing what he was going to find. Earlier he'd hoped that the phone might be out because of weather. But that hope died when he saw that the phone lines had been cut, the box destroyed in a way that would make it impossible to get service without a technician.

For a moment, he stood in the cold dark, watching the snow drift down from the dark sky, suddenly afraid of what he would find next. Someone hadn't wanted them to be able to call out. What were the chances that the person also didn't want them leaving?

He walked down to his pickup hoping not to alert the others. He'd parked off to the side of the lodge but as he approached the truck he could see that the hood was open slightly. His heart raced as he swore under his breath.

Shade knew even before he popped the hood and shined the flashlight down on the engine... He wasn't going anywhere in his truck. Closing the hood, he shined his light in the direction of Brad's vehicle, already knowing that like his truck it wasn't going anywhere.

He headed for Lizzy's SUV but saw before he reached it that, like his pickup, the hood was slightly ajar. He shined the flashlight into the interior on her damaged radio.

The only way to get off this mountain now was on foot and it was a very long walk. Given the storm, they weren't going anywhere tonight.

CHAPTER TWENTY-TWO

LIZZY PICKED UP her tea, cupping it in her hands as she soaked in the wonderful warmth. "Kayla, walk me through what happened."

The young woman looked up at her. She had drunk some of her tea. She still looked in shock but seemed to be more focused. "I went to my cabin for a blanket. After getting the chocolate, marshmallows and crackers from the kitchen, I started back down the mountain toward the fire. I stopped for a moment when I heard the firecrackers go off."

"Did you see anyone leave the fire or come back to it?"

Kayla shook her head. "I was staring at all the sparks flying through the air." They all had been, Lizzy thought. "I started walking again as things died down. I was almost there when I heard someone call my name. That's when I went around the edge of the barn and saw what I thought was a body." She shuddered and finished her tea. "I guess that's when I screamed."

"Did you check to see if Tyler was dead?"

She shook her head.

"Did you know it was Tyler?"

Another head shake. "Why would someone want to kill him?"

"We don't know that they did." Lizzy thought of the diary page in her pocket, anxious to look at it and see what Ariel had written. All of this seemed to come back to Ariel and the hell she'd raised in high school.

Shifting gears, Lizzy said, "I got a copy of Ariel's cell phone calls on the night she was murdered." She studied Kayla's face. Had the woman's eyes flickered just a little? "You didn't mention that she called you the night she died."

The woman looked confused for a moment. "So that was who called. Someone butt-dialed me. I said hello. I could hear music in the background and what sounded like grunting." She shrugged. "I had no idea who it was. I thought it was a prank call from outside the party."

"You stayed on the phone for over a minute on what you thought was a prank call? Kayla, are you telling me you didn't know it was Ariel?"

The woman looked away guiltily and then swallowed before she said, "I recognized the number. I thought she was having sex." She shrugged. "I didn't have anything else to do. I was curious. I could hear what sounded like grunting as well as the music. I remember getting up and looking out the window to see if she was outside and it was just a prank. I think by then everyone had moved into the garage because the wind was really rocking the trees."

Lizzy felt ice race through her veins. She hadn't heard Ariel having sex. She'd heard Ariel being murdered. Maybe she hadn't realized that even now. Or maybe she'd been watching the whole thing from the shore of the pond. If anyone had reason to hate Ariel and some of her other classmates, it was Kayla.

"So Ariel had your number? She would have had to have it to butt-dial you. Had she ever called you before?"

Kayla smiled as if she knew what Lizzy was getting at. "You're wondering why Ariel would have my number in her phone when she barely said two words to me in school unless it was to give me a hard time, right?"

That was exactly what she was getting at.

"We talked after school. Only so she could get the answers to the math assignment or try to pay me to write her papers for her in English class."

This was news. "Did you?"

Kayla looked away. "I guess it doesn't matter now, does it? She paid me to do her homework, her papers. I wasn't busy so I didn't mind and my mother and I needed the money."

Lizzy thought of the thumb drive found in Ariel's purse. "How did you get the work to her?"

"I put it on a thumb drive. She'd give me another thumb drive for the next assignment."

Lizzy thought of all the times she'd seen Ariel popping a thumb drive into her laptop to send her assignment to their teacher.

She heard Shade come back in from outside the

lodge. "Wait here," she told Kayla. "You can make yourself another cup of tea if you want. I'll find out what's going on."

The moment Lizzy saw the cowboy's face, she knew there was even more trouble. They moved to the back of the lounge out of earshot from Tyler and Kayla. "What's wrong?"

"All of the vehicles up here have been disabled and now the snowstorm is getting worse," he said, keeping his voice down. "I think I should walk out. It's about twelve miles down to the closest ranch house and cell service. But I don't like leaving you here alone."

"That's why I should go," Josh said as he came in the back door behind them. He turned to Lizzy. "It's snowing hard now. We need to do something about the rest of them," he said quietly as he glanced toward Tyler lying on the couch. "How is he?"

"He needs medical assistance, but he's stable," Shade said. Lizzy could hear Kayla in the kitchen putting on the kettle for more tea.

"Do you want to try to keep them in here until help arrives or have them go back to their cabins and stay there?" Josh asked.

She looked to Shade. He looked ambivalent as she heard the front door open. Their classmates began to file into the lodge, brushing snow off their coats and heading straight for the fireplace and the bar as if they'd made the decision for them.

"Are you sure about walking out of here?" Lizzy asked Josh.

He nodded and looked to Shade. "I saw you check-ing the vehicles. I checked the old tractor in the barn." He shook his head, a silent message that not even the tractor was leaving here tonight. "I figured the phone would be out as well but I saw your tracks where you already checked it." He turned his attention back to Lizzy. "I can make the walk. But mind if I borrow a warmer coat?"

She could see that Shade felt he should be the one to go, but it was clear he couldn't let himself leave her here alone. She started to remind him that she was the sheriff. She could take care of herself, but she could see the wisdom in Josh making the hike out. They still didn't know what they were dealing with here.

"Come on," Shade told Josh as he headed for the front door. As he reached for a coat on the hook by the door, Lizzy saw him frown for a moment before he handed Josh a different coat.

Still Lizzy had seen what he had. Blood. The coat had blood splattered on the sleeves.

"There are warm gloves in the pocket," Shade told Josh. "You have a cell phone?"

Josh nodded as he slipped into the coat. "I'll get a few things from my cabin, but I'd take a flashlight and some water."

Shade got him water and a breakfast bar from the kitchen. "Stay on the road and good luck."

Josh smiled. "I'll be fine." The highway patrol-man looked at the others huddled by the fire and bar. She followed his gaze. Tyler was sitting up and Jennifer was sitting next to him asking how he was. She heard him say that his head hurt like hell but that he was going to live.

"Good luck to the two of you," Josh said. "You're going to be the ones who need it more than me, I fear."

A PERSON HAS to see the humor in all this, especially if they're already dead. This has to be the worst class reunion in history. I'm sorry, but I can't help finding some satisfaction in the fact that I'm not the only one who made enemies in high school.

And now my killer is having fun using my diary pages to get some form of vigilante justice? Too bad most of what was written in there wasn't strictly fact. But close enough. Facts don't matter all that much when emotion takes over.

But it did give my killer fuel for the fire, so to speak. Or is it subterfuge? Pretty soon they will be at each other's throats—as if they haven't been already.

So don't judge me for being amused. Like they say, what goes around comes around and just keeps coming around, or something like that. Now that I know how my friends really feel about me, I don't care what happens to them. Why should I? Maybe no one will survive this reunion.

At this point, I'm up for wagering who's next. I still have my favorites and could offer suggestions—not that the killer would listen to me. Would I spare anyone in this group?

Maybe one. But I'm keeping that to myself. Can't

wait to see who will avoid the grim reaper now that it's clear that the killer isn't finished.

Good luck, my old friends.

As Shade had reached for a coat to give Josh, he'd seen a dark stain on the sleeves of a coat hidden underneath others on the rack. He'd frozen, but only for a moment. He'd needed to get Josh down the road as quickly as possible and he hadn't wanted anyone else to notice the bloody coat.

Pulling off another large warm coat, he'd handed it to the man. But Josh had seen the blood. His eyes had widened. He'd been smart enough not to say anything. Lizzy had seen it, as well.

Whoever had taken that coat had attacked Tyler. They'd probably thought it wouldn't be discovered, hidden under a larger coat. It would have been easy for them to go unnoticed if they stayed back enough from the fire. Once they came into the lodge, they could remove the coat and gloves and hide them so no one saw the blood splatters.

All he could hope was that a lab would be able to get DNA, fibers, hair, something from the coat to point them to at least the person who'd attacked Tyler. The killer? He could only assume so.

Shade shot Lizzy a look. He carefully pulled both coats off the hook, keeping the bloody one covered, and carried them into his office for safekeeping. When he came back out, he locked the office door. He just hoped they all lived long enough that DNA would matter in this case.

When he looked up, he saw Lizzy watching him. She'd seen enough to come to some of the same conclusions, he knew.

"Did you see who stepped away from the fire before Tyler was hit?" she asked.

He shook his head and did a head count of the people in the room. Everyone was accounted for, he saw with relief, sans Josh. Brad and Christopher were making everyone drinks. Jennifer was helping serve them. Kayla was curled up in a chair with what appeared to be another cup of tea. Tyler looked pale but was sitting up watching all of them. Ashley stood with her back to the fire, seeming not to trust anyone in the room. Her face was tear-streaked. Stephanie stood at the opposite end of the fireplace, her gaze on Ashley as if still upset with the woman.

With Josh gone, there were only nine of them left. He noticed that Lizzy had moved away and taken something out of her pocket. She studied it with her back to the others. From the slump of her shoulders, whatever she was reading was upsetting her. He moved to her and saw that she was holding what looked like a piece of paper torn from a book.

Taking her arm, he drew her farther away from the others. "What is it?"

She seemed to hesitate as if not sure she should be sharing the information. But like him, she must have realized their situation. They needed each other more than ever.

"Ariel left a diary. Someone found it and is using what she wrote about each of them against the others. Some of it is definitely inflammatory. The first one accused Stephanie of driving the car that killed Whitney Clark in the hit-and-run accident that took her life and that Ariel had gotten the information from Ashley. Stephanie swears it's a lie, but she had a DUI arrest the night of our graduation party. She also said she wasn't driving that night, but she took the rap because she was underage and not alone."

He stared at her. "If she wasn't driving, then who was?"

"Ariel's father." Lizzy sighed and held up the diary page she'd been reading. "This one was found on Tyler…" She looked down at the page in her hands before carefully putting it back in her pocket. "It accuses him of being the driver of the car that killed Whitney. Ariel had earlier accused Stephanie of the same thing. Only with Tyler, apparently she was blackmailing him."

Shade let out a curse. "Did you have any idea all that was going on?"

She shook her head. "I suspect there are more diary pages."

"More attempted murders," he said under his breath like a curse. They both turned to look at their classmates who were huddled around the fireplace. "What are we going to do with them?" he whispered.

"I have no idea. I think we're all going to have to stay here tonight until help comes," she said. "What choice do we have? Let's just hope there really is safety in numbers."

LIZZY STARED AT the group in the lodge as outside snow fell in a blur of white against the blackness. When she'd seen Ariel's car being pulled from the pond, she'd thought it had been an accident. She'd wanted it to be a twist of fate that the woman had ended up in that dark, cold grave because of something she'd done to herself.

Even when she'd realized it had been murder, Lizzy had still thought that Ariel had brought it on herself because of the way she'd treated everyone. She'd thought Ariel's death had been an act of retribution, a single incident. Then she'd seen Tyler lying there… and she feared it might be more involved than that.

"Where's Josh?" Christopher asked, looking around the room, his gaze settling on Lizzy. But it was Shade who answered.

"He's left to get help for Tyler."

"Left? But all the rigs are out front." Lizzy saw recognition dawn on the man's face. "Are you telling me he walked out of here? Why wouldn't he take—?" Christopher swore and looked around the room. "You didn't call for help? You sent Josh?"

Lizzy could see no way around the truth. "The phone lines have been cut and the vehicles tampered with," she said. "But there is no reason for panic. Josh has gone for help."

Christopher swore again.

Brad had gone pale. "So someone in this room did this? Attacked Tyler and then made sure we were stranded here?"

"We're safe here," Shade said. "We'll stay in the lodge together until Josh returns with help. It will be at least four hours."

Christopher shook his head and reached for another beer.

"This is not how I thought this reunion would go," Ashley said, sounding close to tears. "Now someone's attacked Tyler and made sure we can't all leave?"

"I think the question we should be asking ourselves is who's next?" Brad said.

"Maybe we should have the slideshow," Kayla said, but no one responded. "Or the dance we planned."

"Seriously, Kayla? Does anyone look like they want to dance?" Stephanie snapped.

"Let's all settle down," Shade said. "We're here for a while so let's try to make the best of it. I'm going to put on a pot of coffee and Buckshot left us some cookies."

"I'm going to my cabin for a sweater," Jennifer said as she put her arm around Ashley. "Why don't you come with me? I think the fresh air would do us some good."

"It's snowing hard out there," Lizzy said, hoping

to keep everyone together so she could keep an eye on them.

Jennifer gave her an impatient look. "We'll be right back."

Lizzy watched them leave, trying to tamp down her worry.

"Restroom?" Stephanie asked, coming up to Lizzy.

She pointed toward the large room at the back where the dances were held and watched as Stephanie disappeared through it.

Shade went into the kitchen to make the coffee, saying, "It's going to be a long night."

Lizzy was the only one who stood at the window watching Jennifer and Ashley until they disappeared in the storm. Turning back to the others gathered around the fire, she tried to relax. Maybe Tyler's attack was all there would be. But then again, she'd thought that about Ariel's murder.

"It wouldn't be our class reunion, unless there was drama," Christopher said, joining her. "Beer?" He offered her one of the bottles in his hand. Lizzy shook her head. "More for me then, Sheriff."

She was relieved when Ashley and Jennifer returned, both shaking off the snow. They discarded their coats on the hooks by the door and joined the others. Jennifer had been right. The walk to her cabin seemed to have done them both good.

Ashley took the glass of wine Christopher offered her and came over to stand by Lizzy. "Did Shade mention that he came by to see me yesterday?"

Lizzy shook her head. She was watching the room, watching her classmates, looking... What was she looking for besides a killer?

"I thought he might have mentioned it," Ashley said and took a drink of her wine. "Maybe we should have canceled the reunion. Maybe our class is cursed."

Lizzy looked over at the woman. "It's a little late for that."

Ashley sighed. "I can't shake this feeling." She shuddered and then tried to laugh it off. "Ariel used to say I pretended to be psychic because I couldn't stand not being special."

"You can see the future?"

The woman shuddered again. "I hope not. Sometimes I just feel things. Like on graduation night. Sitting at the cemetery. I knew Ariel was dead. I just... felt it." Ashley looked away as if fearing she'd said too much. "I know Ariel was mean, but she was also vulnerable and scared. She just hated showing it. That's what gave her such rough edges."

Lizzy laughed. "Rough edges. That was Ariel all right. But I do know what you mean. It wasn't the cruelty in her that allowed her to control us, it was that softer part that we all saw that made us sorry for her at certain moments. It made us want to protect her from herself. We didn't want to hurt her even as she was hurting us." She shook her head. "She was one complicated human being. Even now, it makes no sense why she dominated all of us the way she did."

"But it does make sense. Otherwise, it would mean

that we were all just afraid of her and that makes us cowards." Ashley drained her wineglass. "She should be here." Her voice broke and she covered it with a laugh. "If Ariel was here right now, well, this party wouldn't be so dull, you know?"

Lizzy did know. "You said earlier that you feel something?"

Ashley nodded as if she was sorry to be reminded. "Just a bad feeling that it isn't over." Her gaze met Lizzy's. "Why would someone attack Tyler and make it where we can't leave?" she whispered. "That's crazy, huh? Ariel was the one everyone hated, not the rest of us." Her voice broke.

"I wish I knew."

When Lizzy said nothing more, Ashley seemed to notice the empty wineglass in her hand. "Looks like it's time for a refill."

The wind howled in the eaves. Lizzy looked at the people in the room, finding it hard to believe that any of them was capable of murder and possibly attempted murder. She couldn't imagine that kind of anger, especially spread over ten years.

Why hadn't the killer struck before now? That thought made her frown. Why wait until the reunion? Or had the killer been waiting for Ariel's body to be found?

Lizzy realized with a start that Stephanie hadn't returned. She went down to the large room at the back of the lodge. The tables were still up from where the photographs had been but other than that, the room was empty. She saw that the bathroom door was still closed.

Moving closer, she listened for the sound of running water but heard nothing. "Stephanie?" She tapped on the bathroom door and then tried the knob when she got no answer. It was locked. "Stephanie?"

Shade appeared at her side. "What's wrong?"

"Stephanie. She asked where the bathroom was, but that was a long time ago."

"Stephanie!" he called louder and pounded on the door. Still no answer from inside. "We keep a key in the office for when kids lock themselves in." He left to go to his office.

Lizzy saw that several people from in the lounge had come into the room. She hurried to shoo them into the main lounge and closed the door behind Shade as he returned. He used the key to unlock the door and swing it open.

She rushed forward with Shade right behind her. Stephanie lay on the floor, body convulsing in spasms, her back arching before she suddenly collapsed. Her face was a bright cherry red that appeared to be getting darker. Lizzy knew at once. Cyanide poisoning.

Shade dropped next to her to check for a pulse.

"Is she…?" Lizzy barely got the words out before he was getting to his feet.

"She's gone." As he rose, he handed her a small crumpled piece of paper. She recognized it as another one of the pages torn out of Ariel's diary. "This was lying beside her."

Lizzy quickly read what had been written on it:

Stephanie and my father? Gross. It makes me want to throw up. She really thinks people won't find out? Worse, she thought she could keep it from me? They both did? This is going to cost you, Daddy. And you, too, Steph. Talk about a bitter pill to swallow.

Lizzy glanced up at Shade. They shared a look before they both rushed into the lounge.

SHADE WENT STRAIGHT to the bar. "No more drinks." He realized he would have to watch the food just as carefully until Josh got to where he could use his cell phone and call for help.

"What's going on?" Brad demanded. Glancing around, he asked, "Where's Stephanie?"

"What did Stephanie have to drink?" Lizzy asked. "Is her glass still around?"

They all looked around at each other and then at the drinks in their own hands. Quickly, everyone put down their half-finished glasses and stepped back, looks of horror and shock on their faces as realization began to move through the group.

"I think that's her drink," Kayla said, pointing to a glass on the edge of the coffee table. "She said she wasn't feeling well and was going to the bathroom. She seemed to be having trouble breathing and complained of a headache. What was wrong with her?"

"She's been poisoned," Lizzy said and a gasp went up around the room.

"Is she going to be all right?" Ashley cried and looked from Lizzy to Shade and back before beginning to cry. "Can this get any worse?"

Shade feared it could. Everyone looked shell-shocked and scared. He glanced at Lizzy, wondering how she wanted to handle this.

"I need you to all line up," she ordered.

"Wait," Jennifer said as if she hadn't been paying attention. "What's going on?"

"Someone poisoned Stephanie." Ashley's voice broke.

"*Poisoned* her?" Jennifer repeated.

Lizzy continued as if uninterrupted. "As I come around, I want you to empty out your pockets for me." Shade handed her one of the Native American baskets from the mantel.

"You can't be serious," Brad said when she started with him.

"Everything in your pockets," she said.

"Legally—" Brad began, but Shade interrupted with, "Empty your pockets, Davis. Now!"

Brad complained but emptied what he had in his jeans pockets, which amounted to only change and a couple of receipts.

"I need your wallets and purses, as well," she said. "Don't worry, you'll get them back. Shade, would you frisk the men for me to make sure there is nothing in any of their pockets?"

Brad started to put up a fight but when Shade got in his face, he shut up.

Lizzy continued down the line, keeping each person's items separate from the others as Shade frisked the men. She reached Ashley and handed Shade the basket of items after Ashley emptied her pockets.

"I'm going to have to search you."

"Is this really necessary?" Ashley said, wiping at her tears. "You can't think I would do anything to Stephanie or anyone else. Anyway, Jennifer and I weren't even here." But she lifted her arms.

Lizzy checked her pockets and moved on to Kayla, then Jennifer. All three had paled visibly and Jennifer was crying softly.

She knew that the poison could have been administered to Stephanie's drink numerous ways. And there might have been only one portion so the killer would no longer have any evidence on him or her.

"I'm going to have to interview each of you separately."

"You can use the dining room," Shade said. "I can close the doors. I'll check the coats by the door, as well."

"Thank you," she said, having forgotten about the coats. Maybe they would get lucky. "Ashley, why don't you come in first?"

"Why would anyone want to kill Stephanie?" Ashley cried the moment they were seated in the dining room, the French doors closed.

"Did you know where Stephanie was the night of our graduation party?"

"I already told you—"

"But I thought you might want to change your story, given what has happened. You knew about the man Stephanie was seeing, didn't you?"

Ashley looked away for a moment.

"Ariel knew."

Ashley let out a bitter laugh. "Of course she did."

"Ariel traded in secrets to keep her friends in line. We've already established that. But was she blackmailing some of you?"

"Not me," the young woman said too quickly. "And if she was blackmailing Stephanie, I knew nothing about it."

"But you knew about Stephanie and the man she was seeing."

Ashley finally met her gaze. "Ariel recorded them making love in her bedroom."

There was *another* video, other than the one Ariel had left for Shade? "Coach told me that she'd recorded the two of you, as well. Is it true?"

Another bitter laugh. "She said she had a video of us, but I never knew if it was true or not. Until now." She shook her head in disgust. "Let's face it, we were all getting sick of Ariel by the end of our senior year and for good reasons, you included. Stephanie was over her and I didn't blame her."

"Who was the man in the video with Stephanie?"

Ashley gave her a shocked look. "You didn't know? Stephanie was sleeping with Ariel's father."

Lizzy had suspected as much before she'd read the diary page. The two had been pulled over graduation night and Stephanie was cited with a DUI. "Was it serious?"

Ashley rolled her eyes. "Maybe Stephanie thought it was but not Mark Matheson. It would have destroyed his career since Stephanie was underage and his daughter's friend. But he destroyed his career anyway, didn't he? And now Stephanie…" She began to cry again.

"Who at the reunion would want to hurt Stephanie?" Lizzy asked.

Ashley shook her head. "I don't know."

Lizzy knew she had to ask her about the earlier diary page. "Did you tell Ariel that Stephanie was driving the car the night Whitney Clark was killed in a hit-and-run?"

Ashley's head jerked up, her eyes widening. "Is that why she was so upset with me?"

"Ashley, if you know something about that—"

The woman buried her face in her hands. "I was angry with Stephanie because of something that happened at school." She looked up. "It was stupid. I wanted to hurt her, but I wouldn't kill her."

"What do you know about Whitney's death?" Lizzy asked.

Ashley cried for a few moments before wiping her eyes and pulling herself together. As she pushed open the door, she glanced toward the lounge where Tyler was lying on the couch complaining of a headache, but alive. "I promised Ariel I would never tell."

"Ariel's dead and now so is Stephanie."

Ashley grimaced and looked as if she would burst into tears again.

"Tyler," she said in a hoarse whisper. "He was driving the car. It was an accident. Stephanie was fooling with him while he was driving. He didn't see Whitney until it was too late."

Lizzy shook her head. "Why would you promise Ariel not to tell?"

"Because she needed the money. Well, not needed it, but she wanted it."

"She was blackmailing Tyler."

Ashley nodded, wiping at her tears. "I kept her secret."

"Who knew about this besides you?"

The woman shook her head.

"How did you find out?" Lizzy asked.

"Ariel had forgotten to lock up her diary."

CHAPTER TWENTY-THREE

DEPUTY JOHN "ACE" TURNER took the call from the highway patrolman. The sheriff was in trouble up on the mountain at her class reunion? He had to laugh as he disconnected. One person attacked and all the vehicles sabotaged? Send reinforcements? What had poor Lizzy gotten herself into?

Since finding the photo of her up at the guest ranch, he'd tried to find out more about her. But there was little to find. What surprised him was that he found nothing about her parents. Wouldn't there have been an obit, if they'd died?

All that aside, he had to decide what to do now. He had more seniority than anyone else in the department. Rightfully, he should have been sheriff. If he had been, he wouldn't be trapped up on a mountainside right now. He could call for backup and go up there like gangbusters to save the day. Hell, he could call in a SWAT team if he wanted to.

But why let anyone else get credit for saving the sheriff? He could handle this himself. Save the day all by himself. Save the sheriff.

The thought made him laugh. Voters would realize what a mistake they'd made. That was if the sheriff didn't get herself killed before he got there. That option would work, too, since he would be next in line. He'd already applied for the undersheriff position, but the thought of working for a woman turned his stomach.

Ace grabbed his hat as he headed for the door. He'd drive up to the guest ranch and take care of whatever trouble there was. It all sounded pretty straightforward. A class reunion gone awry. Probably too much booze, old grudges and someone with a temper. Though the highway patrolman hadn't said that the sheriff had a perp in custody. Was it possible she didn't know who had done the killing?

Clearly the woman needed him. He imagined the write-up in the newspaper as he drove out of town. "Deputy Saves Sheriff at Her Guest Ranch High School Reunion." He grinned to himself as he left town behind and started up into the mountains.

The highway patrolman said to watch for him on the way up to the ranch. The man would be hiking back up the road from a neighboring ranch and would need a ride.

Like Ace was going to let a highway patrolman steal his thunder, he thought with a laugh.

LIZZY RUBBED HER TEMPLES. Her head ached. She checked Tyler. Fortunately they'd been able to stop the bleeding on his head wound. It didn't appear to be that bad since, other than a headache, he said he was all right. Still, she was anxious to get him to the hospital. Anxious to get out of here as much as the others.

Not that it would be over for her. She had a killer to catch. This case had already taken too many twists and turns. There had been so much more going on her senior year than even she'd imagined. Worse, she felt as if she'd only skimmed the surface. Her greatest fear was that the killer wasn't finished.

"I need you to be honest with me," she told Jennifer when she was brought in for questioning. "What do you know about who Stephanie was seeing our senior year?"

She frowned. "I didn't think she was dating anyone. Did you ask Ashley?"

"I did."

"Well, what did she tell you?"

"The truth."

Jennifer glanced down for a moment. When she looked up, there were tears in her blue eyes. "Why bring all this back up now? Stephanie's dead. What's the point? She made a terrible mistake but she probably isn't the first girl with a daddy complex who turned to an older man."

"I'm bringing it up because someone killed her."

"Not because of who she was seeing ten years ago," Jennifer argued.

"Then why?"

The woman blinked big blue eyes at her. "I have no idea."

"Someone poisoned her and that someone is here

at the reunion. So who in that next room had reason to want her dead?"

Jennifer shook her head and wiped her eyes, her voice breaking when she spoke. "I honestly don't know, but I'm scared. It's like the person wants us all dead. I keep thinking about what I might have done or said to one of them back in high school that was so awful that they want to kill me."

"And what have you come up with?"

Her eyes were dry again, her stare cold and calculating. "Kayla. You know how she's always watched us all. Ariel was horrible to Kayla and so was Tyler. Did you know she asked him to our prom and he turned her down so brutally that even he felt bad about it later? And Kayla was the one to find him. Everyone else was around the fire."

Was that true? Lizzy couldn't remember who'd been around the fire before or after the fireworks had gone off. Any one of them could have used the distraction to attack Tyler. Any one of them could have doctored Stephanie's drink.

But whoever tried to kill Tyler had covered up the bloody coat. At least that was the theory.

She let Jennifer return to the lounge even though she suspected the woman hadn't been completely honest. When she called in Kayla, the young woman still looked in shock as she took a seat.

"Kayla—"

"I didn't hurt anyone. I liked Tyler. He could be

an ass, but when it was just the two of us, he was…
kind to me."

"And Stephanie?"

"Stephanie? You think I poisoned her?"

"Did you?"

"Of course not. Why would you think that?"

"Was Stephanie kind to you?"

Kayla looked away. "She ignored me as if I was
invisible. I always wished that Ariel had." As if realizing what she'd said, she quickly added, "I didn't
kill her either. I don't care enough about any of these
people to…dispose of them."

Lizzy heard honesty in her words. "High school
was hard for you."

Kayla shook her head. "It was hard because my
mother was sick and I had to take care of her. High
school is hard on a lot of people."

"You had a crush on Tyler?"

The woman dropped her gaze and when she lifted
it again, tears filled her eyes. "I knew he didn't feel
the same way about me. I was certainly not his type."

"Who was his type?"

Kayla's face clouded. "Ariel. Not that she noticed.
She was too busy destroying Christopher's life and
every other man who crossed her path."

Lizzy realized with a start how much Kayla knew
about everything that was going on. Of course, being
the wallflower, she'd been invisible to most of them
and all the while, she'd been watching. "Who was

Stephanie involved with?" She saw the answer at once on the woman's face.

"Ariel's father."

"And Coach, our history teacher?"

Kayla met her gaze. "Who didn't he sleep with?"

"Ariel?"

She nodded. "She slept with him to get back at her father."

The video, the dress, Ariel's bedroom. "Coach swore he didn't sleep with Ariel."

Kayla made an and-you-believed-him face.

Lizzy felt sick inside. Which meant Ariel could have been carrying the man's child. Everyone knew all this was going on except her? Three classmates were dead and she didn't feel any closer to the truth.

Lizzy proceeded to question one after another of her classmates. All she got was more of the same. Everyone was scared, her included.

SHADE HAD SENSED the growing unrest in the room while Lizzy was interviewing each of their classmates.

"I don't know about the rest of you, but I'm not staying here," Christopher said as Lizzy came out after finishing her interviews. "This is insane." He looked around the room as if trying to decide who was the most dangerous. "Waiting here for the killer to strike again? Wondering who's next? No, thanks." He headed for the door.

"It's pitch-black out there and blizzarding," Shade pointed out, even though he doubted it would do any good. Christopher was fired up and half-drunk. Another reason it was foolish for him to take off on foot. "You can't really think walking off this mountain in the middle of the night in a snowstorm is the smart thing to do under any circumstances, but especially these."

"Shade's right," Lizzy said. "Josh has gone for help. I think you're making a mistake leaving here tonight. At least with us all together in here—"

Christopher let out a bark of a laugh. "We were all together when Stephanie was poisoned. It didn't stop the killer, did it? We don't know that Josh even made it down the mountain for help. Or that he isn't the killer and he's been sneaking back here to kill us all."

"That does seem like a stretch," Brad said from the corner he was sitting in. "How would he have poisoned Stephanie?"

"Christopher's right," Ashley chimed in. "I'm not staying here either. I'd rather take my chances out in the storm on the road. At least I'll be doing something, not sitting around waiting for the killer to strike again. Can I go with you?" Shade saw the man hesitate. "Seriously, Christopher?" she demanded.

"I'm going, too," Kayla said, jumping to her feet. "I don't have to walk with you two if you don't want me to."

Christopher groaned. "I'd rather you walk with us so I can keep my eye on you."

Kayla didn't seem insulted. "Sorry, but I'd rather walk alone because I have no reason to trust either of you." She grabbed her coat off the hook and pushed out the door.

"Hurry up, Ashley. I'm not staying here a moment longer," Christopher said and stepped outside.

Ashley scrambled after him. "I have to get my things out of my cabin."

From the window, Shade watched through the storm. Kayla went toward the road and the other two headed toward the row of cabins. The snow had let up some. In the cabin's porch light, he saw the two emerge with Ashley's rolling overnight bag. Apparently she planned to drag it through the snow and down the mountain. Christopher was looking around anxiously and clearly hurrying her along. Shade had lost sight of Kayla.

Turning back to the others, he caught Lizzy's eye.

She looked resigned as she shook her head. "I can't keep them here. But I have faith that Josh got through and is on his way back with law enforcement," she said, turning to look at the three left: Brad, Jennifer and Tyler. "Help should come across the three of them if they stay to the road."

"I want to leave, too," Jennifer said and began to cry. "I'm sorry. I have no idea what's going on or who's doing this but I don't want to stay here either." She glanced at Brad.

He laughed. "You think I'm the killer? The only reason I'm still here is because I'm a newsman and this is one hell of a story."

"Until you're the one who's dead," she said. "Fine, I'll go alone. It's safer than staying here."

Brad scoffed. "How far is it to the first house? Twelve miles. In a snowstorm? In the dark? Go for it."

"I shouldn't have to walk that far. Like the sheriff said, Josh is getting help. Law enforcement will pick us up and we'll be safe."

"*If* Josh got through. *If* he's not the killer out there waiting for you. *If* you don't freeze to death before they reach you." Brad sat back down on the fireplace hearth and folded his arms. "I'm not going out there with all those lunatics."

As Jennifer left, Shade moved to the door to lock it behind them. "Then I guess it's the four of us." He glanced at the large clock on the wall. It was almost 2:30 in the morning. "It's only a matter of hours before it gets light. We'll stay here and we should be fine. Brad, why don't you help me with the coffee? I think we'd be wise to stay awake until help comes."

Brad rose slowly from the hearth. "I should warn you that I'm armed. I have a gun."

Shade groaned. "Great. Try not to shoot yourself with it. Or worse, one of us."

"I'll check the back door," Lizzy said and headed for the large room at the back of the lodge.

As she entered the back room, she glanced toward the bathroom where Stephanie's body still lay in the spot where they'd found her. She quickly averted her eyes. The smell of death followed her to the back door.

She felt helpless. She was the sheriff. She had taken an oath to protect. She'd failed miserably after only days of being in the office. How could she not question if she was right for this job? She'd thought she could handle it, but if this was any indication...

She was almost to the door when she stopped as she realized something. She'd just assumed that all this began with Ariel's death. But now she realized with a chill that this all began with Whitney Clark's.

Whitney had befriended Lizzy *before* Ariel. She remembered Whitney saying that Lizzy had to watch out for Ariel. But that wasn't the only one she'd warned her about. Stephanie.

"ARIEL RUNS EVERYTHING. She has two sidekicks, Stephanie and Jennifer. Stephanie is an Ariel wannabe. Jennifer's all right, when you can get her away from Ariel. I actually like her when she isn't pretending for Ariel's sake that she can't stand me." Whitney had laughed. *"Just watch Ariel. She's vicious."*

LIZZY THOUGHT OF the diary pages naming Tyler and Stephanie in the hit-and-run. And Ariel, who'd known and used the information to squeeze money out of Tyler and keep Stephanie in line.

Her heart began to beat harder as she realized that Ashley had also known who'd killed Whitney and had kept it to herself.

For a moment she almost started back to the lounge to tell Shade what she'd figured out, but first she had to lock the back door. Then she would tell Shade. Ashley was in danger. And Christopher, too, if he'd read the diaries and kept silent. This had all been about Whitney Clark's death.

As she reached to lock the back door, the lights went out.

There was that moment of surprise, then total disorienting blackness. She heard Shade call her name. Heard the panic in his voice moments before she heard running footfalls. She opened her mouth to call back as she reached for her weapon strapped on her ankle. Fingers closed over her arm before she could reach it. She struggled to fight them off when she felt the pinprick of a needle jammed into her.

She let out a small cry before a hand clamped over her mouth. The fight she put up was both futile and frail. The drug rushed through her veins so quickly that her knees buckled under her. She could hear Shade looking for the flashlight he'd had earlier as she was dragged out into the darkness and the cold night air.

Her eyelids felt too heavy. She fought to keep them open, fought to see her attacker, already knowing who it would be. Opening her mouth, she tried to call out to warn Shade, but her mind had disconnected from her body. She couldn't move, she couldn't speak.

As she was dragged through the cold, snowy blackness, all she felt was the biting grip of fingers digging into her flesh as she was taken away.

SHADE FINALLY FOUND the flashlight and snapped it on. The beam skittered across the floor in front of him as he raced toward the back room of the lodge. "Lizzy? *Lizzy!*" He screamed her name, his voice breaking. He shined the light around the large empty room and into the bathrooms, the beam freezing on the open back door and the snow falling outside.

His heart in his throat, he ran to the gaping doorway and was hit by the cold, the snow and the blackness. *"Lizzy! Lizzy!"* His voice was hoarse with fear. The flashlight beam flickered on the ground directly outside. He could see footprints and drag marks in the snow.

Running, he followed the drag marks into the trees only to have them disappear. Had the killer picked Lizzy up to carry her?

He shot the beam out into the dense, dark pines. Nothing. No movement. As he tried to catch his breath and still his thundering heart, he shivered, realizing he'd run out without a coat. He also hadn't come out with something he absolutely had to have: his gun. He'd also forgotten about Brad. He sprinted through the snow back toward the lodge.

Shade told himself that Lizzy couldn't have gotten away that quickly. The killer had no way to get her off the mountain. Lizzy was still here. Somewhere. He just had to find her before—he refused to let his mind go down that trail of thought. If the killer wanted her dead, Shade would have found her lying in the lodge's back doorway after taking her last breath.

For some reason, the killer wanted her alive. Shade tried to assure himself that she would stay that way.

Lizzy was strong, she was smart, she would be fine. But even as he told himself that, he was reminded of the others who had died. This killer was relentless, diabolical, determined and certainly not done.

He shined the flashlight ahead of him as he reached the back of the lodge. As he stepped in, he heard a sound and froze as he recognized it. The front door lock making a snicking sound and then the door opened and slammed shut. His heart began to pound even harder.

"Brad?" In his terror to find Lizzy after the lights went out, he'd completely forgotten about the newsman and Tyler. No answer. "Brad?" He swore under his breath as he followed the beam of his flashlight through the lodge. It didn't take long to realize that Brad was gone. Now he was out there somewhere with a loaded weapon.

Shade swore but didn't have time to worry about Brad right now. Strapping on his holster, he checked the pistol to make sure it was loaded, then grabbed another clip just in case. His fingers trembled as he slipped the gun into the holster, grabbed a coat and, taking the flashlight, headed for the back door to follow the drag tracks into the pines and beyond. He would find Lizzy. He would find her before it was too late.

CHAPTER TWENTY-FOUR

DEPUTY ACE TURNER took his time driving up the mountain. As much as he wanted to save Lizzy and be the hero, he wanted to give her time to really hang herself. According to the highway patrolman, she already had one wounded man. And a dead body, if you counted Ariel Matheson.

He smiled to himself, enjoying how screwed she must be feeling. Hell, by the time he reached the guest ranch, the tally could be even higher. This was going to look so bad on her record. He almost felt sorry for her. Maybe the county would impeach her. That's if she didn't cry uncle and give up. If it was him, he would step down. Well, it would never have been him since he certainly wouldn't have gone up to that class reunion with a nutcase on the loose.

Dreaming about how he'd take over the department after he saved her, he noticed that the snow seemed to be letting up. It had rained in the valley, so the only snow was up here in the mountains. But even that was ending as he left town.

As he came over a rise, he saw a man walking up the road in the dark. He recognized him in his head-

lights. Ace had been pulled over by that same patrolman a few weeks ago for a broken headlight. The
guy had been a dick. He shook his head and chuckled
since the tables had turned. The highway patrolman
had said that he'd walked almost all the way down
the mountain until he got cell phone service. Now he
was halfway back and still had miles to go before he
reached the guest ranch.

Ace knew he'd get in trouble for not picking him
up, but since he had no idea who the killer was, didn't
it make sense not to stop?

The patrolman, hearing the sound of a vehicle behind him, turned and waved a hand. Ace got a kick out
of the expression on the guy's face as he sped on past.

"Sorry, sucker," he said, grinning as he glanced in
his rearview mirror. The highway patrolman didn't
look happy. Let him think that other law enforcement
vehicles would be coming along to pick him up soon.

As his headlights cut through the pines lining both
sides of the narrow road, Ace thought about what he'd
find when he reached the guest ranch. Mayhem probably. But then again, this was what he lived for, the
excitement, the adrenaline rush as he saved the day.
He really did love this job at moments like this.

SHADE HAD LOST the drag trail only yards into the
woods but picked it up again as the pines thinned.
Now, the trail had petered out again. Fear paralyzed
him for a moment. He stopped to catch his breath and

listen, turning off the flashlight as he stood stone-still in the dark.

The snow had stopped. Only a few isolated flakes drifted down. A breeze moaned in the tops of the pines as they swayed against the black sky. Somewhere in the distance he heard an owl hoot, making him start.

He tried to still his nerves even as he felt the urgency of finding Lizzy. Whoever had taken her hadn't killed her outright. That gave him hope that maybe the killer had another plan for her that didn't include death. At least not right away. Because they knew he'd come looking for her?

Of course the killer would set a trap for him.

The darkness seemed to close in on him. He thought of Lizzy and his daughter he hadn't gotten a chance to get to know yet. He wanted both so desperately. If he didn't get off this mountain alive, Maisie would have no one.

Snapping the flashlight back on, he began to search the ground again for any sign of tracks. It took a few frustrating, heart-pounding minutes before he found them again. But when he did, he thought he knew where the killer was headed.

The tracks though were no longer drag marks. Had the killer picked Lizzy up? Was he or she now carrying her? Was that why there were deeper scuff marks in the snow?

He followed the tracks as they crossed the mountainside toward the last of the cabins farthest from the lodge.

COMING IN AND out of consciousness, Lizzy tried to open her eyes wider but her eyelids were too heavy. She could only make out a dark figure standing over her. Opening her mouth, she tried to speak, but still nothing came out. Her throat felt so dry that it closed. She fought to breathe. Had she been poisoned like Stephanie?

The figure leaned over her, blocking her view for a few moments. She held her breath, trying to hide the fact that the drug was wearing off. This was how her life was going to end? But as she braced for death, she felt her fingers being opened, something being shoved into her palm, and her fingers closed over it.

Her heart beat harder, more painfully in her chest as she realized what she now held. *A diary page.* Her attacker had pressed the page into her hand so that when she was found dead, everyone would know why. Each secret that Ariel had written down in her diary was now being revealed as the killer took yet another life. Another debt paid?

So why wasn't she already dead?

The figure above her seemed to freeze at a sound that Lizzy hadn't heard over the pounding of her pulse. She listened as she tried to fight off the drug. She couldn't feel her body, couldn't move a muscle. Panic made her heart beat faster. She had to let out the breath she'd been holding.

A hand was suddenly clamped down over her mouth. She felt her eyes widen in alarm only an instant before she heard the gunshot.

AS ACE ROUNDED a curve in the narrow road, his head-lights picked up something ahead. "What the hell?" He threw on his brakes as he realized what he was seeing. A body lying beside the road.

He skidded to a stop. In the glare of his headlights, he could see that whoever it was, they weren't moving. He looked around but past the body there was noth-ing but snow-covered pines on each side of the road. The darkness was so intense it would be impossible to know if there was someone lurking there, lying in wait for him to come along and get out of his cruiser so they could attack.

Ace felt a chill shudder through him. The person lay on his or her side, back to him. He stared at the figure, pretty sure it was a man. He honked his horn. The fig-ure didn't move. From this distance, he couldn't tell if the person was still breathing or not. He guessed not. Whoever it was, he told himself he couldn't help. Getting out and endangering his own life would be a waste.

Why did it have to be so damned dark up here in the mountains? He looked out at the black sky. Only a little snow drifted down. He could almost feel the cold, black October night just outside. Sitting in the warmth of his patrol SUV cruiser, he waited, feeling as if he was in one of those zombie movies. If he opened his door to get out to move the body, the zombies would come out of the trees and he'd be a goner. He knew it was crazy, but he still couldn't shake the feeling that someone was out there, waiting for him to do just that.

He swore, cringing as he hit the gas, refusing to look back. But he hadn't gone more than a few yards before he saw another body lying beside the road. He felt ice claw its way up his spine as the breeze lifted a lock of blond hair from beneath a knitted winter cap.

Call for backup. Don't be a fool. Call. Now.

CHAPTER TWENTY-FIVE

SHADE GLANCED DOWN the mountain. He'd lost the tracks again. Now he wasn't sure where to go. The killer had been carrying Lizzy. She wasn't that heavy, but deadweight— Another thought he shoved away. Lizzy would have been incapacitated in some way for the killer to take her. What if the killer had gotten too tired to carry her any farther and had changed plans and headed for a cabin closer?

He could see tracks by the back of the cabin below him in the woods. He had to check it even though he knew he might be wasting valuable time. But if he went all the way to cabin nine and she wasn't there—

Shade reached the back of the cabin when he heard the gunshot. It was quickly followed by a second shot. Brad? He slipped in through the back of the cabin using his master key. It was empty. At the front of the cabin, he moved to the window and looked out.

In the large yard light, he saw the pines sway in the breeze. Snow fell from the branches in large white clumps that formed pockmarks in the smooth surface of the covered ground. Past the pines, he saw something move into the shadows down by the barn. Tucking the flashlight into his belt, he pulled his weapon and eased the door open. The cold breeze stole his breath for a moment. He couldn't see anyone.

The silence of the October night weighed on him. He had no idea who'd fired the shot—just that Brad had said he had a gun and Brad was also now missing.

Shade had to find Lizzy. He closed the door and went back through the cabin. He could feel time slipping away from him. He couldn't bear the thought that he and Lizzy might not get their chance. He couldn't let that happen. He'd find her. Or die trying.

THE KILLER WAS BACK.

Lizzy heard someone enter the cabin and lock the door. She could hear heavy breathing and the shuffle of footsteps across the floor as if every step was an effort. The killer stopped in the other room. She imagined the person looking out the window. Looking for Shade?

Was that what they were waiting for? She knew he could come for her and the thought pierced through her like a bullet. He would be walking right into a trap. She couldn't bear the idea of him being harmed. She thought of the gunshot she'd heard. Maybe it was already too late.

Forcing away the image of Shade lying dead back at the lodge, she tried to concentrate. She could hear the killer moving around in the other room. Was the person having second thoughts? Murder had to get to even a psychopath at some point, didn't it? But she knew all too well the criminal mind worked in its own warped way. Few killers thought that what they were doing was wrong and then stopped.

She suddenly realized that she could feel the diary page in her hand. Her fingers began to open of their own volition, and she tried to move the rest of her body. If Shade was still alive and coming for her, she had to warn him somehow.

It took all her mental strength, but she was able to move her leg a fraction of an inch. Her right arm jerked just a little. Whatever they'd given her, it was wearing off. But was it wearing off quickly enough?

She heard whispering in the other room, although she couldn't make out the words or tell if it was one person or two. Maybe the person was talking to themselves.

Lizzy felt her pulse leap.

Or maybe there was an accomplice. A second killer.

SHADE QUICKLY MOVED toward the other cabins down the row. He wanted to turn on his flashlight but knew it would only make him a sitting duck if he did. His heart raced as he tried to keep his wits about him. Panicking right now would do Lizzy no good. He had to believe that she was still alive, waiting for him. He had to use his head. She was in one of these cabins with the killer. All he had to do was figure out which one and then what?

He didn't know. Create a diversion? Go busting in like a one-man SWAT team? As he moved cautiously along the edge of the pines toward cabin two, he realized that if Josh had gotten through, the cavalry should have been here by now. Either Josh hadn't made it... Or he was the killer, just as Brad had suggested, and Josh had circled back.

Shade told himself not to think about that right now. First he had to find Lizzy. He was convinced that the killer had carried her to one of the cabins. But in the back of his mind, he also knew that the killer could have dumped her somewhere.

He had to believe that the killer had kept her alive for a reason. Because the killer had known Shade would come after her. It didn't matter. He would do whatever he had to because in his heart Lizzy was already his. His hope. His dream. His future. His future and Maisie's.

For a moment he let himself imagine the three of them as a family. He could see it. He and Lizzy holding Maisie's hands as she skipped along between them. A family. *His* family. The image buoyed him as he reached the next cabin, opened the door and quietly stepped inside. It only took him a few moments of searching before he moved on to the next cabin and then the next.

At cabin six, he thought he heard a vehicle engine in the distance. *Please let it be law enforcement coming to help.* But he felt a sliver of dread pierce his heart. He had to find Lizzy first. He had to save her if possible before the law arrived. He couldn't chance that the killer would panic and finish her off before he could reach her.

The thought drove him harder. Only three to go. All his instincts told him that she was in one of them. The killer had carried her all this way looking for a place to hole up. Beyond cabin nine, there was nothing but wilderness, no real place to take a stand with a hostage.

He opened the back door of cabin seven slowly, more cautiously than before, his weapon drawn. The door screeched and he froze. He heard a sound from inside. He'd been right. The killer had weakened from carrying her and hadn't made it to the last cabin after all.

Listening, he heard it again. The rustle of movement.

The killer?

Or Lizzy?

ACE WAS DRIVING FAST, throwing up rocks and snow and ice as he ascended the mountain. He saw the lodge ahead in his headlights. Cold darkness. There were no lights anywhere, nothing but blackness and the sound of the wind swaying the snowy pines. He slowed, feeling a chill clear to his bones.

He'd never seen anything like this. He felt as if he really *was* in a zombie movie. He thought about turning back but had a growing fear that he would never reach town. If anyone was still alive at the guest ranch—

But even as he thought it, all his instincts told him to run. This was beyond anything he'd ever had to deal with. Whatever was going on up here, he wanted nothing to do with it.

As his cruiser came flying over the last rise, he saw a man standing in the middle of the road. He slammed on his brakes, his heart in this throat. This one wasn't dead. Not yet anyway.

He picked up his radio. It squawked. "Need an ambulance and coroner. Need backup. Sterling's Montana Guest Ranch. Urgent."

His hand shook as he put the radio back. He'd thought his greatest fear was driving up here and finding everyone dead. But with a start, he knew his worst nightmare was that one person was still alive, still looking for fresh blood and waiting for him up here in the dark of night on this isolated mountainside.

The thought sent a wave of terror through him. He wished now that he'd picked up the highway patrolman on his way up the mountain. Or let someone else take the call.

He gripped the wheel tighter. His nerves were so raw he wasn't sure he would be able to pull his gun to defend himself. Worse, he feared his bladder would fail him if he had to get out of his cruiser.

His fears seemed to multiply as the man staggered toward the cruiser, holding out a bloody hand.

SHADE HELD HIS breath and let his eyes adjust to the darkness inside the cabin. He knew he wasn't alone.

He could hear someone breathing within a few feet of him. The movement he'd heard had grown still. Had the killer heard him come in the back?

He knew the layout of these cabins by heart after growing up here and helping get them ready for guests since he was a boy.

This one was a two-bedroom with a short hallway that led past the bathroom and into the living room. The bathroom was off to his right. A door to a bedroom a few feet ahead off to his left. Farther up the dimly lit hallway would be the door to the second bedroom before the hallway opened up to the living area.

The noise he'd heard had come from the living area where he had to assume someone—possibly with Brad's gun now—was waiting for him.

He edged along the hallway in the dark, weapon drawn, until he was opposite the bathroom. He couldn't see anyone in there, but he could hear them struggling to breathe. Lizzy? He wanted to rush to her, but first he had to deal with whoever had taken her. He prayed that she would keep breathing until he did.

As he started past the bathroom door, he heard movement inside. He froze and tried to see into the dark bathroom.

Lizzy.

She was trying to move. He realized that she could see him in the dimly lit hallway. He held his finger to his lips and the movement halted. He signaled he'd be back and heard her try to speak.

With his back against the wall past the bathroom,

he cautiously headed for the living room, knowing he might only get one chance, one shot. He had to make it count.

LIZZY WANTED TO SCREAM. But she could barely make a sound. Shade. She saw that he was armed, but he had no idea what he was about to encounter in the other room. Her heart had surged at the sight of him. She'd known he would come, dreading it and yet feeling her heart swell with love for him. Of course, he would come looking for her. The killer had planned it that way.

She wanted to call out to him, to warn him, but her throat seemed to have closed from the drug they'd used on her. Her lips felt like rubber. All she could do was breathe and keep trying to get her muscles to work again.

She'd managed to shift her legs some and could now feel her fingers flexing. The drug was wearing off. Just not fast enough. She strained to hear as Shade moved cautiously toward the living area. The killer was out there waiting for him. Of that she was sure. But she feared the person wasn't alone.

Lizzy thought she heard a vehicle. Josh should have called for help by now. She'd expected the ranch to be crawling with law enforcement. Unless someone had stopped him from making it down the mountain. Unless he hadn't gone. Unless—

"Don't come any closer," she heard someone say in the other room.

She frowned in confusion. She'd been so sure that she'd figured out who the killer was. But she'd been wrong.

A flashlight beam came on, some of the ambient light making its way down the hallway. She blinked, even that little bit of light blinding her for a moment.

"Put the gun down." Kayla's voice came from the living room. "I don't want to kill you but I will."

CHAPTER TWENTY-SIX

THE BLEEDING MAN stumbled into the side of the cruiser. Ace's gaze locked with eyes like deep holes in the pained face that appeared at the window. With a shock, he recognized Brad Davis, the newspaperman who'd befriended him during the race for sheriff.

"Help me," Brad said as he pressed a bloody hand against the driver's-side window, leaving a print. Ace told himself he should wait for backup. For all he knew, Brad was the killer. But he could see the man's blood-soaked coat where it appeared he'd been injured.

He cringed as Brad began to pound on the window. He knew he had no choice. He grabbed the door handle and, throwing open the door, drove the man back as he pulled his weapon.

"Help me," Brad demanded as he clutched at his side, blood oozing out between his fingers. "I need... help." He seemed about to lose consciousness. "Kayla," he managed to say as he grabbed Ace's arm with one bloody paw. "She has my gun."

As Brad started to pass out, Ace pushed him into the back of the patrol car. "Stay here," he said. "Help is on the way." His mind was whirling. All of this was happening too fast.

The sound of a gunshot pierced the night air, making him turn to look in the direction the sound had come from.

That's when he saw the light in the cabin. It flickered. A flashlight beam? His heart jumped. Someone else was still alive down there. The killer?

SHADE DIDN'T LOWER his weapon as he looked into the barrel of the gun pointed at him, and then at the woman holding it and a flashlight. "Kayla."

She sat against the wall. He could see from where he stood that she was wounded. Her coat was soaked on one side. Had Brad shot her?

"What's going on, Kayla?" he asked quietly. In the ambient glow of the flashlight beam, he told himself he shouldn't be surprised. They'd all considered her the weirdo. But still he was. She looked...scared.

"Where are the others?" Kayla asked, sounding like she was in pain.

He frowned. "I don't know."

Kayla glanced toward the door but quickly returned her gaze to him. The gun in her hand stayed pointed at his chest.

"What did you do to Lizzy?" he asked. "If she's hurt, we need to get her help. What did you do to her?"

Kayla shook her head. "I don't know what you're talking about. I haven't seen Lizzy."

He stared at the woman, worrying that she was completely deranged, that all of this had been too much for her. She must have lost contact with reality. Except for the gun in her hand.

"You need to put down the gun, Kayla. This is over. By now, help will be on the way."

She shook her head.

"You really need to get medical help," he said, the barrel of his weapon still pointed at the woman's heart, just as hers was pointed at his. "I can understand why Ariel—"

"None of you did anything to stop her. You let her bully everyone. I never understood why you didn't stand up to her."

Shade shook his head. "It wasn't just you. She put all of us through hell."

"It doesn't matter," Kayla said, sounding close to tears. "I just want it to end…" She waved the flashlight across the room and back. But the gun stayed pinned on his heart.

He saw the change in her eyes. She knew she was going to die. Which meant… He dived as she pulled the trigger. He heard the bullet hit the wall where he'd just been. The report echoed in the small cabin, and a shower of Sheetrock dust fell over him an instant before the second shot. This one caught him in the side, exploding in hot pain.

Stars danced before his eyes and dimmed, making him fear he'd pass out before he could stop Kayla from killing him.

THE DRUG WAS wearing off, but there were still parts of her body that weren't cooperating. Lizzy struggled to roll to her side and climb to her hands and knees. She'd been working on getting blood flow back into her limbs when she heard the gunshot.

Dizzy and still weak, she forced herself to her feet and had to grab the sink to keep from keeling over. How was she going to be of any help to Shade in her condition? She didn't know, only that she had to try.

Running her hand along the wall for stability, she exited the bathroom and started toward the living room. The only light was coming from the large flashlight lying on the floor ahead of her. Shade must have dropped it. In her fogged state, she picked it up. It was heavy and cold to the touch.

She shined the light on Shade. He was wounded and bleeding badly. She dropped down beside him.

And then she saw Kayla, slumped against the wall, her chest and hands soaked with blood as she raised her gun.

ACE QUICKLY CLIMBED back into his cruiser and shut off the engine, killing his headlights. He sat listening to the *tick, tick, tick* of his cooling engine as he waited for backup. The snow had stopped but now lay as a white blanket that shone in the darkness.

Nothing moved. He'd never felt more alone. It was as if the world had ended and he and whoever had that flashlight down at that cabin were all that were left.

Brad had either passed out in the back seat or died. Ace didn't want to check.

Either way, he was alone on this mountain with a killer.

Then he heard more gunshots.

Do something! Here's your chance. You came up here to play hero. If you just sit here, someone else will get credit for ending this. Backup is coming.

And yet he couldn't move, paralyzed with fear. It was a totally unique experience for him. He'd always jumped in with both feet, loving the thrill of the fight, the chase, the arrest.

He stared out his windshield, ignoring the bloody handprint on his driver's-side window. He had no idea how many people up here were dead and wouldn't unless he got out and did a body count.

He couldn't take his eyes off the cabin with the light still shining there. Knowing that was where the gunshots had come from.

Making up his mind, Ace threw open his door and ran through the dark stillness that lay between him and the light. He prayed for the sound of sirens. He should have called for backup sooner. He should have done a lot of things differently.

But there wasn't time to worry about that now, he thought as he neared the cabin. He had to stop the killer.

He was almost there when he saw a shadow move next to the cabin. He raised his gun, but the shadow disappeared so quickly, he thought he'd only imagined it.

Racing up onto the porch of the cabin, he threw open the door, his weapon ready.

LIZZY WOULD REMEMBER feeling as if she was moving in slow motion and everything else was happening way too fast. Kayla had her gun pointed at Lizzy, only to swing it toward the door as it banged open. The woman's eyes widened at the sight of the deputy and the gun in his hand. Kayla pulled the trigger.

Deputy Ace Turner let out a grunt before dropping his gun and crumbling to the floor. Kayla fired again at the doorway. The bullet lodged in the woodwork next to the door. She was aiming to fire again when another figure appeared.

A bloody, disheveled Jennifer filled the doorway.

"Kayla, no!" Lizzy cried, her words coming out hoarse. She strained for Shade's gun on the floor next to him. But Jennifer grabbed Ace's service revolver and turned it on Kayla. The report echoed in the small cabin as the bullet struck Kayla. She toppled over and then lay still.

"Drop it!" Lizzy called to Jennifer, her voice growing stronger. She raised Shade's gun and aimed it at the woman in the doorway. She could hear the sound of sirens coming up the mountain.

Jennifer, looking as if she was in shock, hesitated, her gun pointed at Lizzy. Then she slowly lowered the weapon and let it drop to the floor.

"Lizzy," Shade said, his voice breaking.

"It's all right," she said as she heard the sound of sirens coming closer and closer.

Jennifer leaned against the doorjamb, her face lit by the flashing lights of law enforcement racing toward the cabin. Over the sirens, Lizzy could hear Jennifer making a keening sound. The high-pitched cry sent a chill through the room.

Within minutes there were uniforms everywhere. Lizzy stayed with Shade until he was placed in the ambulance. The drug had worn off enough that she could take control of the situation on the mountain. Still, it all felt so surreal, like a bad dream that was never going to end.

It wasn't until later, on the way to the hospital in one of the patrol SUVs, that she reached into her pocket and took out the diary page that had been pressed into her hand. She smoothed it out, recognizing Ariel's curlicue writing.

And then there is Lizzy, who has the biggest secret of them all.

CHAPTER TWENTY-SEVEN

"CAN I SEE SHADE?" Lizzy asked the moment she arrived at the hospital. She was told she would have to wait. Both Brad and Shade had been taken into surgery along with Jennifer, who had minor injuries including a few defensive knife cuts on her arms, and Tyler with his head injury. When Josh arrived, he gave her the bad news about Christopher and Ashley, both stabbed to death down the road sometime after they left the guest ranch.

"Kayla?" Josh asked.

"Dead," Lizzy said. "Brad said he shot Kayla when she came at him out of the dark. He tried to get away from her but fell. He said that must have been when she stabbed him." Lizzy had told state investigators, back at the lodge as bodies were taken away and crime scene tape spread around the guest ranch, how Kayla had shot Shade, killed Ace and attempted to shoot Jennifer.

She didn't know how long she'd been in the hospital's waiting room before the doctor came out. "Shade's just come out of surgery," Dr. Bullock told her. "So he isn't awake."

"It doesn't matter. I want to see him."

The doctor nodded and gave her a patient smile. "Just for a minute."

She walked down the hallway, pushed open the door and froze. Shade lay in the bed, his normally tanned face pale. Lizzy swallowed the lump in her throat and stepped to him. She'd almost gotten him killed. She'd almost gotten all of them killed. As it was, almost half of her class was dead.

But by the grace of God, Shade was alive. If Kayla had shot him again... Lizzy knew she shouldn't be thinking like this. Shade was going to be fine. Brad, Tyler and Jennifer were somewhere in the hospital, also going to make it. It seemed that if Kayla had had her way, none of them would be alive.

Lizzy pulled up a chair closer to him and, after studying his face for a few moments, picked up his hand and pressed it to her lips. She felt hot tears run down her cheeks and splash on his large, sun-tanned hand.

Wiping her eyes, she looked down at his fingers tangled with her own. She realized she'd never looked at his hands before or seen the tiny scars that came with being a rancher. She smiled as she rubbed her thumb over them, thinking of how brave he'd been. He'd come to save her against all odds. She hated to think what would have happened if he hadn't.

Her gaze shifted to his handsome face. "Hey, cowboy," she said, her voice breaking. "You're going to be all right. Good as new." She nearly choked on the lie. Would any of them ever be the same again? But Shade had to be. He was a father and there was a little girl who needed him. Maisie wasn't the only one.

"I want to meet your daughter," she whispered as she squeezed his hand. "I want to meet Maisie once you're well."

SHADE OPENED HIS eyes and blinked. For a moment, he didn't know where he was or what had happened. He lay perfectly still, listening to his own heartbeat, his own breath, as he remembered.

Lizzy. He tried to still his pulse. She was all right. He'd seen her as the ambulance door closed. Their eyes had met. That memory warmed him. He thought about his daughter. His daughter. He still couldn't believe it. He recalled everything he had to live for.

He could feel the pain medication making him dull-witted and drowsy. A doctor came in, followed by a nurse. He closed his eyes and let himself drift as they worked around him. Then there was blessed quiet again.

Lizzy. He let himself dream about their future. Once he was healed, once he did what he had to do, once he and Maisie were a family. He thought of Hannah. He'd been so angry with her for deceiving him and for keeping his daughter from him for two years.

But almost dying seemed to soften every emotion, especially anger. He had too much to live for to be angry with her anymore. She was about to lose not just her life, but the daughter she clearly adored. His heart went out to her. In the end, she'd come to him and told him the truth. She'd given him the chance to be Maisie's father.

For that, he would always be grateful.

With luck, things would work out with Lizzy. If they ever got to go on a date.

"I FIGURED I'D find you here," the former sheriff said when he walked into Lizzy's office Sunday morning.

She smiled at Sid, then her eyes filled with tears and she rose from her desk.

He limped to her and hugged her tightly. "I was so afraid that I'd lost you. Lizzy, you've always been like a daughter to me."

She nodded against his shoulder, a lump sealing her throat. They stayed like that for a few moments before stepping apart. "I'm not sure I can do this," she said, finally voicing the words that had been in her head since coming off that mountainside. Now standing in her office with the former sheriff and her mentor and the man she'd loved like a father, she felt she had to get the words out before they choked her.

"You're scared," Sid said, nodding as he took a seat.

"I failed miserably," she said. She dropped into her desk chair. She'd gotten it all wrong. She hadn't thought the killer was Kayla.

She told the former sheriff everything she'd found out. The car that had hit her on the road coming back from the guest ranch was found in Stephanie's grandmother's garage. Her husband had come forward with a note Stephanie had left him before the reunion, confessing to breaking into the guest ranch, taking some of the photos and almost getting caught. She'd apologized to her husband, saying she could understand if he wanted a divorce because there could be more coming out about her. Eric Tanner had been devastated by his wife's murder and upset that she would think he couldn't handle secrets from her past, including her affair with Ariel's father.

When Lizzy hadn't been able to reach Kayla's mother, she'd sent deputies over to their house. They'd discovered the mother dead. The coroner said she'd been dead from natural causes for almost a week. Her bedroom was filled with air fresheners.

Ariel's diaries had been found under Kayla's bed, with some of the pages ripped out. Most of those had been retrieved from the scene.

Both Christopher's body and Ashley's had pages with them. Jennifer and Brad had gotten away from Kayla before she could leave a diary page with them. Lizzy realized that Kayla must have found the diaries when she went over to Ariel's mother's house to pick up the prints and digital photos for the reunion.

"Don't be so hard on yourself," Sid said. "You're not clairvoyant or superhuman. You did your best."

"I still feel like I should have figured it out." She didn't tell him that it had kept her up all night. It didn't feel finished. She kept thinking that she'd missed something. Somehow it all felt too cut-and-dried.

"You just do the best you can, and remember, the

criminals are doing everything possible to keep you from finding out the truth. They're working against you. You already had two strikes against you when Ariel's car was found. It was a cold case, the hardest ones to solve, and you had hardly any time after that before the killings began again. No wonder you feel overwhelmed. But you're going to be fine."

"Am I? I wouldn't say this is the best start to my career, don't you think?"

"If Deputy Turner had followed procedure, you would have had fewer casualties."

She thought about Ace. He'd probably just wanted to show the county they'd hired the wrong person for the job. Lizzy still thought he might have been right.

Lizzy thought about what Sid said, that the killings had started up right after Ariel's body was found. When Kayla found the diaries and read some of the things in them about her, it must have led to what happened up at the guest ranch. Kayla had been a secret cutter and Ariel had ridiculed her in the diaries, saying things like the girl should cut her own throat.

The diaries helped tie up Lizzy's case and solve Whitney Clark's hit-and-run, as well. Ariel had said that Tyler was driving the car the night Whitney was killed. She had known because Ashley had told her and mentioned that Stephanie was with him. On the DL, Ariel had helped him get his car fixed by her uncle down in Missoula, but then had been blackmailing him ever since.

But that wasn't all that was in the diaries.

Brad had cheated on his exams, trying to hide the fact that he wasn't as smart as he thought he was. Christopher had a drinking problem. He'd broken into a liquor store their senior year and never been caught, and Ariel had used the knowledge against him. Josh sold weed. Jennifer was a kleptomaniac.

The only one Ariel had spared was Shade. Because she'd really cared about him? Or maybe she just hadn't been able to find something to use against him—until she realized that he liked Lizzy.

The last page of the diary was Ariel's own big secret. She was pregnant with Coach's baby.

"Often something precipitates this kind of mayhem," Sid said. "Most of the time we never know what the trigger was. But this time the signs are all there. Kayla was a loner who spent her life taking care of her mother. The woman's death had to leave Kayla at loose ends. She'd lost her life's purpose, but finding the diaries with everyone's secrets, she must have seen a new purpose."

Still, even knowing what might have triggered Kayla, Lizzy had trouble believing it.

"The worst part is that Kayla was right," Lizzy told him. "I didn't do enough to protect her from Ariel." Her laugh came out in a huff. "What am I saying? I couldn't even protect myself from her. But I was so busy worrying about myself back then that I never gave a thought to what someone like Kayla must be going through because of Ariel."

"You know it's much more complicated than that,"

Sid said. "It wasn't just that Kayla was bullied in high school. Ariel bullied all of you, and the rest of you didn't become killers. You couldn't have stopped it any more than you could have if Kayla had walked into your classroom at Progressive and opened fire with a semiautomatic weapon," the former sheriff said. "We don't know what possesses people to do the things they do. But whatever drove Kayla, it wasn't just high school. The people she killed were just easy targets."

"I should have never let them have the reunion. At one point, I was sure that all of it was happening because of Whitney's hit-and-run death. But I can't see that as Kayla's motivation. She wasn't close to anyone in high school, certainly not Whitney, who was good friends with Jennifer and Stephanie before Ariel got jealous."

Sid shook his head. "Trust me, it was a combination of things."

She still felt she needed to make sense of it. That she should have seen it coming. "Ariel's car turning up seems to have set it all in motion."

"Probably," he agreed. "It didn't help that when Deputy Turner got the call, he decided to go John Wayne and didn't call for backup until it was too late. I spoke with Highway Patrolman Josh Adams. He told me that Ace drove right past him." Sid swore under his breath. "He might have played a part in this, but he was no hero."

Lizzy said nothing, because there was nothing to say. Ace was dead. In her mind, he died saving her and Shade, although indirectly. He would be remembered as a hero.

"I figured from the beginning that Ariel's death was because of the way she treated all of us. But there were so many suspects," she said. She felt close to tears with exhaustion and the knowledge that she'd failed badly.

Sid sighed. "I know you're thinking about quitting."

She looked up at him and swallowed.

"Because I've been there. When things go to hell, you think you should have known, you should have somehow been able to stop it. But if that were possible, criminals would never be able to get away with anything. We're human, Lizzy. But that is also what makes us the best defense against this kind of evil, our humanity. You might not realize it right now, but you will. Just give it some time. Don't give up. I promise it will get better," Sid said as he left.

She doubted that as she closed up the office and drove home to find Aunt Gertie cooking up a storm. "Are we hosting an army?" she asked, peeking over her aunt's shoulder at all the food on the stove.

"I was in a cooking mood and decided to go with it," Gertie said with a laugh. Wiping her hands on her apron, she turned to face her niece. "I'm going to freeze some of it. Have you heard from Shade?"

She nodded and began to set the table. "Shade says he doesn't know how long Hannah has before she's gone and he will be a full-time single father for Maisie." She could feel her aunt studying her as she finished setting the table and then dropped into a chair. Lizzy and Shade had talked briefly about this after she'd returned from the guest ranch.

Gertie pulled out a chair and sat down facing her. "How do you feel about an instant family?"

"We haven't even gone on a date yet. We've only shared a couple of kisses."

"And yet you're in love with him," her aunt said.

Lizzy smiled, tears in her eyes, and nodded. "It scares me. What do I know about raising kids?"

Gertie laughed. "No one goes into it knowing how to raise a child, believe you me. When you were dropped on my doorstep…" Her aunt seemed to catch herself. "Just a figure of speech," she said hurriedly.

"No. That *is* what happened, isn't it? My mother rang your doorbell and ran, didn't she? You don't have to deny it anymore. I know." She thought about Ariel's diary page and Lizzy's big secret. Not hers exactly, but definitely about her.

"How long have you known the truth?"

"I found out in high school that my parents hadn't been killed in a car wreck."

Her aunt nodded, looking sad. "I could tell you weren't happy. I thought it was public school. That's why I decided to send you to Progressive. I thought a smaller school would be better for you. I'm so sorry. I never wanted you to know. You have to understand. Your mother was so young and alone and scared."

"How can you keep making excuses for her? She didn't want me."

Gertie pursed her lips for a moment. "It wasn't like that. Your mother was too young, too immature, too afraid to raise you. And because of that, she missed so much of your entire amazing life. What a terrible loss. It ruined her life, leaving you behind. I know that's why she got on drugs."

"You should have told me."

Gertie nodded. "But I thought a little white lie—"

"What about my father?"

Her aunt looked away for a moment. Clearly, she'd hoped never to have to tell her any of this. "I never knew who he was."

"And my mother, is she really dead or was that also just another little white lie?" She saw how her words hurt her aunt and quickly reached for her hand. "I'm sorry. I'm not angry with you. You saved my life in so many ways. Thank you for raising me. I know it must have been hard and I'm sorry about that. I know I was difficult at times."

Her aunt smiled and wiped her eyes with the hem of her apron. "You brought incredible joy to my life and purpose. For me, it was the best gift that anyone could have given me. But it's true. Janet's gone. An overdose. It wasn't just you she couldn't handle. It was life." She met Lizzy's gaze. "You're nothing like her. You're strong and determined and there is nothing you can't do. You and Shade will have a happy life together and you'll both love that little girl as if she were your own."

Lizzy couldn't help but smile. "The glass is always half full with you, isn't it, Auntie?"

"Honey, it's the only way to go through life."

SHADE OPENED HIS EYES. It took a moment for him to focus on the woman standing by his bed. He tried to hide his disappointment. He'd been hoping to see Lizzy.

"How are you feeling?" Hannah asked as she moved closer. "When I heard…" Her voice broke.

He could see the fear in her face. If something had happened to him, with her dying, what would have become of Maisie? Hannah had told him years ago that she had no close relatives. Her parents had died before she went to college in separate car accidents over a three-year period. She'd been alone in the world and soon her daughter would be, too—if Shade were gone.

"I'm going to be fine," he assured her. "How are you doing?"

"That's something we'll need to talk about once you're well enough to get out of here." She looked around the hospital room. He saw her swallow. "The doctor gave me a few months." Her gaze came back to him. "But during a lot of that, I won't be able to take care of Maisie. Shade, I wouldn't blame you if you didn't want to take this on. It is so much to ask, especially after what I've done to you."

"Stop." He reached for her hand. It was ice-cold. "I will do whatever has to be done. You can count on me, Hannah. I promise."

She nodded but didn't look convinced. "I have a home in Arizona. That's where my doctors are—"

"Then that's where I will be."

Her eyes widened. "You'll come to Arizona and live with us until…?"

He nodded. "I will. I'll be there for you and Maisie."

Tears began to roll down her cheeks. "I can't tell you how…"

"I know. Maisie is my daughter. I'm just glad you came to me and told me what was going on. I'll raise her, Hannah. When it's time, I'll bring her back to Montana and I'll raise her on the ranch with my family. She will be loved. I can promise you that."

LATER THAT DAY, Lizzy approached the hospital bed. Shade's eyes were closed, but he didn't look as pale as the other times she'd come by. There were no longer a lot of tubes and wires hooked up to him either. The doctor had said he was doing so well that he would be released soon. She felt a wave of relief to see him looking so much better.

His eyes opened and settled on her, then he broke into a smile. His blue gaze seemed to light up as if delighted to see her. She couldn't help but smile in return. The handsome cowboy she'd fallen for was back.

"How are you?" she asked as she stepped up to his bedside.

"I'm going to live, just like I told you. You can stop looking so worried. It was just a flesh wound."

It was a lot more than a flesh wound and they both

knew it. The gunshot had missed any vital organs. He would have a scar but then they all would, some of those scars less noticeable than others.

"It was quite the reunion, don't you think?" Shade joked, clearly more of his old self as he tried to lighten the mood.

"The doctor said as long as your wound doesn't get infected, you should be out of here in a few days," she said, in no joking mood.

He nodded, solemn again. "About the date I really want to take you on—"

"We don't have to talk about that now."

"We have to," he said, suddenly so serious she felt her stomach drop. "Hannah came by… Her cancer… It won't be long now. She needs me to come down to Arizona until…" He locked gazes with her. "The last thing I want to do is put off our date, but—"

"It's all right," she said quickly, even as her heart squeezed. "You have to take care of your daughter and her mother right now. Don't worry about me."

"Just promise me that when I get back…" His words seemed to falter. "Promise me that you'll be here."

"Where else would I be?"

He eyed her suspiciously. His hand brushed hers, sending that charge of electricity skittering through her veins. "Lizzy?"

She rolled her eyes. "I promise."

Shade lay back on his pillow, letting go of her hand. She could see that he was still in pain, still weak, still dealing with everything that had happened just as she was.

"It's a date, then." His gaze came back to hers, but she could tell he was having trouble keeping his eyes open. "Sorry, Doc just gave me something to help me sleep."

She put a hand on his warm, strong arm. "It's a date," she repeated as his eyes closed. She stayed like that while he dozed, tears in her eyes, as she watched the steady rise and fall of his chest.

CHAPTER TWENTY-EIGHT

LIZZY HADN'T SEEN Shade since the coroner's inquest, but he'd called to give her updates on what was happening down in Arizona with Hannah and Maisie. Early winter had come on the heels of autumn, covering the landscape with a thick blanket of snow and stretching out all the way to March.

She'd hardly noticed, keeping busy tying up all the loose ends from the case.

Spring came like it always did. One minute the sun was out, the next snow began to fall and kept falling until the sun came out and melted it all over again. For months, Lizzy trudged through the snow and slush to do her job. Every day, she thought of Shade in sunny Arizona. Not that she would have traded him places.

Every day, she thought about quitting. But then she would get up the next morning and go to work. Sid had promised it would get better. She stood in the snow at funerals, hired a new deputy and advanced one of the more seasoned deputies to undersheriff. She did what had to be done, waiting for things to get better.

The new deputy she'd hired to take Ace's place

was a woman who'd worked for the police department in Missoula.

"Ace would have loved it," Sid said when he heard.

That had made her smile, realizing how untrue that was.

Every night when Shade called, she heard the exhaustion and worry in his voice. His calls were the only thing that warmed her as December turned into January and January into February and then March headed toward April.

"Hannah is fighting to stay alive for Maisie," Shade said. "But it's a losing battle even as determined as she is. Maisie is watching her slip away. It's breaking my heart."

"I'm so sorry, Shade. I wish there was something I could do."

"The treats you sent have been a real hit. I've told Maisie about you. I love the way she says Lizzy with her little lisp. It's so dang cute. She says you bake good cookies."

"Gertie baked them," she blurted. "I cannot tell a lie."

He laughed. "It's our secret. How are you doing?"

"Hanging in there."

Every night when he called after Maisie had been put to bed, they talked about everything and sometimes nothing. Even the silences felt right.

Sid and Dorothea had moved their wedding to June. They'd said they'd changed their mind about a Christmas wedding because of the weather, but Lizzy suspected it had more to do with her and Shade and Maisie. Dorothea was hoping Maisie might want to be a flower girl.

Everyone was waiting for Shade and Maisie to come home. Especially Lizzy.

SHADE WAS HOLDING Hannah's hand when she passed. Before that, he'd relieved the hospice volunteer and had sat with Hannah, promising to take care of Maisie, to love and protect her and make a home for her.

"With that sheriff of yours?" she'd whispered with a smile.

"She's not mine yet, but if I have anything to do with it…" He'd smiled. "Yes."

"I'm so glad you're Maisie's father. I know I'm leaving her in good hands." She'd closed her eyes and after a moment, her hand had gone limp in his.

He carefully laid it on the bed beside her and, leaving the room, made the call to the coroner before going down the hall to Maisie's room.

His daughter was curled up in her big girl bed, a pink-and-blue comforter over her. Her blond hair was splayed across her pillow patterned with characters from a kids' movie he'd now seen a dozen times and would see a dozen more. Hopefully with Lizzy present.

He looked down into her sleeping, peaceful face and prayed that he would have the words to tell her that her mother was gone. The last months he and Maisie had bonded, spending more and more time together as Hannah became more and more sick. And yet he was terrified even at the thought of the responsibility he felt for his daughter's well-being. He was a cowboy and had more experience with horses and cows than children.

After the coroner arrived and Hannah's body was taken away, Shade called Lizzy.

"Maisie and I are coming home in a few days." His voice broke. "I can't wait to see you. I'll call you when we get back after the funeral arrangements have been made." He realized it would always be *we* now.

Shade couldn't believe it. He and Maisie were finally back in Montana. He pulled out his phone to call Lizzy. He had imagined this moment so many times that he shouldn't have been so nervous. But then again, this was nothing like anything he could have imagined—not in his wildest dreams.

Lizzy picked up on the second ring.

"Hey," he said, feeling like a teenager again.

"Hey," she said lazily. He could almost see her lie back on her bed to settle into his call as she had for months. He'd loved those phone calls after he'd gotten Maisie to bed and Hannah settled in for the night with the live-in nurse.

They'd talked about everything from bigfoot to aliens from another planet, from furniture to favorite vegetables, from pet peeves to perfect days they remembered. By now, they knew practically everything about each other, including their favorite colors, who was a morning person and who wasn't, and what made them happy and what made them cry.

Shade hadn't cried since he was a boy when he'd broken his arm trying to ride a bull that his father had told him to stay clear of. But he'd definitely teared up a lot lately when he looked at his daughter and felt for Hannah and what she was about to lose.

"About that date," he said now.

He heard her sit up. "You're home?" The concern in her voice made it clear that she knew what that meant.

"My family had a room all ready for Maisie in my wing of the ranch house. Wait until you see it. They went all out."

"Oh, Shade. Is she all right?"

"She knew her mommy was sick and in pain. It could be rough for her for some time but she and I have been pretty inseparable for months, since Hannah was bedridden so much of it. We've talked about her mommy going away to a place where she isn't sick, but at her age… These months with Maisie, I wouldn't take anything for them. It's strange how things work out."

"How are *you*?"

"Better than I thought I'd be. I can't tell you what it was like to feel that jet touch down in Montana again. I have missed it so much. Missed you so much."

"I've missed you."

A comfortable silence fell between them. "I'm having Hannah buried back here. She has no family and her ex is fine with it. I hope you understand.

I want Maisie to have somewhere she can go to visit her mother in the years ahead."

"Of course you do. It's the right thing to do."

He let himself breathe before he said the rest. "It's going to take a little bit for us to get settled in at the ranch. But once we do…" He sighed. "Lizzy, I'm dying to see you. Tell me you still want to go out with me."

She laughed. "Shade, nothing's changed."

He laughed at that. "*Seriously?* We were both almost killed and now I have a two-year-old daughter. I'd say a lot of things have changed."

"Do you think any of that changes how I feel about you?"

He couldn't help but grin. "How *do* you feel about me? No, don't tell me. Save it for our date." He chuckled, finally starting to relax a little. He knew this woman. "I'll call you soon."

"I can't wait to meet Maisie and see you."

"You sound tired. How is the job going?"

They talked for a while about the day-to-day problems that came with being sheriff of a growing county.

"How are things at the ranch?" she asked.

"Will and Garrett are pretending they couldn't run the place without me. Actually, I don't think they've missed me at all. Will and Poppy will soon be heading up to the guest ranch to get ready for another big season."

"You said you were booked solid? I guess the murders didn't turn anyone away," she said, sounding surprised.

He laughed. "They say even bad publicity is good.

Apparently so." He heard her yawn. "You should get some sleep. I'll call you soon for our date. If you still want to."

"I still want to."

Those were the best words he thought he'd ever heard. "Then it's a date."

"Give Maisie a hug for me."

He disconnected and found himself smiling. The big hurdle was yet to come though, he reminded himself. *The date*. The one he'd wanted for so long. What if he blew it? Worse, what if Lizzy and Maisie didn't hit it off? What if—?

He cursed himself, knowing he needed sleep, needed to have faith, as Dorothea always told him. He was home and Maisie would settle in. And he would finally get to go on that date with Lizzy.

Dorothea had already offered to babysit. Maisie had taken to her right away. She wasn't so sure about his brothers, but who could blame her, he thought with a laugh.

CHAPTER TWENTY-NINE

LIZZY COULDN'T HELP being nervous about the date. It had been so long in coming. They'd built it up so much. What if neither of them could think of anything to say?

"You look beautiful."

She turned from the full-length mirror in her bedroom to see Gertie standing in the doorway. "This dress isn't too much?"

"Not hardly," her aunt said with a laugh. "If it was any less... I'm kidding," Gertie said, stepping into the room. "It's a perfect fit. Although you look a little thin to me."

Lizzy laughed. "You've always said that." The emerald green dress seemed to accentuate her curves, proving she hadn't lost an ounce.

"That color brings out the dark of your eyes and hair," her aunt said. "You're a vision." She wiped at her cheeks. "But it needs something." Gertie reached into her pocket and took out a heart-shaped silver necklace. "It was your mother's." She motioned for Lizzy to turn around so she could put it on her.

Lizzy felt her eyes sting as the cool silver brushed her skin. "My mother's?"

"It was her favorite. She tucked it into your blanket the day she left. She wanted you to have it."

Lizzy had to wipe her tears as she turned again to look at herself in the mirror. The silver heart shone against her olive skin like a light. She touched the solid silver heart and tried to swallow the lump in her throat.

"She loved you, never doubt that, and she would have been so proud of you," her aunt said and hugged her.

Lizzy's phone rang. She checked it, fearing it would be Shade, canceling. Instead it was her office.

EXPECTATION WAS RUNNING HIGH. Too high, Shade thought as he dressed for his long-awaited date with Lizzy. He didn't like the way it was already beginning. Lizzy had called to tell him that she had to go to her office. Something had come up at the last minute. She would meet him at the restaurant.

That didn't bode well, he told himself as he stood in front of his closet trying to decide what to wear. Dorothea knocked and came in to see how he was doing.

"I'm thinking about wearing a suit. What do you think?"

"Have you fallen on your head recently?" she snapped. "You're going to be nervous enough since you've made such a big deal out of this date. Wear something comfortable that's more you." She handed him a pair of clean, newer jeans, a nice pale blue shirt and a navy jacket. "Wear your lucky boots."

"My old boots?"

She laughed. "Wear your good boots. I've put a good luck spell on them. You have nothing to worry about tonight. It's going to go great."

He wished he could believe that. She was right. He'd put too much importance on this date. He wondered if Lizzy felt the same way. With all the months of talking to each other at night, he'd thought they wouldn't be uncomfortable around each other.

But as he dressed, he feared it would be just the opposite. They'd been apart for so long and for such an unusual reason. He just wanted to get this date over with, for it to go well, and for them to move on to what he hoped would be the good stuff.

He said as much to Dorothea after he'd dressed and found her in the kitchen with Maisie. The two were making cookies, Maisie sitting on the counter playing with a handful of dough.

"The good stuff?" Dorothea said and cut her gaze to the child.

"Get your mind out of the gutter. I want us to be a family." He went over to plant a kiss on Maisie's adorable nose. The child laughed and offered him cookie dough. "I think I'll wait until it's baked. But thanks."

Dorothea laughed. "Shade, stop worrying. I promise you, it's all going to be fine."

"Because of the spell you put on my boots."

She cocked a brow. "Because the two of you are

already in love with each other. Now go. You look very handsome. You'll sweep her right off her feet."

He gave Dorothea a kiss on the cheek. "Thanks."

"He's going to blow this," Will said, coming into the room.

"Don't tease him," his wife, Poppy, said right behind him.

"How's my Maisie?" Will asked her and he kissed her cheek and she giggled.

"Precious," Poppy said. "Can I help make cookies?"

Maisie nodded and offered her some of the dough in her hand.

"Go," Dorothea said to Shade. "We're going to be fine."

Will walked him into the living room. "I think there's something you might want to take with you." He reached into his pocket. "I've hung on to this for you. It's our grandmother's engagement ring." He pulled out a small velvet box and handed it to Shade.

"Doesn't this seem a little fast?" Shade asked.

"Up to you, but given what the two of you have been through…"

Shade opened the box and looked down at the beautiful pear-shaped diamond ring. "Wow, it's gorgeous. Do you think Lizzy would like it?"

"She'll love it!" Poppy and Dorothea called from the kitchen in unison and laughed.

Shade smiled, pocketed the ring and hugged his brother. "Thanks." As he stepped back, he sighed and said, "Wish me luck."

"You don't need luck, you have that adorable face and all that cowboy charm."

"Right," Shade said, heading for the door.

"Don't blow it," Will said behind him.

LIZZY TOOK CARE of the emergency at the sheriff's office, telling herself that she wasn't going to let anything ruin her date tonight with Shade. She glanced at her phone. She still had plenty of time to get to the restaurant before he got there. She could go into the ladies' room and freshen up. Or maybe have a little wine to calm her nerves before he arrived.

She stepped out into the spring night, breathed in the fresh pine-scented air and felt herself relax a little. The night was cool and clear but the weatherman had warned of a rain shower later. There was nothing like spring in Montana, she thought as she walked the few blocks to the restaurant.

It was early so there were few people seated as she pushed open the door and headed straight to the ladies' restroom. She wove her way through the empty tables to the back of the old downtown building. This was her favorite restaurant so of course it was the one Shade had chosen.

She pushed open the restroom door and, with a start, recognized Jennifer Fox at the sink drying her hands. Lizzy hadn't seen Jennifer in months, not since the woman had been released from the hospital and come by the sheriff's department to give her statement.

"How are you?" Lizzy asked, noticing that the cuts had healed on Jennifer's arms. There was barely a scar.

"Good, how about you?"

"Good. Are you having dinner here tonight?" Lizzy stepped up to the mirror to check her makeup. She hardly ever wore makeup so she really wasn't very good at it.

"No, I was actually here looking for a job," Jennifer said.

That surprised Lizzy. She looked over at her and noticed for the first time the purse slung over her shoulder. And recognized it.

"There's a waitress position open that I'm applying for," Jennifer said. She turned from the mirror and gave Lizzy a shrug. "I should get going."

Lizzy nodded as she watched Jennifer start toward the door. On impulse, she pulled out her phone and called a once familiar number.

Jennifer was almost to the door when the phone in her purse rang. The ringtone stopped her dead.

"You have Ariel's ringtone?" Lizzy asked, almost too shocked to speak. Because it wasn't just the ringtone that had sent a chill up her spine. "Oh, my God. Jennifer. It wasn't Kayla."

The woman slowly turned to face her. A feeling of dread moved ghostlike through the room.

The blood had drained from Jennifer's face. "What? Because I have Ariel's ringtone, you think I killed her?"

"I didn't until I saw Ariel's purse slung over your

shoulder. It was her favorite but it wasn't the one found in her car the night she died. It didn't hit me until just now that Ariel had her favorite purse at graduation and again at the party."

"I always liked this purse," Jennifer said. "I liked her ringtone, too. I should have thrown the purse away along with my own after I dumped the contents of hers into it, but I couldn't. It wasn't like Ariel would miss either one. Ten years is a long time. The phone didn't make it, but I saved the ringtone."

Lizzy shook her head, seeing what she'd been missing before. "You idolized Ariel. That's why you kept her purse and her phone, why you use her ringtone. It makes you feel closer to her. You can't stand it, can you?"

"Can't stand what?"

"Not getting the credit for what you orchestrated," Lizzy said.

Jennifer laughed. "Prove it."

"You idolized Ariel. You wanted to be her."

"Who didn't? She was rich and spoiled. She got whatever she wanted."

"But that's not why you killed her."

"No?" Jennifer mocked.

"It was about Whitney Clark." She saw at once that she'd hit upon the truth—just as she'd suspected that night up at the guest ranch. "I guess I never knew you and Whitney were that close."

"We'd known each other before she came to Progressive," Jennifer said. "We were best friends. But

Ariel was jealous of her. She didn't want her in our group. Told me not to talk to her." Jennifer shook her head, but her eyes had narrowed, her lips parting in a sneer. "I hated Ariel when she turned on Whitney. I hated her worse for making me choose."

Lizzy saw it now. "You chose Ariel."

Jennifer looked away, her eyes filling with tears. "I hurt someone I cared about to stay in that group." She shook her head. "I regretted it and was going to talk to Whitney…"

"But she died in the hit-and-run before you could." The woman nodded.

"Why kill Ariel graduation night?" Lizzy asked.

Jennifer smiled. "I guess I'd finally had enough of her. She announced at the party that she was going back east to college, her parents had saved money for her and were paying for all of it. I'd been turned down for a scholarship to the University of Montana in Missoula. It seemed so unfair. Ariel was always throwing around money, lording it over me."

"Something else must have triggered it at the party," Lizzy said.

Jennifer hesitated for a moment. "Ashley told me about Ariel blackmailing Tyler. She said it was all in some diaries that Ariel kept. I couldn't believe it. They'd all kept quiet about Whitney's death? But Ariel was the worst. She'd actually used it to get even more money. Her greed appalled me. I wanted her to pay for everything she'd done."

Jennifer chewed at her lower lip, the sneer gone as

her eyes shone with bitter, angry tears. "She could be such a bitch." With a swipe at her tears, Jennifer shook her head. "I think at first I was just going to scare her. But then…" She shook her head again. "She was so sure I wouldn't kill her."

"You found the ski rope in Brad's garage. You helped yourself to a knife in the kitchen, cut a couple lengths of rope and then climbed into the back of her SUV to wait. And once she drove far enough from the party, surprise her."

Jennifer's laugh was almost a sob. "I thought it would be nice if she begged for her life. But you know how she was. She said she'd rather die and mocked me, calling me names. Saying if I betrayed my friend Whitney, it wasn't her fault."

Lizzy saw the woman's pain, heard it in her voice.

"You tried to kill Tyler because he was the one driving the hit-and-run vehicle. But the others?"

"They knew. I found it all in the diaries after I killed Ariel. I went to her house. I'd been there so many times, I could just walk right in. I found the diaries."

"The diaries you later hid in Kayla's house."

She nodded as if lost in what she'd read in those pages. "They all knew and they kept quiet. Whitney deserved so much better than that."

Lizzy could see it all now. "You tried to frame Stephanie for Ariel's murder. And Kayla…you just used her?"

"She would have talked if I hadn't killed her. I

found her after Brad had shot her and told her to go hide in the cabin where I had you drugged and bound in the bathroom. I told her to kill anyone who entered. Except for me."

"And you would have killed me and Shade if I hadn't picked up his gun and aimed it at you. I thought you were in shock, but you knew exactly what you were doing."

Jennifer chuckled, but it held no humor. "At that point, I figured I had nothing to lose. I could kill you all. But in retrospect, I needed you and Shade alive so you could tell them that it was Kayla who shot Shade. She was so scared, she would have shot anyone who came through that door and I knew it. She almost killed me."

"You played the victim very well. Right up until you grabbed my deputy's gun and killed Kayla." Lizzy realized what had been bothering her all these months. The piece that hadn't fit in the puzzle.

"She would have killed you and Shade if I hadn't stopped her," Jennifer said.

Lizzy shook her head. "How did you get to the cemetery that night after you killed Ariel?"

"I moved my car at the party. All I had to do was walk from the pond, staying in the trees. I really did see Snake on his motorcycle. He gave me a ride to the cemetery and later Ashley gave me a ride to the gas station near Brad's where I'd left my car. I told her the same story I told you."

"Ariel called Kayla before she died."

Jennifer laughed. "She butt-dialed Kayla. I didn't realize what was happening until I heard Kayla's voice and dug out Ariel's phone before I pushed the car into the pond. Fortunately I put my hand over Ariel's mouth in time or Kayla would have heard the whole thing."

"Were you the one who set up the meeting at the cemetery or was that Ariel?"

"Ariel. She sent the text as she was roaring away from the party. I didn't realize it until I was walking back to my car. That's why I was twenty minutes late getting to the cemetery. By the time I got there, Ariel was swimming with the fishes."

Lizzy shook her head. "So Kayla wasn't in on any of it. Brad shot her when she came out of the dark toward him, thinking she was the killer. She stabbed him with a knife from the kitchen she must have gotten when she was in there making herself another cup of tea earlier that night. You really did set something in motion, poisoning Stephanie after framing her, trying to kill Tyler. What a busy night you must have had going after Christopher and Ashley, then making it look like you yourself had been attacked by Kayla."

"I definitely got my exercise that night. It's amazing how easy it was though."

"You realize that I'm going to arrest you, right?"

Jennifer scoffed. "You have no proof. It would just be your word against mine and based on what?"

"You have Ariel's ringtone and her purse."

"You could never get a conviction on such flimsy evidence."

"Are you sure about that?"

"I'm sure because it will never come to that. I was willing to die up on that mountainside if that's what it took. I guess instead it will end here." Jennifer's voice sounded strange to Lizzy's ears. She watched the woman reach inside the shoulder bag and pull out the gun. "I spared you once, but not this time."

Lizzy had her own purse gripped in her hand, but tonight of all nights she'd left her gun at home. She flung the purse at Jennifer's face and dived for the first open stall.

CHAPTER THIRTY

SHADE COULDN'T BELIEVE what had been a beautiful spring night was now clouding up to rain. He told himself it wasn't an omen as he parked behind the restaurant and started in the back door. He couldn't wait to see Lizzy. It had been way too long.

The report of a gunshot at first made him think he was having a flashback. But before he heard a second shot, he was running toward the sound. He hit the ladies' bathroom door with his body and barreled inside. He rushed toward the woman with the gun poised to fire into one of the stalls—Jennifer Fox.

Suddenly a foot lashed out of the stall.

Shade had a pretty good idea who belonged to the strappy high heel that struck her in the face. Jennifer stumbled back, and the shot went wild. She didn't have time to fire again before Lizzy lunged out of the bathroom stall at her. She grabbed the gun that was still held high in the air and twisted it out of Jennifer's hand. She shoved her back against the sink, and Jennifer lost her balance and started to fall. Shade reached the two of them and grabbed hold of Jennifer before she went down.

"You are under arrest for the murders of…" Lizzy was breathing hard and she unloaded the weapon into her hand. "Christopher Drysdale, Kayla Harrison, Ashley Houston, Stephanie Curtis Tanner and Ariel Matheson. You have the right to remain silent." Lizzy stopped long enough to make a call to the sheriff's office for backup before she continued with the Miranda warning.

The restaurant owner, some of the staff and several diners had come to see what was going on. Shade shooed them out as he held on to Jennifer.

She glared daggers at him as she spat out, "I should have killed you and Lizzy when I had the chance."

Several deputies pushed their way in. Shade turned Jennifer over to them.

"The only place you're going is prison," Lizzy said. "For a very, very long time. That's if you don't get the death sentence."

Jennifer shot her a hateful look as she was led out in handcuffs. "Ariel never liked you," she called back. "She made fun of you all the time. If she knew you were the sheriff…" The rest of her words were lost as she was taken away.

Shade looked at Lizzy and smiled. "Sheriff, you are one kick-ass woman."

She smiled back at him and looked down at her high heel. "I think I broke it on her face."

He laughed. "This is definitely not the way I thought our first date was going to go."

Her new undersheriff stuck his head in the doorway. "Can you come down to the office and make a statement?"

Lizzy looked at Shade. "I will first thing in the morning. Book her for multiple murders. Tonight, I have a date."

"WHAT DO YOU want to do?" Shade asked in the ladies' room as the rest of law enforcement left the bathroom and everyone else went back to the dining room.

"I think along with my broken heel, I might have ripped my dress." She turned to show him the tear up the back seam, exposing her panties.

"Not a problem," he said and he took off his jacket to tie it around her waist. "Nothing showing that shouldn't be." He looked down at her broken heel that was barely keeping her upright. "I'll understand if you want to cancel dinner under the circumstances."

"Would you mind if we skipped it?" she asked and saw disappointment take some of the light out of his blue eyes before she added, "Skip dinner and get right to the good stuff?"

"The good stuff?" he repeated, his voice husky.

She smiled and closed the distance between them. "The good stuff." Standing on her wobbly heel, she leaned up to kiss him. He caught her with an arm around her waist and practically lifted her off her feet as he deepened the kiss. They stayed like that until they heard the bathroom door open.

A woman stuck her head in. "I'm sorry, is this restroom still in use?"

Shade broke off the kiss without looking at the woman. "There's a hotel across the street. Think you can walk on that broken heel that far?"

Lizzy grinned. "Watch me."

Laughing, they left the bathroom to the woman and limped out through the dining area with the owner asking who was going to pay for the gunshot damage. "Call the undersheriff," she said over her shoulder as they stepped outside, Shade's arm protectively around her.

Rain fell in a torrent, pinging off the overhead metal awning like shotgun lead. Water puddled in the street and splashed up as an occasional car swished past. Shade looked over at her. "I'd say let's make a run for it but—"

Before he could finish, Lizzy leaned down, pulled off her heels and took off running barefoot through the rain. She splashed through the puddles in the street, laughing as she was drenched from head to toe, until she reached the entrance to the hotel.

Shade ran after her and swept her up into his arms at the hotel's front door. "You're crazy, you know that?"

Crazy in love, she thought. "I'm alive. We're both alive."

His gaze locked with hers. "Yes, we are. Shall we make the most of it?"

"Definitely," she said, and he pushed the door open and carried her into the hotel, the two of them looking like drowned rats.

THEY WERE BOTH laughing as they rode the elevator up to the top floor and padded down the hallway, leaving wet footprints to their room. When he opened the door, Lizzy caught her reflection in a mirror on the wall.

"I actually fixed my hair tonight for this date," she said. Now it was straight and dripping.

"I think you look beautiful," he said as he kicked the door closed with one lucky boot and took her in his arms. "But we have to get you out of these wet clothes."

She grinned up at him. "I couldn't agree more."

He stepped into the bathroom. She heard the shower come on before he turned back to her. "Do you mind?" he asked as he gestured to her dress.

Lizzy felt her pulse leap. She shook her head and he untied his jacket from around her waist and let it drop to the floor. He reached behind her, his eyes never leaving hers, and slowly unzipped her dress. It, too, fell to the floor.

She unbuttoned his shirt and drew it off his broad shoulders, reveling in the muscles, and dropped it to the floor to join her clothes. Peeling his wet jeans off took both of them, which had them laughing again. Dressed only in their underwear, Shade drew her into the steamy shower and under the powerful warm spray of the two showerheads.

He kissed her slowly as he removed her bra and then slipped her panties off to drop them on the shower floor. His underwear followed until they were both naked, standing before each other. She ached to press her wet body against his but he held her at arm's length for a moment, as if taking her in with his eyes.

"You are so beautiful," he said, his voice hoarse. She leaned her head back as he kissed his way down her throat to her hard, aching nipples. He gently pushed her thighs apart.

With a start, she heard him remove one of the showerheads and shuddered as the warm water caressed first her breasts, then her stomach and then lower until she thought she wouldn't be able to stand it. She leaned back while he held her hips with one hand and the showerhead with the other. She let out a cry of intense pleasure before he took her in his arms again.

It all felt like an erotic dream. Shade's big hands lathering her body with bath gel. Her hands on him. And finally, her legs trembling from the most pleasurable shower she'd ever had, he turned off the water and carried her to the large king-size bed with its wonderfully silken sheets where he did what he called a proper job of making love to her.

Later, sated, Lizzy looked over at Shade. His eyes were bright as she leaned up on one elbow to study his handsome face. "I suppose I don't have to tell you that I've never had a first date like this one."

He smiled. "Me either."

"It's the best date ever." Lizzy ran her finger down the length of the scar just above his hip and looked up into Shade's blue eyes. He'd come so close to being killed. They both had and yet here they were.

"It's over," he whispered and drew her close to kiss

her. "You and I are just beginning." He pulled back to look at her. "That is, I hope we are." Letting go of her, he rose from the bed. "I want you to know that I planned to do this earlier at the restaurant wearing clothing."

He dug something out of his jacket pocket and turned to hold it out to her. She stared at the tiny velvet box, wet from the rain, and felt her eyes burn with tears. Naked, Shade dropped to one knee beside the bed.

"I never forgot you those ten years we were apart. The timing was always off. But now… I know it's crazy quick. But all it took was that one kiss on graduation night."

"You do realize you're going to make it difficult to tell our children about this moment," she said, her voice breaking.

"Elizabeth 'Lizzy' Conners, would you be my wife, a mother to my daughter and a faithful partner to me for the rest of your life?" He drew back the tiny box for a moment. "If you need more time—"

She shook her head. "Yes, I would love nothing more than to be your wife, to be Maisie's second mother, to spend my life loving you."

Shade broke out in a huge grin as he opened the velvet box. Lizzy let out a delighted gasp when she saw the ring. "It was my grandmother's. Will gave it to me tonight."

All she could do was smile, tears cascading down her cheeks, as he slipped it on her finger. It fit perfectly.

Shade climbed back in bed with her. Spooning her, he whispered in her ear, "I'm starved. What do you say to room service?"

THEY ATE BURGERS and fries with chocolate milkshakes and watched a movie cuddled in bed together. Shade had never felt this kind of contentment. He looked over at Lizzy. She was admiring her ring, her dark eyes bright with the same love that she showered on him.

The date had definitely not gone as he'd planned it, thank goodness. It hadn't been awkward. It had been perfect. But Lizzy was right. They would have to change a few things when they told their children about the night he asked their mother to marry him.

He thought of Maisie and couldn't wait for Lizzy to meet her. That was really the last hurdle, he thought.

Later, when he realized that Lizzy had gone to sleep in his arms, he retrieved one arm to turn off the movie and snuggled down in the bed next to her to get some sleep. He couldn't remember ever being this happy.

But as he started to close his eyes, they flew open again. He remembered Lizzy trapped in that bathroom stall while a woman with a gun tried to kill her. He was marrying the sheriff.

A very capable, smart woman, he reminded himself. Would he have it any other way? He knew Lizzy wouldn't, so that was good enough for him.

This time when he closed his eyes, he drifted into a peaceful, tender sleep.

CHAPTER THIRTY-ONE

THE NEXT MORNING, Lizzy couldn't believe how comfortable she felt around Shade—even naked. They'd made love again, slow and sensual, before first light, then had breakfast in bed.

A knock at the door surprised her, and she looked over at Shade.

"Not room service again," she said, frowning.

He wrapped a towel around his waist and went to the door. At the sound of his brother Will's voice, she jumped up and ran into the bathroom. What was Shade thinking, inviting his brother to their hotel room?

She listened until she heard Shade tap on the door and tell her it was safe to come out.

"What was Will—?" But she didn't get to finish the sentence, coming out of the bathroom to find dry clothing lying on the bed—his and hers.

"I asked him to bring us something to wear out of here." He shrugged. "We didn't exactly hang up our clothes to dry last night, not to mention your dress being torn."

Lizzy eyed the jeans, T-shirt, underwear and

sneakers that were distinctly hers. Her gaze shot up
to Shade's. "He got these from my house?"

"Your aunt was kind enough to get them for you,"
he said sheepishly.

She groaned. "She *knows*?"

Shade let out a laugh. "She's eighty-two, she knows."

Lizzy had to laugh. He was right. If anyone would
understand, it would be Gertie. "I should get home
though. She's going to want to hear all about it."

He raised a brow.

"Not all about it. Just some of the good stuff."

He chuckled. "Do you think you can stop by the house
later? Maybe come for lunch? We could order pizza."

Lizzy felt her heart do a little dip and then her stomach followed. "What if she doesn't like me?"

"Maisie? She will love you." He closed the distance
between them. "Just like I do." He kissed her slowly,
wonderfully, deliciously. "Around noon?"

She nodded. She'd been so anxious to meet the girl,
but now she was worried. And it wasn't just that she
had no idea how to be a wife, let alone a mother. She
had no idea how to be a sheriff either. If she'd been a
better sheriff, she would have figured out that Jennifer was in on it. She was anxious to get down to the
jail to talk to the woman.

But first things first. Gertie. Then Maisie. Then
Jennifer. It was going to be a rough day, she thought,
until she looked down at the engagement ring on her
finger, then up at Shade.

It was going to be a wonderful day.

SHADE WENT HOME to find Maisie sitting at the kitchen table eating a bowl of cereal and Dorothea telling her a story about when she was a girl. He hoped it didn't involve witch's brews and spells, but Maisie seemed to be enjoying it.

Maisie smiled when she saw him. He gave her a kiss on the cheek and joined her at the table. "Can I have a bite of your cereal?" She held out her spoon and he pretended to take a bite. "You'd better eat it so you grow big and strong."

"I am big," she said and went back to her cereal.

He glanced across the table at Dorothea. "Any trouble last night?"

"None here. How about with you?" She apparently couldn't hide her knowing grin.

"It was the perfect date." As he said it, he realized that for him and Lizzy, it had been.

"Anything exciting happen?" Dorothea prodded.

He pretended to give it some thought and started to shake his head, but instead laughed. "Oh, I did ask Lizzy to be my wife and she said yes. You mean something like that?"

She swatted at his arm playfully. "You're awful, you know that?"

Maisie laughed as if following the conversation and repeated the word *awful*.

"Nice," Shade said to Dorothea. "We're really going to have to watch what we say around here."

"Good thing I'm getting married and moving out."

He'd forgotten about that and felt his smile fade.

"But you'll come visit every day. If you think you can get away from all of us that easily, you are sadly mistaken."

"Like I'll miss the lot of you," she said, but he saw her tear up before she rose to get more coffee and offer him a cup.

"I invited Lizzy over for lunch. I thought we'd order in pizza."

Dorothea turned abruptly from the kitchen counter. "You will not. I'll make something special. This is the first time…" She indicated Maisie with a nod.

"Yes," he admitted.

"Then it has to be special. Let me give it some thought. Noon?" He nodded and she clasped her hands together in obvious delight. "I'm assuming you gave her a ring."

"Grandmother's."

Dorothea nodded in approval. "Good job," she said, smiling. "It was the spell I put on your boots, wasn't it?"

Maisie glanced at his boots and said, "Do your boots smell?" in her cute little lisp. They all laughed.

WHEN LIZZY WALKED in the door, she found Gertie, where else but in the kitchen. "What is that wonderful smell?" she asked.

"Your favorite brownies," her aunt said, turning to smile at her. "I wanted to bake something special." She gave Lizzy a wink, her eyes glittering with mischief.

Lizzy shook her head. "You continue to surprise me."

"I shouldn't. We've known each other long enough."

"Then this won't come as a shock to you, I suppose." She held out her left hand. The pear-shaped diamond caught the light.

Gertie let out a gasp. "What a beautiful ring. So your night went like that, did it?" She clasped her hands together, and tears filled her eyes. "I am so happy for you." She threw her arms around Lizzy. "I've dreamed of this day," she said as she pulled back to wipe her tears. "Let's celebrate with brownies." She turned away.

Lizzy stared at her slim strong back and felt her heart drop.

She'd been so happy that she hadn't given a thought to what this would mean for her aunt, who'd taken care of her since she was a baby. Gertie would be all alone in this large house. How could she desert her eighty-two-year-old aunt?

SHADE WAS TRYING hard not to be nervous. He kept telling himself that this was going to go fine. Even if Maisie was a little standoffish to Lizzy at first. Dorothea kept telling him the same thing.

"Stop pacing," she said. "You're going to wear out the floor."

After breakfast, he'd bathed Maisie in the tub and dressed her for the day. While Maisie and Dorothea worked on cooking lunch in the kitchen, he'd taken another shower and dressed. But still he couldn't believe how nervous he was. So much was riding on this first meeting. Kind of like his and Lizzy's first date, except for the fact that they had known each other for years and had crushes on each other almost as long.

He groaned and raked a hand through his hair before going in the kitchen to see if he could help. He and Maisie played a variety of games involving trucks and baby dolls and wooden blocks with rules she seemed to make up as she went along until he heard a vehicle drive up.

"That's Lizzy."

"Lithie," his daughter said. "Cookies."

He laughed. "You would remember that, huh. I'm not sure she's bringing cookies today. I want you to meet her."

Maisie went back to her playing as he stepped to the door. When he opened it, he saw the same nervousness in Lizzy's face. He drew her to him and kissed her. "It's going to be fine." He was starting to sound like Dorothea.

She smiled, but he could tell something was wrong. He told himself it was just nerves. Once she met Maisie...

"Come on in." They walked into the living room where Maisie's toys were spread across the carpet. She had a doll in one hand and a block in the other and appeared to be talking to both. "Maisie, this is Lizzy."

The little girl looked up. "Cookies," she said and smiled.

"Yes, she sent us cookies," Shade said. "Why don't we sit down?"

Lizzy took a seat. "What are you playing?"

"Houth." She held up her doll and then went back to stacking blocks so the doll could smash into them and knock them over.

"Can I get you something to drink?" Shade asked. "Lunch should be ready soon."

"Water would be wonderful."

LIZZY'S THROAT HAD gone dry. All the way over here, all she'd been able to think about was her aunt and how she couldn't leave her. She couldn't imagine how marriage to Shade would work with him on the ranch and her still living with her aunt, unless they could talk her aunt into moving, which seemed impossible.

She felt sick. Looking at the floor, she saw that Maisie had quit playing. The adorable blond, blue-eyed two-year-old was staring at Lizzy as if finally really seeing her.

"You wanna see baby?"

Before Lizzy could answer, the little girl crawled up onto her lap and handed her the doll. "She's beautiful. Just like you," Lizzy said, admiring the naked doll. "Where are her clothes?"

"Falled oft."

Lizzy laughed. "Shall we see if we can find them?"

Maisie slipped off her lap and sat down again on the floor. Lizzy joined her. "Shall we put her clothes back on?" she asked, having found them in the pile of toys.

Maisie shook her head. "She doesn't like 'em."

"Well, then, we better build her house, don't you

think?" Lizzy began to stack blocks. Maisie watched her for a few moments and then began to pile more on.

As Shade stepped back into the room, the doll rammed the house, blocks flying, and both Maisie and Lizzy laughed.

IT WAS THE best sound that Shade had ever heard. He stopped partway into the room, a glass of water in his hand and a juice packet for Maisie. He watched the two of them playing on the floor. Lizzy was going to make a great mom. This was going to work. He thought of the children they would have together.

Dorothea called them in for lunch and he took Maisie to wash up. He realized she'd had an accident and he'd have to change her clothes, probably toss her into the tub, as well.

Hannah had been in the process of potty training. She'd told him that it was really about training himself at this stage. *"You just have to remember to take her often."*

This was his future, he told himself as he undressed his daughter and got the water going in the tub. He just hoped that Lizzy was all right in the kitchen with Dorothea. He knew the woman would be wringing everything out of his fiancée about the murders and last night's date and he groaned to himself.

"WHAT'S WRONG?" DOROTHEA asked the moment she and Lizzy were alone.

She started to deny that anything was wrong, but

realized she couldn't keep this to herself. She'd have to tell Shade, too. It was breaking her heart. "I love Shade and I want to marry him, but what about Aunt Gertie? I can't leave her, especially now. She needs me."

"Do you know your aunt at all?" Dorothea demanded. "She would love to see you married off where she is free to do whatever she wants."

Lizzy looked at her in shock. She didn't believe that for a moment. "What does she want to do that she isn't already doing?"

"I heard from Sarah who works at the travel bureau that for the past few years in the fall, your aunt comes in and asks for cruise brochures from around the world."

She felt herself start. Could this be true? "She's never said anything about traveling."

"Not to you, since she feels she can't leave you because you need her."

"That's ridiculous. I don't need her taking care of me. I'm there for *her*."

Dorothea laughed and shook her head. "I think the two of you really need to talk. But I can tell you right now that your aunt would have a fit if she knew you put off Shade and your future because of her."

WHEN SHADE AND Maisie made it in to lunch, he could tell that something had happened. He gave Dorothea a questioning look and she made an *it's all fine* wave of her hand.

He put Maisie into her high chair and sat down beside Lizzy. When he took her hand, it was ice-cold. What had happened while he was getting Maisie ready? Something, no matter what Dorothea indicated.

Lunch was a seafood quiche and fruit salad. It amazed him how well Maisie ate, especially compared to him and Lizzy. They both picked at their food, lost in their own thoughts.

Conversation was stilted. If they hadn't had Maisie to entertain them, it would have been pure hell. He was glad when it was over and Dorothea told the two of them to run along. She'd take care of everything, including getting Maisie cleaned up yet again and down for her nap.

"I'm sorry, but I have to go," Lizzy said as they left the kitchen.

"What did Dorothea say to you?" Shade demanded, trying to keep his voice down. Everything had been so perfect this morning. Lizzy and Maisie had hit it off. Everything had looked as if it was going to work out for all of them.

"I can't talk about it right now," she said. "Please, I have to go, but I'll call you later. I promise."

He watched her go, cursing under his breath before he went to find Dorothea.

"GERTIE?" LIZZY FLEW into the house calling her aunt's name. She had to talk to her. This couldn't wait. If what Dorothea had told her was true…

She stuck her head into her aunt's room and started to close the door when she saw the brochure on her nightstand. She stepped into the room. It was for a cruise around the Mediterranean. The brochure looked as if her aunt had nearly worn out the pages looking at it.

She felt her heart break. How could she have not known? She'd had no idea that Gertie had wanted to travel. Why hadn't her aunt said something? For the same reason Lizzy thought she couldn't accept Shade's proposal.

Lizzy heard the front door open and her aunt calling her name. With the brochure still in her hand, she stepped out of Gertie's room. "You want to travel?"

Gertie looked from the brochure to her. "I've thought about it."

She laughed. "Auntie, why didn't you tell me? You have to go. This one is this summer. I want you on this boat. In fact, it is going to be my gift to you."

"Most certainly not," Gertie said indignantly. "I have plenty of money to pay for the trips myself. I've been saving for the day when…" Her voice faltered.

"When you didn't have to take care of me anymore."

Her aunt shook her head. "No. For when you moved out and started your own family. A few of my friends have been planning a cruise for a while now."

Lizzy shook her head, smiling through her tears. "I thought I was taking care of you and you thought you were taking care of me."

"We've taken care of each other. But now it's time to spread our wings, don't you think?"

She hugged her aunt. "What about this house?"

"It's just a house. I have a place I've had my eye on. I think it's time for me to think about assisted living."

"Assisted living?"

"They have a pool, community dining and they have all kinds of classes. They've talked to me about teaching a cooking class once I move in."

So it had gone that far. Lizzy'd had no idea.

"Why are you looking sad? I'm excited about this next part of my life. Aren't you?" Gertie asked impatiently. "You love Shade, right?"

Lizzy nodded.

"And the little girl?"

She nodded again. "I just met her. I think we're going to be just fine together."

"Then smile. Embrace all of it. If I've taught you anything, I hope I've taught you that."

She did smile and handed the brochure to her aunt. "Tell your friends that you're on for the Mediterranean."

Gertie's eyes shone as Lizzy hugged her again. "Time to spread our wings."

EARLY SUMMER CAME to the Flathead Valley with the scent of blossoms on the fruit trees, green grass and sunshine. Lizzy saw her aunt off to Seattle to catch her cruise ship with her friends. She'd never seen Gertie so excited.

In Whitefish, everyone had anxiously anticipated Jennifer Fox's trial, but at the last minute, she took a plea deal that spared her life and saved the taxpayers the cost of a trial.

In her testimony, Jennifer admitted everything. From her statement it was clear that she enjoyed telling how she'd planned it all once she'd found the diaries. Brad printed the confession in his newspaper word for word, making it the most popular edition of his paper for the two weeks it ran. The part that shocked most everyone in town and had people talking at every café was Jennifer's lack of regret for all of it.

Lizzy was relieved when Jennifer was moved to Montana State Prison in Deer Lodge for her life sentence without any chance of parole and the talk began to die down.

"Did you get the invitation?"

She looked up to find Sid standing in her office doorway and smiled. "Came yesterday. Going to be the wedding everyone in town is talking about."

"I hope not," he said as she waved him in. He closed the door. "Good to see you behind that desk."

It had been hard after everything that had happened at the guest ranch, but Sid had been right. Time had helped. Also finally getting rid of that nagging feeling that she'd missed something important. Jennifer was now locked up, the key thrown away. When that piece of the puzzle had dropped, Lizzy had felt as if maybe she could do this job after all.

"My aunt sends her regrets," Lizzy said.

"Dorothea told me that Gertie's on the cruise of her dreams with a bunch of friends," he said.

She nodded. "First the Mediterranean, and then the world. She said she might get off somewhere and stay for a while. You know her house is going on the market."

"I heard that a young border patrolman has already made an offer on it. He has a wife and two small children."

"And Shade and his brothers are hard at work on our house on the ranch," she said. "It has the most wonderful view of the mountains and there are houses close enough that Maisie will have kids to play with. They're building a new elementary school out that way that should work perfectly for kindergarten."

He laughed. "You sound like an old married woman."

"Don't I though," she said, smiling. She and Shade had opted to get married at city hall before Gertie left. Sid and Dorothea had been their witnesses. Maisie had been there, practicing throwing rose petals as she would soon at Sid and Dorothea's wedding.

The ceremony was short and sweet and perfect, since there would be a new addition to the Sterling family by next Christmas. Maisie asked for a sister or a brother. Shade and Lizzy wouldn't have minded another little girl. But when the doctor told them it was a boy, they were both delighted. Maisie would have a little brother.

Lizzy put her hand over her slightly protruding stomach under her sheriff's uniform and smiled to herself. She'd gotten pregnant on her first date with

Shade—after years of waiting. Some things were just meant to be, she thought as her phone rang.

She picked up, wondering what this day had in store for her.

"Sheriff Sterling," she said and smiled.

OH, JENNIFER. I could lie and say I didn't know how you would react when I told you that you couldn't be friends with Whitney and me. You knew Stephanie and Ashley would side with me. But you did have a choice. So why blame me?

You were so easily manipulated. Until you weren't. I knew that once you heard about the diaries you would find them and then things would get interesting.

I have to hand it to Lizzy though. Once she saw my purse hanging from your arm... You really shouldn't have kept it. And my ringtone? Kind of rubbing it in my face, huh?

I thought for sure that you were going to kill Lizzy, too. I never realized how clever she was.

But you, Jennifer, I always thought of you as a loyal friend. When you popped up from the back seat and put that knife to my throat... I really didn't think you had it in you. You surprised me all right.

Now if it had been Stephanie, that would have been another story. I saw her giving me the side-eye more than once. I knew she disapproved of me. But hey, she certainly had no right to judge given what she'd been up to. Gross.

But, Jennifer, I thought I could depend on you. Just

goes to show, you really have to watch the quiet ones. I think it also proves that there is a cold-blooded killer in all of us.

I know Lizzy wouldn't agree. Lizzy got her killer—and the man of her dreams. I'd wish her and Shade the best, but even death can't make me that nice.

I like to believe that I didn't deserve to die. But maybe I did. Maybe I took too much pleasure in the questionable things I did. Just like my grandmother used to say. Maybe I would do it differently, if I had another chance.

Or maybe not.

* * * * *

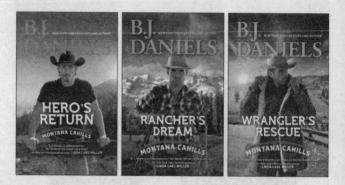

Get 4 FREE REWARDS!

We'll send you 2 FREE Books plus 2 FREE Mystery Gifts.

FREE
Value Over
$20

Both the **Romance** and **Suspense** collections feature compelling novels written by many of today's best-selling authors.